The Gentleman Poet

By Kathryn Johnson

The Gentleman Poet

The Gentleman Poet

KATHRYN JOHNSON

AVON

An Imprint of HarperCollins*Publishers*

THE GENTLEMAN POET. Copyright © 2010 by Kathryn Kimball Johnson. All rights
reserved. Printed in the United States of America. No part of this book may be used
or reproduced in any manner whatsoever without written permission except in the
case of brief quotations embodied in critical articles and reviews. For information
address HarperCollins Publishers, 10 East 53rd Street, New York, NY 10022.

HarperCollins books may be purchased for educational, business, or sales promo-
tional use. For information please write: Special Markets Department, HarperCollins
Publishers, 10 East 53rd Street, New York, NY 10022.

FIRST AVON PAPERBACK EDITION PUBLISHED 2010.

Designed by Diahann Sturge

Library of Congress Cataloging-in-Publication Data
    Jensen, Kathryn, 1949–
        The gentleman poet / Kathryn Johnson. — 1st ed.
            p.   cm.
        ISBN 978-0-06-196531-9 (acid-free paper)
        1. Shakespeare, William, 1564–1616—Fiction.   2. Women household employees—
    Fiction.   3. Great Britain—History—Elizabeth, 1558–1603—Fiction.   I. Title.
    PS3610.E567G46 2010
    813'.6—dc22   2010003347

10 11 12 13 14   OV/RRD   10 9 8 7 6 5 4 3 2 1

Acknowledgments

$\mathcal{M}$any individuals, and more than a few institutions, have had a hand in this novel. They share the credit and none of the blame for what it became. Here are a few . . .

Kudos to wise, nurturing Kevan Lyon of the Marsal Lyon Literary Agency—she's as good as it gets in the universe of agents. Thanks also to Jill Marsal for offering to bring us together. My appreciation to sterling editors, Carrie Feron and Tessa Woodward—without their enthusiasm and insight, this book might not be in your hands today. The Columbia Writers Critique Group—*you know who you are!*—has generously provided practical advice and emotional support to their member-writers for over three decades. I have been fortunate to benefit from a good many of those years.

My everlasting gratitude to Shakespearean scholars the world wide, whose amazing research still awes me and enticed me to weave a fantasy around their hard-won facts.

Thank you, *thank you* to the Folger Shakespeare Library in Washington, D.C., for allowing me access to a breathtaking collection of all things related to Will. The beautiful Folger Reading Room provided knowledge as well as atmosphere to fuel this writer.

No one could have been more gracious or inspiring than the residents of Bermuda. During my research trips there, Michael and Carol Aston provided a delightful room, with a quiet workspace in which to write, at their 1734-built *Granaway Guest House*. (Michael, your breakfasts are to die for!) Hannah at the Bermuda Bookstore offered cultural and historical information as well as introduced me to the spectacular Bermuda librarians, whose names I've totally forgotten but I love you anyway! The Maritime Museum staff helped me visualize the famous wreck of the *Sea Venture* and life in the seventeenth century. Such an exquisite place, Bermuda begs to be written about, and visited.

Finally, there is my husband. Without the peace of mind, encouragement, and love you have shared with me, this story simply would not be.

KJ
Silver Spring, Maryland
February 2010

The Gentleman Poet

Prologue

London, England—1611

*B*en Jonson, overheard speaking to fellow playwright Thomas Middleton, following the premier of William Shakespeare's *The Tempest*, at the Globe Theatre:

Jonson: *"How can anyone believe such unnatural scenes? Will knows nothing of storms at sea and shipwrecks, the man never having left good English soil! And as to the quality of his prose, do you know that the Players have often mentioned it as an honor to Shakespeare that in his writing, whatsoever he pens, he never blots out a line?"*

Middleton: *"And what say you to that, friend?"*

Jonson: *"Would he had blotted a thousand!"*

One

Methought I saw a thousand fearful wracks;
A thousand men that fishes gnaw'd upon.
—from *Richard III*

Elizabeth—July 24, 1609

A storm was coming. For weeks since our departure from Plymouthe, I had been blessedly free of the seasickness that plagued others aboard our ship. Then one cloudless, azure-skied morning, as the gentlest of zephyrs billowed our white sails, demons took possession of my poor head and I began to fear the worst, for here in the middle of the vast Atlantic Ocean we were at the mercy of the elements.

The pain came on so sudden and fierce I thought it might pop my skull like a nutshell between the pincers of a cracker. I could keep down no food. The dull, brassy flickering of lanterns below deck pierced my eyes, so that I had to squint against the painful glare. Never had one of my spells been this bad.

But no sign of concern marked our good admiral Sir George Somers's confident manner when he stooped his tall frame to enter Mistress's chamber with a cheerful "Good day to you, Mistress Horton." He came daily to share news of our progress aboard the *Sea Venture*. The fleet was now eight weeks out of Plymouthe Harbour, with our proud *Venture* as flagship, leading the way.

Mistress Horton, benefactress of the Virginia Company, received the ship's officers' highest respect. When in the mood, she dined at governor Sir Thomas Gates's table. When not, she sent me to the galley to fetch her meals.

Sweet Savior! Elizabeth, do not think of Cook's larded mutton. Nor his greasy cabbage-and-turnip stew, scorched Shrewsbury cakes, or savory purses oozing with over-spiced gravies.

Holding my stomach, I squatted unnoticed in my scratchy fustian cassock behind the largest of Mistress's trunks, desperately wishing myself back in London and on solid, blessedly unmoving ground. Burying head in arms, I tried to shut out their conversation. But the dizzying stink of Mistress's lilac perfume and rocking motion of the ship made my misery worse.

"Captain Newport predicts we are no more than eight days of making Cape Henry," the admiral advised her. The Cape being off the coast of Virginia, New Britannia. Our destination.

I looked up, hopeful. Eight days! Could it be we might outrace the storm?

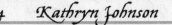

"It cannot be soon enough." Mistress's sour gaze drifted about our tiny compartment. She pursed her lips and huffed. "These accommodations are far less comfortable than promised."

In truth, this private chamber was more than most aboard obtained, lesser passengers and crew being stacked atop one another in the ship's cave-ish innards. *How spoilt you are, old woman*, I thought.

"Now, now, good lady." The admiral patted her withered hand. "Do you not enjoy this fine adventure?"

"I enjoy nothing of this method of travel. If it weren't for concern over my investments I never would have . . ." She cast about the chamber again. "Where is that worthless girl?"

Her words stung, although I'd heard them often enough before, as well as felt a bounty of her quick, harsh slaps. But I would not have a good man like the admiral think so little of me.

I kept to the shadows, praying the old witch wouldn't ask me to bring out her hippocras and biscuits. The mere thought of spiced wine and sweets set my stomach churning again.

I should never have set foot on this ship, came the bitter thought. Unfortunately, I'd had little choice in the matter, given my recent dire circumstances.

Sir George smiled, better at indulging her than either Governor Gates or Captain Newport. "You will soon see how well your money is spent, dear lady. And as to conditions for the crossing, we can ask no fairer weather."

It was true. We had enjoyed only the gentlest of swells and

no breeze stronger than our sails might enjoy. Yet my head reminded me that this fine weather would not last. If only we had been closer to Virginia . . .

We were to be the Third Supply to the Jamestown Colony. Our more than six hundred settlers and soldiers aboard seven ships and two pinnaces sailed with all manner of victuals, tools, weaponry, soldiers, marines, and varied materials sufficient to sustain our company and those who had sailed before us, against famine, weather, and savages. All of London had applauded our brave and exciting enterprise. Throngs of well-wishers had lined the wharves of Plymouthe to hail our departure.

But now, as *Venture* spilled down yet another slippery liquid trough, my insides lurched dangerously. I stifled a sob, clamping a hand over my mouth.

Fearing to offend the admiral with my sickness, I seized my cloak and took the chance to escape while they conversed, scrambling through the common crew's hold, then up, up, up the splintery wooden ladder and out into brisk sea air.

Cloak wrapped tight, I rushed past sailors working on the swaying deck. All, thankfully, too busy to pay mind to an ill serving girl. At a place of solitude near the bowsprit, I heaved up the watery contents of my stomach and clung limp, sweating, spent to the rail. From the intensity of my agony I felt more certain than ever that we were about to sail into the fiercest of maelstroms.

"You are but a natural weather gauge, Elizabeth." My father's words, meant to soothe me during a lesser spell. "Think of your headaches as a gift, if you can. They always pass, and you will never be caught in the rain." It had become our small joke.

I pressed a trembling hand to my temple. It throbbed mercilessly. I drew deep breaths, tucking a stray yellow curl beneath my cap. After a while it became possible to open my eyes again, though I could only squint against the too-brilliant sunlight.

The sky above was the true, honest hue of periwinkles and larkspur. A salty breeze, still soft and steady, filled our sails nicely. The sea spread before me, a composed gray-green endless carpet upon which to ride. Four of our other ships, including our little pinnace leashed to our gunwhales, floated in easy view. Three others I could see more distant. The last, I trusted, lingered not far behind. A peaceful scene if ever there was one at sea.

But when I gazed down into the white spume sliced out of Neptune's depths by our proud flagship's prow, I saw that the dolphins, playful fellows that had frolicked alongside us these many weeks, were gone.

Where to, good friends? A fish's secret sanctuary?

Would that I could swim away with them. I stared at the distant southern horizon where ocean kissed the sky. As I watched, a thin, muddy line appeared although I suspected no land lay there.

I longed to warn our captain. But who would believe a maidservant when not one of our expert navigators antici-pated a monster as treacherous as the many-headed Scylla stalked us?

Worse yet, I should be accused of witchery if my prediction proved true. And anyway, what good would their knowing do?

Closing my eyes against the pain, I swallowed back another mouthful of sour bile and felt the wind go hot and moist against my face. I fingered the hem of my worn cloak, for the comfort it always brought. My mother's rosary I had sewn within, where the pretty beads would not betray me. A score of whispered Hail Marys did little to calm my cursed head or steady my heaving stomach.

"Your mistress calls," a voice said above the wash of waves against our hull.

I turned with a start, dropping the cloak's edge from trembling fingertips.

Behind me stood William Strachey, commissioned to act as our voyage's historian. His long face, shaven chin, dull rust-colored hair shot through with gray were all unremarkable. He wore doublet and hose of a dusty moss-brown hue, quite plain. But in his left earlobe twinkled an exceptionally fine gentleman's gold ringlet, distinguishing him from crew and lesser passengers—carpenters, coopers, farmers, craftsmen, soldiers, and base laborers. It seemed strange, at least to me, that a mere clerk should own such an expensive trinket, but I had no time to give such suspicions further thought now.

"Yes, sir. Thank you, sir." I kept my eyes low and fled past him.

Down through the gaping hatch, like a rabbit into her warren. Back through the dank, grim passage crammed with the governor's guard playing cards. The stench of piss pots, spilled sacke, stale food, and unwashed bodies filled

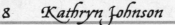

my nostrils. Cloak pressed over mouth and nose, stomach clenching, I rushed back toward Mistress Horton's chamber.

She was alone now.

"Elizabeth!"

I knew not to expect sympathy. Nevertheless, her sharp tone brought me up short, and I stopped well beyond her reach. "Yes, madam."

The old woman's black fish-eyes twitched with anger. "You are never to go above deck without me. How often have I told you?"

I held back my indignation, knowing to voice it would only buy me trouble. Meekness worked better on her. "But I was ill, madam. I wished not to foul your chamber."

"Nevertheless. Those sailors—" She pinched her thin lips and left the rest unsaid.

With so few women, ten only among our ship's total manifest of one hundred fifty, we of our sex watched ourselves well. But I suspected it was less concern for my purity than desire to always be attended that she kept me below.

"I shall have something light to eat now, girl."

I sighed. "Yes, madam."

"And fetch my Bible. There on the largest trunk."

I handed her the deliciously soft leather-bound book, its gilded page edgings catching the lantern's light, even that making my head pound.

At one time, my family had owned a dozen volumes, equally as fine—books by Homer, Virgil, a compendium of cookery beloved by my mother, others as well. The older ones, some in Latin, were illuminated in colors so vivid they took the breath away. Gone. All gone now, I thought bitterly.

Mistress split open her Bible with two blue-veined sparrow claws. When she seemed immersed in the pages, I plucked a twig of lavender from her pomander and crushed it beneath my nose. The fragrance gave ease enough to my roiling stomach to allow me to resume my duties.

From the tin of biscuits I took the largest remaining and placed it on her favorite pewter plate. None for me, even if I had been able to eat; *she* counted out our supply each night. If one went missing, she would accuse me of thievery to the captain. Whatever flavorless fish stew Cook contrived for the guard and seamen's mess waited for me.

I found the small cask reserved for her favorite ale, drained off a measure into a pewter cup then set it aside where it wouldn't topple with the ship's motion. From a fist-sized block of sugar, kept locked in a small coffer beneath Mistress's bed, I scraped a few precious crystals onto her biscuit.

Without warning the ship's steady roll changed to a precipitous pitch. I grabbed for a timber and the cup at the same time. *Now it does begin*, I thought. *Sweet Virgin, save us!* Had my hands been free, I might foolishly have crossed myself.

Caution, Bethy. Take care what you reveal. My mother's final words of warning.

But terror of another kind brought me back to this moment. Ships sank in storms. And when they did, this far from land, all aboard drowned. All. Was my young life to end so early?

Above decks the Master shouted orders. From the creak of ropes and slap of feet, I guessed that sailors were taking to the rigging. The massive sails would be bundled along spars and booms, so as not to pull us over in the coming storm.

"What takes you so long, Elizabeth?"

"It is ready." But my hands were shaking now and I had trouble grasping the cup.

The ship bucked. Ale sloshed in a golden waterfall to the floor. "Oh!" I cried.

My foot slipped on the damp planks, going out from under me. I tried to catch myself, but the plate flew from my hand, the cup too. Clanking empty against the stack of trunks, it rolled away with the motion of the ship.

"Clumsy girl!" Mistress clutched the carved arms of her chair and glared at me. "Your bad luck if you have bent them."

"Your dishes are undamaged," I said from my sore knees, retrieving both. Where the biscuit had gone, I knew not. Luckily, she was too far away to strike me. "I will fetch another."

"Do not bother." She whisked an imperious hand through the air. "I would wait until these tricky breezes cease."

"They will not." I sat up, rubbing my knees through my skirts.

"And how do you know?"

I had not meant her to hear. "I don't," I lied.

She tossed me a look of disgust.

I busied myself with chores until she fell to napping; then I went to sit beneath the nearest small hatch, ignoring other passengers' nervous chatter as the swells built. Here the foulness of the hold freshened, the pain in my head felt less severe. Above me, *Venture's* massive wooden masts soared up into an evil sky.

Although it was not yet five glasses past noon, the heavens turned black before my eyes, then blacker still, than an ironmonger's furnace. There would be no stars to navigate by tonight. No moon. The wind rose, playing an ominous whistle through the rigging, as if a great, ravenous bird perched there waiting to pick our bones. As I sat helpless, trembling, the noise increased to a howl, then an unholy shriek.

"Dear God, do protect us!" a man called out in prayer from somewhere in the hold.

A woman wept aloud. Other voices attempted to comfort her but soon grew silent, catching her fear at the first ominous crash of thunder. I felt as sorry for them as for myself.

Lightning rent the skies. Silver against black. Then the rains came, wind and water shouting down each other, drowning out even the most terrified shrieks of women and men alike as they huddled deeper within the ship's bowels.

Then, as suddenly as the demons had assaulted me, they left my poor head, for all the good it might do at this, our darkest hour.

I stayed at my post beneath the hatch, though the rain poured in and the fear never left me. Peering up at the sails, I watched in horror as they tore partway free of the yardarms. Within moments they were shredded by the fierce wind. The ship rose then floundered, creaking mournfully, heaving upward on each towering wave before pitching downward again.

My insides clutched and tumbled with each desperate lurch and wallow of the ship.

Behind us, I knew, trailed the lively *Blessing,* then *Diamond, Unitie,* the swift *Falcon, Lion, Swallow,* and last of all, sweet *Virginia* and little *Catch.* Eight more tortured vessels carrying our fellow adventurers. I imagined their plight as hopeless as ours. I imagined every single soul drowning in the boiling black seas.

Two

And though she be but little, she is fierce.
—from *A Midsummer-Night's Dream*

The miracle of it was—we did not immediately drown.

For days the ocean swelled to mountains around us, although we could only ever feel them, as no lantern would stay lit and neither sun nor moon nor starlight appeared in the sky, day or night.

Captain Newport ordered all passengers and crew shut below, hatches latched to prevent further flooding. But water trickled constant between her hull boards, filling the bilges waist deep. The admiral divided his men, sending them to pump and bail at three stations below. Useless, I thought as the waters rose, and rose again.

I was astonished to see even the oldest sailors, men not

accustomed to prayer, bending knee to beg God's mercy in our final hour.

I mostly stayed by my mistress, comforting her as I could. Despite my dislike for the old crow, I felt sorry for the terror I saw in her eyes. For myself, I wished a quick end, the sooner to join my dear father and mother, cruelly taken from me by queen and plague—one fate no more merciful than the other. It was as a result of my family's demise that I, daughter of a respected tradesman, was now remanded to the servitude I so despised.

But now the ship's ribs cracked louder than a bear-baiter's whip, making me jump and forget all else but our fate. I felt something hit my head, reached up and plucked a lump of oakum from my cap, spit out from between weakening boards. A steady stream of water flowed from its place. Like a beast foreseeing its own death, our brave *Sea Venture* wept. I looked around for something to plug the hole, saw a gob of rotting meat floating by and tried to stuff it into the gap. But it would not hold. The last of my hope drained away.

Every man, whether sailor or gentleman, soldier or farmer, took turns at bailing and pumping. I saw our historian laboring as hard as any mariner.

But whereas in other faces I saw despair, Mr. William Strachey's eyes gleamed with what one might mistake for excitement. Intent on his task, he rallied the others with shouts of, "Now, men, we make headway. Heave! Heave!" He sounded more like a great general rallying his troops to battle than a ship's clerk.

Despite all efforts, the flood sometimes filled the ship to the spar deck. Miraculously, we remained afloat, though no place aboard remained dry. No deck, bilge, or cubby offered rest. No food stayed unsullied by brine or filth. Casks broke loose and split, cracking against timbers, exploding with a noise that made the sky's thunder but a mouse's squeak. Precious sweet water and beer spilled into the slop around us. The stormy seas reduced trunks, furniture and all other unsecured valuables to splinters and shards. And we passengers became as bruised and battered as the cargo.

After two full days of the maelstrom, the cries and pleadings of our men and women ceased, there no longer seeming a point. Mistress Horton obtained one of the few perches above water level, atop a crate lashed to the staves in her chamber. She lay there, clutching her Bible to her breast. Eyes clamped shut, she prayed, hour after hour, taking no further notice of me, as I was of no use to her.

Left free to roam the doomed ship, I crawled or swam, where I could. If these were to be my final hours, I wished to know every inch of my watery grave.

Where more oakum had split from the boards below deck, Lady Wheaton and her daughter Ann were trying to stuff the openings with pieces of cloth to staunch the flow.

"Come here, you lazy slattern," Ann called out. Her blond hair hung in damp strands around her face, her cap having got lost in the filthy wash around us. "This is your brand of work, not ours." She thrust a dripping rag into my hands and fell back against a broken barrel.

"Hush, Ann!" her mother gasped. "We are all in the same desperate need." She cast me a look of exhausted apology as she clung to a beam to keep the ship from thrashing her to a pulp.

"Of course I'll help," I shouted against the wind's roar, "though I tried before. Nothing would hold back the water."

After some hours we gave up.

"I can't die," Ann whimpered. "I can't just . . . just drown in the middle of—" She collapsed against her mother's sodden breast, sobbing.

"Come," her mother said, "back to a drier place where we can make our peace in prayer."

I watched them flounder away, through the deepening water, hands gripped tight. Wishing I had someone to comfort me, then glad I would never again have to watch another person I loved perish. I had seen too much of dying.

Through a crack in a hatch lid, I peered up at the ribbons of sail caught in tangled remains of our rigging, whipping in the wind and gray, sheeting rain. Our masts had long ago snapped and their upper parts been washed overboard, most of the hemp lines and stays with them.

By the end of the third day, the storm hadn't lessened and Death shadowed every face. I hadn't eaten in days, my strength now all but spent. Few of our company still bothered to pray. God had forsaken us. Some of the men found comfort in the discovery of an unshattered ale cask. They broke it open to toast our brave end then drank themselves to carelessness.

Mistress remained on her perch, inches above the water. Her lips blue, she stared at me as if I were a stranger and no longer spoke, even to pray.

"It must end sometime," I said to soothe her. "We may yet survive." God forgive me for lying.

She turned her pale face away.

I slept not at all, one day to the next. Perching on a crate high up in a hold, I clamped my eyes shut against the terror and, heart racing, worried for our hapless companions in the little supply pinnace we had been towing. As soon as the storm arose we'd been forced to cast her off for fear of her ramming a hole in our hull. And what of the hundreds of settlers and sailors in the other ships in our flotilla? Had they already drowned? Even if the winds ceased, we had been blown miles apart and would be of no help to each other.

"I do not wish to die," I whispered, weeping. "But if You will it, Lord, I beg of you, please let our agony soon end."

"Lighten her load!" came the command from above at morning's light, through the tempest's noise.

I watched men, near unconscious from their shifts at bailing, heave all objects of weight overboard. Along with wasted victuals and furnishings, out the gun ports went the heavy iron cannons, and chests full of fine lace, pewter vessels, porcelain, and silver cups. For what good would any of them do us if we went down?

"Out of the way, girl! Lest we pitch you over with the rest of the rubbish."

I crept with all haste back to Mistress's chamber.

At the end of four nights and three days, without sleep or food, all had remained below deck but for our brave Governor Gates and Captain Newport. The governor, having himself navigated these waters before, stayed at the ship's wheel on the poop deck. Even I, a city girl, knew if we took a single great wave to the breach, *Venture* would surely tumble over, turning hull and keel to raging skies. Then all would be lost. Only the governor's steady hand and calm head had prevented this, thus far.

On that fourth night, Mistress Horton roused herself to ask, "When will our supper be ready, Elizabeth?"

I stared at her. Her cheeks glistened fever bright, her eyes glazed by delirium.

"There is none, madam. Only a small bit of brown bread I've kept dry." I showed her the crust wrapped in oiled paper that I'd tucked up high in the beams.

"Peasant scraps," she spat. "Take it, wench. I shall wait for a proper meal at the captain's table."

I sighed.

"And I will have my pleated ruff and best periwig to wear this evening. You will have them ready."

"Of course, madam."

I shook my head in disbelief as she settled herself with a contented smile on her crate, as though to rest before a royal banquet. Mad, I thought, the mean old thing is ripe for Bedlam.

I flicked off a tiny speck of blue mold from the crust, judging it still quite edible. My stomach clenched at the faint yeasty aroma of Cook's last batch of bread, now nearly a week past. Even with the tossing of the ship, my belly ached for food.

There was, however, someone else who needed it more than I.

The ship rolled wildly, heeling so far on her port side, I was certain, this time, we should go over.

By Our Lord's mercy, we did not.

I made my way to the hatch that would deliver me closest to the poop. Any other time one of the governor's guard would have stopped me, but as all considered us doomed, no one troubled to warn me of the peril of taking to the deck.

Thinking back, I suppose that although I had prayed for our survival, I half wished to be washed over into the boiling sea. Better to die gazing up at an angry sky than shut within a casket of wood and iron—sinking, sinking, sinking . . . At least my last breaths might be free of filth, my ears deaf to the agonized cries of my companions.

Nevertheless, I clung to the lines our mariners had strung as hand holds across the deck. The ship fell over the crest of an immense wave, then plunged into its trough. The rope rubbed my palms raw. No matter the pain, I held on.

Venture seemed to fall endlessly, leaving my stomach far above me. I looked up and gasped, for even as the water receded from the deck and I coughed out mouthfuls of brine, there appeared yet another mountain of water above us. I fell flat against the boards, wrapping my leg around the hemp's rough length, holding fast with both stinging hands.

So I suppose I was not ready to die. Just yet.

The next three waves did not wash over the ship. It had been that way since the storm struck. Only every fifth or so buried us, as if Neptune himself teased our crew, letting them drain just enough seawater to keep us afloat, then filling her up again.

I scrambled up the steps to the poop deck between waves.

Governor Gates stared at me. "Go away, girl. Below! Below!" His eyes were wild and red with salt, skin drenched and puckered with the sea.

I pulled the oiled packet from inside my bodice with shaking fingertips and held it out to him.

"What?" he barked.

"Bread. 'tis for you, sir."

"Take it away."

"Sir, for your strength. Please, if you fail, so do we all."

He was a broad-shouldered man with handsome features, maybe three score years. Although not young, he was still of good health. How else might he have withstood the rigors of his watch?

"Right then. Give it over."

Unfolding stiff layers of greased paper, I took out the crusty chunk. My stomach called out one last time as I held the bread before him so that he wouldn't have to release his hold on the wheel. He took the crust from my fingertips, whole in his mouth.

I waited while he chewed then swallowed.

"Go below, Little Mother, and make your peace with God," he said more gently, the howling wind whisking the words from his crumbed lips. "It won't be much longer."

He was right.

Within two glasses, the wind ceased.

Three

I'll note you in my book of memory.
—from *King Henry VI, Part I*

*T*hat most peaceful of all nights I crawled up onto the deck through the wreckage and found a cunning hole into which I crawled like a little pigeon. The sky was crystal black, and the stars and moon made themselves visible for the first time in days. The air felt cool and pure and sweet. The only sound was of the gentlest waves lapping our sideboards. But the blessed silence made me wonder . . .

Would the storm return? Did God tempt us with hope?

I gazed up at delicate strands of sailcloth caught in the spiderweb remains of rigging, no more useful to catch the wind than lace. Even were there spare sails, as I supposed there might be somewhere in the hold, I did not know how they could be raised without masts and spars. Without sails we could go nowhere but as we drifted.

Without food.

Without water.

Along the ruined rigging, fairy lights flickered against the black, black sky. Saint Elmo's fire, I thought, remembering one of Father's tales from his days at sea, before he married Mother and opened the apothecary. Was this God's beautiful farewell to us? Perchance He was coaxing us toward Heaven by his angels' brilliant wings.

I stared up at the dancing lights, unable to think anymore what would become of us. Truly, I had never wanted to be part of this voyage. But accompany Mistress as she demanded, or be left without home, family, or craft to fend for myself on treacherous London streets—those were my only choices. My chest tightened at the memory of girls, much younger than I, wandering the alleys, taking money to pleasure any man who asked. I had come so close to *that*!

I turned my mind again to the fate of the other ships. Had any survived to continue on to Virginia and tell the colony of our fate? Had some turned back to England? How sad if we all should perish before reaching Jamestown.

I settled back in my nest, glad not to be disturbed. I hated the thought of going below to listen to the complaints of my fellow passengers. It was my duty to see to my mistress's needs. But with no dry clothing to offer her, no food unsullied by brine, and probably no wine, ale, or even her favorite hippocras, there was little I could do for her.

Above my head the fairy fires flickered in the night for another two hours, then slowly, slowly faded.

Lost.

Adrift.

I closed my eyes and, at last, slept.

"Land! Land!"

Blinking up at the long-absent sun, I came gradually awake. My first thought was that God, in apology for his fury, had lifted us up and carried us on to Virginia.

Sunken-eyed figures staggered up through shattered hatches and companionways onto the main deck, bumping into and trammeling one another in their haste. A few tars shimmied up the stump of a snapped-off masthead and pointed into the distance, calling down their estimates of distance.

"Two miles."

"No, less by far!"

"Praise God!" came shouts from all around.

I fell to my knees, eyes filled with tears and lifted toward Heaven. Saved! Could it be?

We drifted with the current, helped by makeshift masts our crew fashioned from tent poles. A damp but whole sail hung from them, catching a spritely breeze. Governor Gates steered us as the captain directed.

I stood at the rail and watched as low, dark shapes on the horizon grew higher, slowly transforming into clusters of wooded islands.

"'Tis no good," a man close by me muttered. "These be the Devil's Isles. W're better away."

"Back to sea?" the woman at his side wailed. "Pray not."

Horrified whispers passed through the company.

"The Devil's Isles—the dread Bermudas?"

"Everyone knows the place is cursed and bewitched."

"Turn back! Turn back for England!" As if we could, broken as we were.

"What are they talking about?" a trembling voice asked.

I turned to see Sarah Bradley, a younger maidservant I only ever saw when we met at the galley to fetch food for our mistresses. She looked deathly thin, her eyes sunken in her pretty face, skin sallow. She wrapped her arms around her damp shift, shivering though the air had warmed with the generous sun.

"My father," I said, "he told me of these islands. If these be the Bermudas, we've stumbled upon a truly evil place."

"How are they evil?" She stared across the water.

I shrugged. "Inhabited by spirits and cannibals and witches, no doubt. 'Tis what they say of all the New World, though the riches be many."

"To be sure," a guardsman nearby added knowledgably, "even certain rocks and trees may capture and hold innocent prisoners within them."

I sighed. "On the other hand, land is land." I smiled at Sarah and clasped her hands in mine. "Anything is better than water. Yes?"

She gave me a weak smile. "Oh, yes!"

I searched for Mistress below, wanting to tell her the good news, but could not find her. To my surprise, when I returned to the deck, she was standing quite ably at the starboard rail I had moments before left. She peered at the lump of dark land rising closer, yet still more than a mile away, her eyes seeming clearer, less mad now.

I glanced down at my hands, chafed raw by my trip to the poop deck with the governor's bread. They stung from the salt. Then my gaze extended beyond swollen fingers to something brown and leathery, wedged in a crack between deck planks where iron stays had torn loose.

Reaching down, I gently pulled the thing free.

"What is it, girl?" Mistress asked.

I turned it over in my hands. "A ledger or journal of some kind." Stamped in gold on the cover were the words: *True Reportory.*

I showed it to her.

"That will be Mr. Strachey's, I suspect."

"The historian."

She seemed to hesitate, then nodded. "Of course you wouldn't understand such things." She snatched it from me, opening the leather cover, as if it were hers to do so. "The pages are only damp; the ink hasn't run. He must have had it on his person after the storm left or it would have been swept away." She gave a dry laugh. "Perhaps William has already given up his task."

"Why should he?" I looked across the deck, then fore and aft, but he was nowhere in sight.

Peering over her shoulder, I caught a glimpse of scratchy black writing with high loops and low whorls—a very distinctive hand and unlike any clerk's neat printing that I'd ever seen. And though I had expected lists of supplies, tables of tides or phases of the moon, or navigation and watch records of some sort, the arrangement of the lines and words appeared as in an ordinary letter or diary.

"Stupid girl," she said, snapping the journal shut before

I could get close enough to read a word. "Why should he bother with records, being as we are? How long do you think we shall live on that forsaken rock if it is the captain's plan to put us there? No food, no sweet water."

"I shall take Mr. Strachey his ledger," I said, and before she could think whether or not this pleased her, I had it in hand and was down the center hatch.

I searched the wreckage of the midship chambers, where most of the gentlemen travelers lodged. He was not there. Without candle or lantern, the bowels of the ship were cast in gloom, impenetrable to my eyes after the glaring sunlight above. I wished I had thought to bring Sarah with me. I did not like being down there alone, where a seaman—or gentleman for that matter, for they were often no better— might catch me.

A sharp curse from nearby startled me. I peered cautiously around the corner and into a narrow chamber.

Mr. Strachey was down on his knees, digging through a leather-strapped wooden chest, one of the few smaller ones saved from being tossed over.

"Excuse me, sir."

He started so violently he nearly fell over then stood up quickly to face me. A look of fear washed from his eyes when he saw it was only me.

"Did you lose this?" I asked, holding up the book.

His eyes immediately brightened at the sight of the little volume. "Ah, good girl! Give it here."

I handed the book to him. He reached for his purse strings at his waist, as if to slip me a coin for my trouble as he might do on a London street. Then his eyes, still a pure and striking blue even in the darkness, lit with amusement, and his hand fell away.

"Neither penny nor shilling will do me much good here," I said, with a smile but averting my eyes as a good servant should.

"I suppose not." He stroked his chin as if accustomed to wearing a beard, though none was there, and looked down at the book in his hands as though it were his child. "Thank you."

I frowned, trying to think why, when the anxiousness left his face, he suddenly reminded me of someone I knew, or should know. Someone more important than a clerk. What if he'd worn a beard, a periwig, or perhaps more luxurious clothing? I shook my head, feeling silly for suspecting him of being anything but what he appeared—a stranger, a fellow voyager, a gentleman.

I might have asked him if there was a reason I should recognize him. But I knew never to address my betters unless asked a question. Still, I felt a little reckless this July day of our deliverance. The storm had made me so. It had put those of us aboard *Sea Venture* into a different sort of community than we were ever accustomed. None of us had or could now hope to have better food or shelter or clothing than the others, because there was none at all.

"Do you keep accounts in that?" I asked, pointing to his book.

Numbers had always interested me. I had learnt them from my father's apothecary business. I had weighed out herbs and medicinals for his customers while he counseled them on their infirmities. I also used the little brass coin weights to check the truthfulness of the tender offered in payment, since a dishonest customer might shave or break off a bit of gold or silver for later use on other purchases. I was very good with measures, so Father told me.

"Accounts?" he asked.

"Yes, of our days at sea and of the conditions of the weather and wind, and our location."

"Ah. I see. Yes, of course." He nodded. "Other things as well."

"What others?" How bold I was!

But he seemed not to mind my questions. "Words, descriptions, ideas." He hesitated. "Do you read, girl?"

I shook my head. A little, but not worth admitting to a gentleman.

"No, of course not." He looked away with a grimace. "What would be the purpose?"

His words hurt, but I bit back a reply. My brothers had attended school; my sister and I did not. But my father had taught us some few things of our evenings at home. Nodding my head, I turned to go.

"Thank you," he called after me. "I would have missed this."

Four

For courage mounteth with occasion.
—from *King John*

*D*uring the course of that day of our salvation Captain Newport guided what was left of our ship closer to the terrifying land. All of our large guns and cannon had been thrown over to lighten her, so we could not fire them to signal or warn off anyone who might hold the islands. One of our guardsmen shot off three rounds from his musket, but no response came.

Captain Newport ordered down our longboat to precede the larger ship. Two crewmen dropped plumb lines from the little boat to ascertain the depth as we slowly made our way in. The waters were of deceptive depth. Wondrous flower-like formations grew upward through the clear water, branching delicately toward the liquid surface.

I heard a seaman whisper nervously, "Coral. She's bloody all about us. Tear the guts out of the old girl, it will."

The reef sometimes blocked our passage, while other places parted to provide a narrow channel no more than a man's hand broader than our hull. Hour after hour I watched at the rail as we tenderly felt our way toward shore until the ship ground to a halt and there stood fast.

"We are wedged," our master said. "Here we stay, like it or no." He looked a grim soul.

But land! I thought. *Sweet Mary, here we have found cherished, dry, unmoving, beautiful land!* I cared not that sorcerers and demons might greet us. I'd rather live in a tree than perish beneath the sea.

All was clamor and haste as the captain made arrangements to transport the company to shore. The ship was still taking on water, none of the joint packing holding, and the rocks that held us had further damaged her hull. How long she might remain afloat I'm sure no one knew. It seemed to me we were still a half mile or more away from what appeared to be the largest island.

A small skiff and the governor's longboat had remained lashed on deck, while greedy waves sucked down the others. Both boats found employ in ferrying to shore as many of our company as safely could fit at a time.

First to leave were the company officers, along with the governor and his wife. Mistress Horton received a place of honor in the skiff. Later trips carried joiners, carpenters, tradesmen, and lesser military officers. The captain remained on board even as most of his crew rowed ashore. Sarah and I, along with the other servants, could only wait our turns.

Sarah clung to my arm the whole time, her eyes growing wilder with fear as another hour passed and the breeze freshened. "Do you think the ship will hold her berth above the wavelets long enough for us to reach land?"

"I don't know," I said, for I worried about that too.

"I mean, God wouldn't be so cruel as to bring us this close, then—"

"God is cruel in ways you cannot imagine." I suppose I sounded as grim as Death itself.

She stared at me, her eyes immense, astonished.

"Never mind," I said, taking her hand. "Let us use our time to gather what items might be useful on land, should we make it that far." And I dragged her back down into the brine and filth, despite her protests, for I did not want to go down there alone.

She grew quickly excited by our treasure hunt, discovering bits of lace and pretty buttons and a small silver cup she stuffed into a soggy muslin sack, apparently thinking she might clean these items up later for her own use.

"It's not stealing," she said when she saw me looking at the cup. "It was left behind to go to the bottom with the ship. It would be a waste to leave them. Maybe," she added, "I will find their owners."

But I knew she would not.

I found a good stout knife with ample blade that Cook had left behind in his galley, perhaps having better. It might be well to keep it with me, in case I found any growing thing I might harvest for myself and Mistress. But I supposed it would be little use against demons or black magic.

Even as we searched another hold, the ship groaned and

creaked, complaining bitterly against her stony cradle. Her weakened hull might be crushed, and down she'd plunge with us in her. Sarah scuttled up ladder after ladder to the deck, myself close behind her. We had only to wait another few minutes before the lowliest of us made the brief passage to blessed land.

The ship did not sink all of that day while we sat on the beach, drying ourselves in the welcome sun, watching as load after load of surviving trunks, barrels, and tools came ashore, to be taken into stock for our common use.

It was nearly an hour after I'd come ashore when I heard, "Elizabeth Persons!"

I sighed at the familiar, needle-sharp voice. "Yes, madam."

She was standing over me, her lips pursed with irritation. "Find Cook and see what he can do about a meal. I am famished."

As are we all. My head felt as light as sea foam, my limbs wobbly from hunger.

"I don't know if anything has been saved, madam." I looked up and down the beach. Nothing out of the brine that flooded bilge and compartments would be edible. And who knew what creatures inhabiting this rock, if any, might serve as sustenance? Or might think of *us* as their next meal.

The men were still employed trying to save the last of our supplies. With only a few candles and little if any lamp oil rescued, we'd have no light once night fell. Fire for cooking, warmth, or light depended upon flints, if they could be salvaged from the wreck.

Fish, I thought. There must be vast, nutritious schools of them in the warm waters surrounding these islands.

But I'd heard the captain's orders. No one was allowed to fish or hunt until he declared that all valuable materials from the ship had been salvaged. And that might take well until dusk.

I sat in the wet sand, my stockings torn, toes poking naked through them; cassock, apron, and skirts still sticky-damp from their many dousings in seawater. The fabric clung to my limbs, weighing me down. Were it not such a hot day, I would have been shivering. My bruised flesh itched with dried salt. The sun blazed from above. I felt bone weary.

"Food, you lazy girl! Go to Cook now!" Mistress glared at me, kicking me in the side. I had forgotten she was there, I was so tired.

"Yes, madam," I whispered.

I found Cook sitting the other side of a dune, his wide back pressed against the trunk of a tall tree that sprouted feathery fronds of leaves only from the very top of its single straight trunk. I remembered seeing smaller versions in Mistress Horton's London hothouse. A palm of sorts, I assumed, but a very large one.

Cook too was very large. He had nearly filled the ship's galley with his broad shoulders when I went for Mistress's meals, and he was a head or more taller than even the admiral. Nearly two heads over most of the seamen and as strong as any of them. Rarely did any man dare to complain about the food he was served.

Today, Thomas Powell's face was red from the sun or drink—which, I couldn't say. His thick lips appeared nearly black, they were so parched. Untamed dun curls shot out around his sweaty face. But the most troubling aspect of him was what lay beneath his beard-stubbled chin. To my embarrassment he had removed his shirt and lain it to dry in the sun. Feeling short of breath at the sight, I quickly looked away from his naked chest.

"Excuse me, sir," I said, focusing for a moment on the sand between my feet and his before meeting his eyes.

He looked up at me with little comprehension, as if still dazed by our unexpected rescue. Slowly, his eyes cleared and he studied me with lazy curiosity.

"What is it then, girl?"

"Mistress wants her dinner," I said meekly.

His eyes widened. Suddenly he looked fully alert. "What?"

"Mistress Horton. She wants to be fed. And everyone is hungry. What will you do?"

He laughed, shaking his head as if I'd just told the merriest of jokes. "Do you see anything on this beach worth eating?"

I looked pointedly toward the far end of the sand where our few pigs and goats had been brought over in the skiff and were wobbling around as stiff-legged as we all were, finding our land legs.

"Can't slaughter 'em. Altogether they'd make one or two meals. Then what, lass?" He groaned and scrubbed his bewhiskered face with his big palms. It struck me that, beneath the grime and salt and unkempt beard, there might be the possibility of a pleasant face. "Anyway, gov'nor says we need to reconnoiter for game, soon as ever'thing is off the ship."

"And none of the stores at all have survived?" I asked.

Standing up, he scooped his shirt off the sand and pulled it on—which gave me some relief. He seemed less intimidating fully dressed. "Meat's all spoilt. Flour's gone. No verjuice, herbs, vegitives, or bread. What remains of our pantry must be kept 'til we know how far it need stretch."

Weeks, I thought. *Months. Years?* The Bermudas being so cursed and avoided by mariners of all nations, there was little likelihood of another ship coming our way.

"I can't go back to her with nothing," I whispered.

He shrugged. "Tell the old witch she can suck my—" He looked sheepish—no doubt noting the sudden flush that burned across my face. "Just tell her, lass, I'm waitin' on Captain's orders."

I turned and marched away before he could say anything else crude. *Sailors*, I thought.

Behind me I could hear him chuckling to himself.

Great rust-and-white petrels, fat as hens, shrieked, "*Ca-how, ca-how, ca-how!*" circling overhead as I marched across the sand, my face still hot with shame. They laughed at me too.

"Stupid birds," I muttered. I thought I might catch one, if I could, and roast it. But how to go about it?

I looked along the crescent of pale pink sand at our sorry assemblage. I could sit with them on the beach or go off to explore. No cannibals had yet greeted us. Perhaps they were waiting in the trees to surprise the first English to venture into the brush. And if not savages, other wild creatures must live in those lush leaves. Possibly very large ones. I shivered at the thought.

The wiser thing to do seemed to be—lie in the sand, feel the sun on my face, and let someone else discover the residents of our new home.

Five

Here's neither bush nor shrub to bear off
any weather at all, and another storm brewing;
I hear it sing i' th' wind.
—from *The Tempest*

I was suddenly wet again, and cold despite the sun. *Tide must have come in while I slept.*

Shivering, I rolled over, nose brushing the sand. A smattering of bubbles pierced tiny mauve grains as the water withdrew.

I frowned at them.

Another wave lapped in, then left. More little bubbles.

A glimmer of hope lightened my heart. I started digging with my hands.

The pink–gray sand, soft as powder, yielded easily to my fingers. Six inches down I came upon the first clam. A small one, but I forced it open with the tip of my knife, rinsed it in the surf, and ate it there and then.

It was sweet, salty, and delicate. I dug up three more, ate all, and felt a surge of nourishment steady the world around me. I went in search of a pail.

"Clams!" Someone shouted.

I had collected a tin basin full to the brim of the lovely pale-shelled mollusks. Enough for my mistress and three other diners besides. But I knew, even in her present state of hunger, she would not eat them raw. I marched across the beach, weaving between bedraggled figures sprawled in groups upon the sand.

"Lookit what she got, clever wench!"

I pushed away curious sailors, my mind fixed on how to prepare my treasure.

The admiral's guard had lit a fire and were using salvaged metal from the ship to serve as a grate across it. Cook stood over a cauldron of boiling sweet water he must have rescued from an unbroken cask. He looked at a loss for what to put in his water stew.

I gave him an innocent smile, set my pan of clams in their seawater bath over the flame, and squatted down to watch them steam, release their fragrance, and pop open to reveal their luscious, silky bodies.

The succulent aroma brought a crowd. I pointed to the place where I had dug. Soon the beach was covered with kneeling bodies, up to their elbows in muck.

That first night we spent on the very beach where we had landed. Soldiers stood watch for intruders of whatever kind might occupy or have arrived at the islands before us. Come dawn, the sailors and men from among Somers's and Gates's companies continued salvaging from our wrecked and wretched ship all that could be saved.

Most important were the materials of a building nature— staves, nails, tools, rope, all manner of iron grips, bolts, fixtures, and axes. For as soon as we accounted all one hundred fifty of us safe, talk began to circulate among some of the men of building a new ship to carry us the remaining way to Virginia.

All victuals, and the little untainted water and beer remaining, were gathered into one store. A stockade was erected around it, fashioned from saplings growing on the verdant hillside. The governor put all supplies under guard, to be apportioned among the company as might be fair.

"There is enough for all, but only for one week," I overheard Cook complain to Mr. Strachey, as Mistress and I passed them by that first land-blessed morning. "We shall all starve before the governor has his boat built."

"Perhaps," Mr. Strachey allowed. He turned to us. "Good morn', Mistress Horton."

"Good morning, sir, and to you, Thomas Powell." She nodded at Cook. "Such talk I hear. No one wants to stay on these Devil's Isles, yet I can't say that I am ready for another voyage of the like we have just endured."

"You would stay here with the demons?" Mr. Strachey asked. And I thought I saw the beginnings of a smile at the corners of his lips.

She huffed. "You believe in demons, sir?"

"I believe in all things fantastic. How dull would our lives be without our fantasies—good and evil!"

She shot him a look. "Of course, *you* would think that!"

He stared at her, his gaze suddenly brittle, and a silent message passed between them. What it meant I couldn't say, but he no longer looked comfortable swapping pleasantries with her.

Thomas Powell frowned, appearing as puzzled as I was.

She waved an indifferent hand at the historian. "Never mind. Perhaps you can use your fantasies, to find us some of these demons and make of them slaves to bring us whatever delicacies they have hidden on these islands."

Mr. Strachey's gaze drifted toward me for a moment, as if to determine how much of their conversation I understood. I looked away.

"As a stockholder in the Virginia Company," Mistress continued, "I believe we should concern ourselves less with demons and spirits than with real and more probable dangers."

"What might these dangers be, madam?" Cook asked.

"Heathen and, of course, pirates. Then there are our natural enemies, the Spanish. A fort is our first responsibility, not another ship."

"Aye. For shelter as well as for protection." Thomas nodded emphatically. "Another good storm may wash us clean off this beach."

Captain Newport and Admiral Somers apparently were in agreement with them. Later that morning, arms and powder that remained unsullied by salt and damp were passed around to their men and orders given for our protection. The admiral commanded all to remain close together and on the beach until he himself might reconnoiter the island for dangers.

★ ★ ★

"Elizabeth." Mistress sat in the shade where I'd made her comfortable. She whisked a palm frond fan before her flushed face. The day had grown over warm, and the breeze had died to nothing. "Do go to Cook and see what he prepares for the day's meals."

I didn't like starting conversations with Thomas Powell when no one else was around to curb his rudeness . . . or make him keep his shirt on. Neither did I care for crossing the long, sunny beach to his driftwood fire. Sailors, no longer preoccupied with their duties, having no ship to sail, had begun to take embarrassing interest in our women, be they married or not. Their sloe-eyed observations and sly grins made my skin itch worse than the crusty sea salt.

"Elizabeth?"

"I see Mr. Strachey over on the point. Maybe he knows." He seemed lost in contemplation, gazing out across the sea. Was he hoping to spot a rescue ship? Or one of our own lost flotilla limping toward our islands?

"Stay away from that man," she snapped. "He is trouble, that one. He will only involve you in his—" She broke off her words, as if she'd started to say something she shouldn't have. "Never you mind. Just go talk to Cook."

I sighed. "I heard Mr. Powell tell some of the men to bring him fish, of as many kinds as possible."

Mistress wrinkled her nose and fanned herself faster. "I fear we'll tire of the sea's abundance. Fish may be all we ever have to eat here."

"Only if we're lucky enough to catch them." I stretched

my legs out on the sand, happily warming them beneath my skirts. "Look at those fools."

Mistress squinted into the sun at the sailors splashing about in the water's edge. "What are they doing? Dancing?"

I laughed. "Trying to catch a meal, but they are afraid of the fish biting them."

Even at a distance I could see how many and large the creatures were, leaping above the waves, swimming between the men's legs. More likely in pursuit of shrimps or bream than men.

She scowled. "Have they no hooks or nets and such to fling into the water?"

"Lost in the storm," I said.

"We are doomed."

But then as we watched, the men grew braver. Some took up staves from our wrecked vessel and employed them to bash one of the larger fish over the head as it breached a wave. Having thus stunned the creature, they dragged its glistening, flopping body by the tail up onto the beach. Soon they had amassed a pile substantial enough to feed all.

"Go see what Cook will do with them," Mistress Horton said, wetting her lips. "I think a lovely salmon couched in butter pastry would do me well."

I just looked at her. How might that happen without a speck of flour or spoonful of butter?

She glared at me. "Go, I say, you idle girl. Else I'll report your rebelliousness to Governor Gates."

With reluctance, I stood and set off across the beach.

As I passed the sailors' catch, I saw it was made up of different sorts of fish, many I recognized from shopping with my mother at the Stocks Market: pilchard, cabally, snapper, and hogfish of good and generous size. What Cook didn't use for the day's messes, we should salt and dry.

I was halfway across the beach when I felt something rough slip under my skirt from behind and creep, tickling, between my thighs. A spider, I thought, and shrieked, dancing away and shaking my skirts. But it was no spider.

With a cry of disgust, I glared at the three men close behind me. A sailor, whose name I knew was Robert Waters, for I had heard the first mate shout him out of lethargy enough times, waved his poking stick while his mates howled with laughter at my distress as I rushed off down the beach.

I decided from then on I would avoid their like entirely, unless the captain or his mate was nearby to temper their behavior.

I nearly ran the rest of the distance across the beach, even though my palms sweat and a lump grew in my throat at the thought of another meeting with Mr. Powell of the foul mouth. In truth, he was no worse than many of the others. They would not speak so vulgarly in front of Mistress Horton or the other ladies. But a servant girl deserved no restraint.

Mr. Strachey seemed different, though, a kind man and uninterested in tormenting me or others, despite Mistress's warning that I should avoid him. My father had been that sort. Gentle, never profane. Then, of course, there were our governor and admiral, both older and refined gentlemen who commanded obedience with as few words as possible, often with no more than a simple nod of the head.

I knew little more about them, or any of the other passengers for that matter. A face here, a name there. Even Sarah was a stranger to me. We spoke a few words in passing; neither of us dared tarry long for fear of punishment.

But now I must face Thomas Powell again. Whenever I had visited his galley on the ship to fetch Mistress's food, he always was drenched in sweat and smelled of onions, beer, and grease. And his immense, strong hands frightened me more than I could say. Although he sometimes tried to get me to linger and pass a few words in conversation, I felt nervous around him and made away as soon as possible.

Now, even though I cared not in the least how I appeared before a common cook, I smoothed my skirts and brushed wisps of hair from my face, tucking them back into my cap to make myself more presentable.

I approached the thatched lean-to Gates's men had erected as a temporary galley on the beach. Thomas Powell stood at a stump-turned-chopping-block, wielding a cleaver, forearms slimy with fish guts. He looked up quickly when he heard me approaching, then away as if he'd already decided I wasn't worth his time.

I stood silent, watching him behead and gut one fish after another. Two swift strokes of the blade: Down the belly, scrape out the innards, toss the whole fish—head, bones and all—into his rescued iron cauldron.

Guts and blood spattered across the sand. A cloud of raucous seabirds fought over the entrails.

"Unless y're good with a knife, go away. I have no time for idle chatter," Thomas said without looking up.

"Mistress Horton wishes to know what our meals will be today."

"Fish stew," he said, "long as our good water holds out. Then just fish."

I peered into the briny mess of raw flesh separating from bones, floating in a murky liquid covered with a sludgy gray froth. "There is nothing at all to thicken your broth or sweeten it?"

"No flour. No vegetives or sweet herbs. No parsley, hyssop, pennyroyal, rue, mint, parsnips, carrots, onions nor anything but fish, lass. A fistful of peppercorns, yes, but that is all. Not even a handful of salt."

I giggled.

He looked up sharply. Then his eyes shot through with humor for just a moment before he lowered them to his labors. "Yes, well, salt enough in the cursed sea all around us, lass, but not of the digestible kind. We shall have to dry our own."

It seemed to me he spoke a good deal finer than most of the crew. I wondered if he, like my brothers, had been schooled.

"Maybe herbs grow wild here?" I ventured.

He laughed. "You won't be findin' me in that brush until Sir Somers returns with reports of savages, if there be any. Meantime, we'll not starve."

I nodded and turned away.

He said, "You are Miss Elizabeth?"

"Yes. Elizabeth Persons."

He nodded then went silent. After a moment I started to move away, but he called after, "Just tell your mistress it is fish stew for the day."

And so, I left him to his work.

Six

Ships are but boards; sailors but men:
There be land-rats and water-rats,
land-thieves and water-thieves.
—from *The Merchant of Venice*

*W*alking back across the beach, I stayed alert and watched all that was going on around me. If any man dared approach with pole, sword, or bare hand to assault me, I would see him in time and raise an alarm. I felt for the knife tucked within the folds of my skirt. I was glad I hadn't pulled it out to threaten the tar who had assaulted me with his dirty stick. Far better to keep it against more serious deeds.

Soldiers had started erecting another larger stockade above the tide line, near the edge of the trees. Several of the governor's men were building a cabin of sorts within it, thatched with the same palm fronds as topped Cook's shelter. No one appeared interested in my progress across the sand, but I was unready to let my guard down. I pulled my cloak around my shoulders. Though the sun was warm and I could have easily cast it off, it felt a welcome shield from unseen eyes.

Before I reached Mistress, a glint of something bright among the dunes caught my eye. I squinted into the sunlight. Mister Strachey sat among the grasses, ledger propped on his knees, writing. His earring, I thought, how bright it shines! It must be wonderful to be able to afford a bit of gold to pretty up dull old clothes.

I wondered if he kept count of the fish caught, or of the men who labored hardest against those who loafed in the shade. He had spoken of ideas and descriptions—but of what sorts? Was it a particular interest to him that the sand here was a peculiar pinkish shade, that the tallest trees had no branches but for their crowns, that neither fish nor fowl we'd encountered seemed fearful of men? Did he record our governor's and captain's bravery through the storm and write glowing words of praise for their bringing all one hundred fifty aboard safely to this foreign shore, losing not a single soul to the sea?

More troubling to me yet . . . whom did William Strachey report to? Was that why Mistress had warned me away from him? Was he a spy for the captain, the Virginia Company or, most terrible of all, for His Majesty King James? This was not inconceivable. Hadn't our neighbors, though they pretended to be our friends, spied for the queen when she was alive?

They had reported my father as a Papist. They had watched his execution, by Her Majesty Queen Elizabeth's decree, and then brought my mother cakes and ale and condolences, as if they had done nothing at all. I hated them. Hated their pretended regret and grieving.

Even as I stood watching him, Mr. Strachey's eyes lifted from his writing and turned in my direction. He neither smiled nor frowned. I wasn't even sure he saw me at first, so remote and impassive was his blue gaze. But as soon as I took another step, he sat up straighter and waved me over.

"What do you say, girl?" he called out. "Is this not a most remarkable adventure?"

I scowled. "An adventure, you call this calamity?"

"Truly, it is." He heaved himself up and strode down the dune, sliding in the sand but keeping his balance remarkably well, as if in his younger days he might have been an acrobat or player. "We read about such happenings—the great explorers and gentlemen adventurers, Sir Francis Drake and his like—but how can we truly understand what they have known without feeling the wind on our cheeks or the sting of the sea?"

"I have had quite enough of the sting of the sea," I said, making him smile. "But if I could afford adventurers' accounts and were able to read them, I would."

"You do not want stories of your own to tell your grandchildren one day?"

"I think I will not have grandchildren as I have no intent to bear children. Nor will I have a husband to make it otherwise."

"Truly? You wish to have no mate?"

"Never," I assured him.

"Why, girl?"

How could I tell him things of so personal a nature, of the terrors of my heart? One question always leads to another. There is peril in revealing too much to strangers, even to those we ought to be able to trust.

"I suppose if I did have children," I said to satisfy him, "I would tell them favorite tales from my own childhood."

"What tales are those?" he asked.

"Ones my father used to read to us."

Not from the Bible; that was for the priests. But there came a time when all of our priests lived in fear of the gallows. They fled to France or Spain, or went into hiding. After that we no longer had them to guide us spiritually.

I was very young and hadn't understood, back then, that my family might be in as dark a danger as the Holy Church's servants.

I closed my eyes against the memories and willed myself not to weep.

"My father read to us from *The Aeneid*. He said it was the most exciting story in all the world."

Strachey nodded. "Quite fine, yes. But Ovid was my favorite writer, in my boyhood." His voice had turned wistful. "And your mistress, does she read to you or tell you stories of her life?"

"Mistress Horton?" I let out a sharp laugh, then clapped a hand over my mouth, though too late. "Pardon, sir, she finds pleasure in her Bible, in silence, sweets"—I considered—"and in a perfectly pleated ruff."

His eyes twinkled, the creases at their sides deepening like sun's rays on the most brilliant day. "Ah, yes. But I cannot accept that you've no stories at all to tell me. Where did you live in London? What of your family? Are they country folk or city people? Craftsmen or farmers? Paupers or merchants?"

"There is nothing to tell," I assured him with a shrug I hoped was convincing. "My family is too common to be of interest to you or anyone. I have lived fewer than twenty years, and all of them on Three Needle Street in Cheapside. Nothing ever happens to someone like me."

He studied me for a moment, sighed his disappointment, and then looked away. "Everyone has stories. Go away now, since you won't amuse me."

"But, sir, I—"

"Leave me." He waved a hand in dismissal, no longer kind or inviting. I had angered him but did not know how.

As I walked away, I tried to think of other things, though the historian's cold treatment had wounded me. I had few chances for companions among our company, and he was at least interesting and willing to talk with me, not as a servant girl but as a person.

I put aside his harsh words and tried to think how to offer my mistress a better supper than Cook's tiresome turtle or fish soups. I had found some goodly oysters without much effort at low tide. Perhaps a simple oyster stew would do for her?

It was then, when no longer fretting over it, that the real reason for Mr. Strachey's irritation came to me.

I did have a story, of course: the tragedy of my family's demise. Somehow, he either knew my tale or sensed that I held back this terrible secret.

Yet I dared not call up dangers of the past for fear, as the wise often say, of their returning to the present. Superstition or not, I would say nothing of those grim days to anyone. Not even here in this remote place. Not even to Mr. William Strachey.

Spies, I thought. *Spies have always lurked where we least expect.* Why should they not lie in wait here too?

Elizabeth Person's Oyster Stew

Stranne new-dug Oysters, about two pails, saving their licker. In fresh water boyle one Onion, two blades of Mace. Throe in oysters and licker, and do gentle boyle more. Add in a goodly amount of butter, but that lacking change this for hog fat-backe to sweeten and flavour, with Flower suffice to thicken. Salt and Pepper to taste.

At the last, pour in a pint of thicke Cream. If cow's milk is unavailable, then goat's milk shall suffice. If not goat's then swine's. Oysters will turn plump and nice with curled edges.

Seven

I am amaz'd, me thinks, and lose my way
Among the thorns and dangers of this world.
—from *King John*

"Hogs!" came a shout from the woods.

The entire assemblage within our new stockade rushed to the gate to see the reason for the commotion.

Now ten days after the wreck, our company had been divided in two. The governor's men, and the few wives and servants they possessed, claimed the main island for their home, building cabins and soldiers' barracks upon it. Sir Somers's men and the remaining craftsmen, sailors, and settlers, as well as Mistress Horton and I, took for ourselves the next-smaller island. It lay across a narrow strip of water we called Somers' Strait.

Creating our little villages required great industry from all, but we were comforted to have shelter, though it be of the rudest sort. Even Mistress Horton seemed as content as she ever was, for Sir Somers had ordered a small cottage—*he* called it a cottage though it seemed little more than a hut— constructed for her alone.

"Is it to please her, or to put her at a better distance from his lordship?" Sarah whispered, a mischievous glint in her eyes as we passed in the yard.

"A little of both, I suspect," I said.

Thomas Powell was kept as Cook by the governor on his island, and there arranged twelve messes for each meal, feeding all of us from both islands. To break our fast, there was neither bread nor beer, and so we mostly ate a bit of fish in the mornings. Dinner came at noon for the officers, at one of the clock for those of lesser standing, and it was the main meal of the day. We supped at five and six of the clock, oftentimes nourished by the remains of the midday meal, though in lesser quantity. We seemed already to have established an order to our lives in exile.

But now, two of the braver of Somers's men were emerging from the wood, shouting and gesturing at what they'd found. A third fellow herded with a stick one of our she-pigs. Lumbering after her came a huge wild hog they must have collared after the brute was lured out of hiding by our dainty miss.

This monstrous good boar would make a fine feast, I thought gleefully. Three times the size of our own, he alone would feed the entire company for a day.

All gathered around hogs and herders, shouting questions.

"By the hundreds they forage in the wood," one of the beast's keepers shouted joyously. "They eat the berries off the palms and on the ground around them. We won't lack for meat, not ever we stay here."

Indeed, within a few days more fine news raised our spirits. Sarah came to me, as she often did, to exchange gossip.

"Sir Somers has made a complete plait of the main island and several of the lesser surrounding ones," she said. "My master was employed to assist him." She swelled with importance, as if it had been she who was elected to the important task.

"It will be our entire world for the time being," I remarked. Or perhaps forever? "Did he find any cannibals along the way?"

"No." She looked a little disappointed, as if her story had been pointed out to lack drama. "But besides the hogs he found birds so tame and curious they flew down to his whistle to investigate, landing on his head or nearby branches. Whereupon, with club or gunstock"—she stood up to demonstrate, swinging her arms viciously from side to side—"his men knocked them down and brought them by the dozens to Thomas for cooking."

I smiled. "Mistress will be pleased. The menu changes from fish to fowl!"

"Also," she continued, "turtles of immense size and number came onto the beaches at night, drawn by our fires."

These too provided excellent sustenance during the weeks and months to come—both in their sweet meat and from the eggs carried by the females. Their oil proved as good for cooking as for lamps to burn.

Only harmless creatures, it appeared, roamed the islands. No savages, witches, or human-devouring monsters lurked in the woods. Not even a single snake or vermin had been seen by any of our company.

It seemed in those first days that we had, by God's hand, found Paradise.

Paradise it might be, but I soon grew restless. I longed to roam the forests, glades and beaches, to see for myself the gentle creatures Sarah had described, free and alive, not stacked like logs as the turtles were, awaiting their butchering for our table. As necessary as it was that some die to feed us, it saddened me that so many should perish to our needs.

Two of our men working together through the night sometimes captured and slaughtered as many as fifty turtle, with thousands of eggs rounder and larger than a hen's. I saw fowl of all type killed by the score, each day more than before, to the point where we often had more to eat than could be consumed before it spoilt.

"Let all be advised," Governor Gates announced at our daily service, "that we shall limit our take of game to what we might comfortably use at one time."

But even with the wealth of provisions we'd discovered, the company soon tired of Thomas Powell's roast pig and watery fish and turtle soups. No, we'd never starve, but the gentlemen among us were accustomed to London dining and fine, complex menus, for which our ship's cook had no patience or proper ingredients.

One day, all of that, along with my life's course, changed.

Thomas Powell's Turtle Soup

Kille the turtle in daylight if Summer. (At night if of the Winter time.) Hang to bleed out, catching its juice to save for a Pudding. The next day, scalde it whole then scrape the Skinne off of the Shell with care to burst not the Gall. Breake shells and put pieces in pot. Lay by the Fins, Eggs, and delicate pieces. Put rest into pot with shells and as muche water as to feed the Company.

Boyle all up.

(Notice to cookes: Had these not been spoilt by the Storme, the following would now be added: Onions, Parslye, Thyme, Salt, Pepper, Cloves, Allspice.)

In the time of one glass before serving, it is necessary to thicken the brothe with Brown Flouer and Butter, but lacking these I macke do with adding the Eggs and Flippers and organs and, for Officers' mess only, a glass of our last Madiera.

Eight

Are not these woods
More free from peril than the envious court?
—from *As You Like It*

*A*dmiral Somers arrived at our door, knocked and peered in past me when I greeted him. "Good day to you, Mistress Horton. How goes your tatting?" He gestured toward the spools of thread and needle-thin hook she held, working a lace edging for her pillowcase.

"I can hardly see my stitches, so poorly do I sleep." She sighed, then seemed to remember her graces. "Come in, Admiral. Please, will you take refreshment? I have a little Corsican wine left to offer you, or my lovely hippocras if your taste is for something sweet." She flapped a hand in my direction, and I went for her cups.

Two small kegs of wine she'd kept in her chamber on

board *Venture* had been saved. Probably because, when so much else was being tossed into the sea, she lay unconscious atop the crate containing them.

The admiral might have been stepping into Horton Hall on Gracechurch Street instead of this rustic shelter that sweaty sailors had lashed together from palm fronds. He bowed graciously through the low doorway, looked around and pulled up a barrel as his chair. "Wine, if you please."

I poured the deep red wine for him, hippocras for her. Again pewter cups, for Mistress's delicate Murano glasses, prized by all fashionable ladies even over goblets of silver or gold, had been smashed to pieces in the wreck.

The admiral sipped his wine, nodded his approval and then took a breath as if in preparation for a difficult speech. "I have come," he said, "to beg of you a great favor on behalf of our stranded company." He reached for her hand and gave her his most charming smile.

I stood back and watched, most curious. For some reason, my stomach tightened into a knot, as if sensing that whatever he was about to say involved me.

She tilted her head in a coquettish attitude, thin, dry lips lifting at the corners, eyes sparkling. "Sir, whatever you may require, it is yours."

"I appreciate your sacrifice, madam." He nodded gravely. "It appears Mr. Powell has taken ill and is unable to prepare meals until he improves. The governor hopes that will be in a day or two."

Ill? Thomas, ill?

I moved a little closer the better to hear. Not that Cook was special in my mind, of course, but any sickness might spread with furious speed across the islands. The list of fevers, agues, plagues, poxes, pestilences and various forms of consumption that had coursed through London in my own short lifetime had taken away, some claimed, near a third of our populace.

Mistress lost her smile. She studied the admiral, her eyes narrowing. "I do not cook, sir."

"No, no." He laughed. "Nor would I expect you to, dear lady." He patted her hand, sipped his wine. To my dismay, his eyes flickered briefly toward me. "But the governor has ordered all able men from both camps to construct a proper shipyard. I do not wish to take any from their tasks to prepare food, yet all must be fed." He hesitated, as if searching for the right words. "I notice that your maidservant has little to do when she is not tending to your personal needs."

Mistress Horton appeared suddenly strained. "You would take her from me?"

"Only for a portion of each day. When you can most easily spare her."

I said nothing, the knot ever tighter in my stomach. I knew what this meant. I would have to work more than twice as hard, for the same compensation: a place to lay my head and a servant's scant meals.

"Elizabeth does not cook well," Mistress snapped. "She is clumsy and slow and would never do for you."

"A pity." For the second time since he'd entered the tiny cottage, Admiral Somers looked directly at me.

I lowered my eyes. Maybe I wasn't the best servant, not being bred to the task, but she was wrong about my being unable to cook. I remembered my mother's wonderful meals and our shared times at the hearth. If asked I could probably make as fine a Banbury cake or brown bread as she'd ever done.

"I can bake a loaf more than passable," I blurted out, pride making me want the admiral to know I wasn't simple and useless, as Mistress so often complained. "My mother, daughter to a baker, showed me the mysteries of tarts, loaves, pasties and cakes when I was but a young girl." By the age of ten I could turn out crusty peasant bread or flaky tarts. At my father's instruction I also had learnt to mix a potion to cure a headache.

"You've watched Cook at his cauldron," Sir Somers said.

I nodded. "Yes, sir." In fact, I'd seen no more of Thomas than was necessary to collect Mistress's meals, for something about the man made me wary, nervous, timid, but in a way that was very different from the way I felt around the likes of Robert Waters. Still, go to him I did, as Mistress disliked crossing the little channel between our islands on the ferryman's raft.

"Do you suppose you might do us a mess of Cook's good turtle soup?"

I had grown to loathe the blandness of Thomas's broths, but of course said nothing. Even when he once asked what I thought of his soup, I'd lied and said it was as good as any I had tasted.

I cast Mistress a quick, defiant look. "I can do as well," I told the admiral. *Better,* I thought.

"Good girl. We shall move some of Mr. Powell's equipment over to our beach so that you will not need to be far from your mistress." He turned to her. "When the girl is done with her morning chores, release her to prepare our sustenance. I do appreciate your sacrifice, good lady."

He kissed her fingertips, leaving her looking stunned and confused after he had gone. To refuse the admiral would have been unthinkable. But now she had been forced to surrender her one servant, even if for only part of the day.

"I suppose it must be," she murmured, lifting her chin with an air of brave suffering. "Perhaps little Sarah can be obtained to stop by and make my toilet?"

"I shall prepare your toilet before I leave each day."

"My collar must be laundered and ruff pleated."

"It will be done."

"And the sweeping—"

"Yes, madam."

She sighed deeply. "I shall report this problem to the Virginia Company on my return to England. Sending a single cook for so many is insufficient."

While completing her list of chores, I thought about cooking. How warm and safe I'd felt, even as a young child, standing on a stool beside my mother in our kitchen. She let me break the eggs. "You do that very well, Bethy. Not a shell in the bowl!" I poured fresh cream for pudding, mixed in plums and currents and forced meat. The luscious smells as the pudding steamed filled our sweet house.

I missed our hearth.

I missed my mother.

If she had lived, we might have kept my father's shop and our home above it.

I decided instead of making turtle soup I would prepare

a different kind of meal. Something of home and hearth, to comfort and soothe our troubled stomachs and anxious hearts. But since no shops existed on Somers' Island, and our supplies were near depleted, I would need to search out my own ingredients.

When Mistress nodded off on her pallet of palm fronds, I took my knife and a hemp sack for collecting whatever herbs or wild vegitives I came upon. I could count on being safe on my own, so early in the day. All of the men were employed at the boatyard, run by Mr. Frobisher on the main island. None were allowed to remain idle so long as our new boat needed building. And the wild hogs, the only other dangerous creature on these islands, could be avoided.

Indeed, I felt safer in Bermuda's wilderness than at the hands of any man. But when I passed by the hut where Sarah sheltered with the other women on our island, out she popped, wanting to know where I was off to.

I explained about my new job.

She glanced back at the rude, reed structure. "I'll be catchin' the Devil for it, but can I go with you? I can't stand another minute of their complaints, you know."

"Come," I said, "I can use the company."

We walked down from the stockade to the beach, where the men had caught in trammel nets and by line great numbers of fish, then restrained them in a pond for our later consumption.

"Slimey, awful things," Sarah commented, wrinkling her nose. "I cain't abide Cook's stinky stew."

"Don't worry, I know how to make better." Surprised at

my own confidence, I decided on the best of the snappers; then we continued on our way, up from the beach and into the woods.

It wasn't long before we came across no less than a dozen herbs of healthful and practical use, for my father had made many of these familiar to me, along with their medicinal properties.

"Chicory," I said, plucking a goodly bunch.

"What's that good for?" Sarah bent and tugged up several handfuls.

"Bitter herb for a fine sallet," I said. "But I can infuse it to treat our scabby, scaly skin." I pointed to the dry patches revealed on her arms where her sleeves had worn ragged and pulled up, our flesh having been so abused by sea and sun. "It also makes a nice tea."

To my surprise I found wild allspice growing on the southern edge of the wood, although Father had told me it was only to be found naturally in the West Indies. Its green berries, ground in a mortar, made a delightful seasoning for sweet or savory dishes. Consumed in quantity it slowed many dire diseases, though not the Black Death, for which there was nothing. As to the leaves, I would dry them as treatment for fevers. Adding them crumbled to a broth, they'd suffice for bay leaves, which I despaired of finding.

"There is a little lemon grass," I pointed out, "so good with poultry."

"How d'you know so much about plants, Lizzy dear?" She was shaking her head as she pinched off the slender yellow-green shoots. "I can hardly tell one from the other!"

"My father was an apothecary."

"He ain't no more?"

"He died."

"Plague I s'pose. Like me friend Mary." She sighed. "Weren't last summer the worst?"

My throat swelled so all I could do was nod. I tried to focus on the herbs and the life all around me.

A little further along at the edge of a field I spotted Alexander, whose seeds and grated root in a poultice eased painful joints. I offered a leaf to Sarah, and we munched as we moved on, while I considered Alexander even better for a sallet than chicory, perhaps with dandelion should I find any.

Deeper into the woods we came upon the tallest stand of cedar trees I'd yet seen, their berries hanging in clusters from the tips of feathery olive-gray branches. Leaving the lowest branches to the wild hogs, I reached up high and plucked as many of the tiny green berries as I could, filling one entire pail with Sarah's help.

"'Boiled down to a syrup,' my father used to say, 'cedar berries make a fine remedy for winter ailments.'"

"You think we'll be here that long?" Sarah asked, her eyes wide and nervous as a captured seabird's.

"Ships take time to build, and our brave *Venture* is gone to us."

I considered another use for the berries. Mistress's hippocras was all but spent, and there was no more ale or beer to be had. So I would steep the cedar berries in water and leave the mix four or so days to become wine. With luck this would satisfy her and make her sleep sounder at night.

Palmetto berries, rich and black and almost wheaty in taste; wild rhubarb; blue berries of a sort I could not name but tiny, sweet and tangy—all of these we took samples thereof. Fennel, though I could find it only in small quantity, should be enough to flavor my fish today. Infusions of the same, my father swore, purified the liver and provided a healthful tonic.

Lastly, Sarah discovered the prize of our day's search. "Look at that ugly thing!" she cried, laughing. "Is it an odd vegitive or what?"

"A fruit of some sort, maybe?" I approached the mother plant cautiously. I had never seen anything like it.

Long, dangerous looking spines covered thick, fleshy leaves; thus discouraging, I imagined, creatures from foraging upon them. Along the edges of some of the fattest leaves grew fist-sized fruits the shape of a Catherine pear in brilliant red and pink shades, and off of these fruits grew smaller purple berries. If I were quite vigilant and cautious, I found I was able to knock the whole fruits from the plant then scrape off the thorns.

Sarah looked on with a scowl. "You ain't goin' to try to eat that, is you?"

I gingerly bit into a berry, made a choking noise, and clasped a hand to my throat. When she leaped back in terror, I laughed and handed her one. "Try it. Even raw it is delicious!"

The fruits themselves, though juicy, were the texture of mulberries but more bitter. Still, I thought, if stewed and mixed with something sweet like honey, or boiled into a sugary jam, I expected they'd make a fine companion to our fish and pork.

And so we returned to our stockade, laden with edible

treasures to provide a grand meal for our men. I planned it in my mind as I peeled the prickle pearlets, contentedly sitting in the sun outside Mistress's little hut: Cedar-planked red-fish with lemon grass and fennel, palmetto berries in place of our beloved bread, and a sallet of bitter and sweet greens and barberries we had plucked while walking back to camp.

My mouth was already watering.

Nine

One fire burns out another's burning,
One pain is lessen'd by another's anguish.
—from *Romeo and Juliet*

*T*homas recovered his health, but things were never the
same after that. The governor and admiral determined that
ferrying either of their people across Somers' Strait for meals
proved too cumbersome. Thus, each community would
now obtain its own food from the larder, and by gathering
nature's bounty as its inhabitants could. But preparing two
separate sets of messes left us short one cook.

At first Admiral Somers appointed two of his guardsmen,
who claimed some acquaintance with the preparation of
victuals. But their meals were not as well received by the
men as mine had been. Mistress Horton refused to consume
anything at all they made after she ate a coddled turtle egg

that must have gone bad in the nest, sickening her near to death.

"I will have your cooking before theirs," she told me three days later, after her stomach had settled with the help of my decoctions of chamomile and mint. As if I were her last, most desperate resort. "You will find more of those excellent clams for us, Elizabeth."

"Yes, madam."

"And this wild mint for tea. It soothes my stomach."

Would that it soothed your temperament as well!

She had grown obsessed about her ruff and farthingale. The whalebones of the latter had become bent or broken in the turmoil of rough sailing and held her skirts not wide enough to please her.

"This would not do in court," she fussed. She never ventured from her cottage without being thoroughly pinned into her bodice and skirts, though she now appeared to me somewhat comically lopsided.

Her neck ruff had become dingy with grime and salt, and she required that I wash, starch it (though the only stiffener I must make from cassava root), pleat it by hand, and set it to dry in the sun to bleach and become suitably rigid, the entire process requiring half a day's tedious labor.

But the worst of her complaints had to do with her periwig. Whereas the officers had abandoned their periwigs for the more practical and natural arrangement of their own hair, she persisted in demanding her ornate, curled "hairs." She was growing a bald pate and refused to go out into the day without her tower of blond curls, tinted as it were to a bright yellow with marigold blossoms, arranged as elaborately as if she were attending court. Unfortunately, the hair had faded in the sun, becoming matted and tangled and caked with salt, so that no matter how I tried to comb or rearrange it the foolish thing came to look more like a petrel's nest.

As she never was happy with anything I did for her, I found excuses for escape.

Happily, I had discovered another source of herbs growing along a sunny hillside on the south shore of our island. I went there daily, with or without Sarah, saying I must return for the freshest mint. On each trip I found and gathered many other useful growing things: wild mustard seed, mullein, gingerroot, cow's tongue, chamomile, plantain, thyme, rosemary, mint of two sorts, field poppy, and father john.

What would not do for brightening our food, I employed as decoction, poultice, or infusion to heal sores to the gums, soothe and relieve Mistress's dry skin, to purge, comfort, or assist the body as a whole. I only wished I could have found a bit of precious saffron to strengthen my heart, aching so for my lost family.

Meanwhile, the admiral appointed four of his men to hunt and scavenge for as much food as the cooks required to feed us each day. Others of our party were to tend guard duty. And each day those not otherwise employed went off, willingly or not, to work on the ship all hoped to deliver us to Virginia.

In this way we became independent of our fellows on Governor Gates's island. Only on the Lord's Day did we all assemble there. Every man, woman, and child was required, under threat of dire punishment and public humiliation, to attend services performed by Master Bucke, our minister.

Orders, I suppose, that were necessary, for sailors are not by nature churchgoing men.

Aside from an inbred lack of godliness, some few of us had other reasons for not attending the king's worship, though I prayed the admiral would never discover mine. For how could I be sure that my father's cruel fate would not visit me here, even on this remote rock in the middle of a great ocean? But, at least for the time being, our governor was more concerned with food than defense of the monarchy's religion.

Somers' Island hunters stalked various fowl by night and fish by day. The cahow proved the easiest birds to catch, I heard the admiral tell Captain Newport.

"My men discovered if they went out by dark, whistling and shouting to make as much noise as possible, the curious birds came to them to investigate."

"And did they then shoot them down?" the captain asked.

The admiral shook his head. "We do not use our ammunition so lightly. No. The birds land on their arms and heads, whereby the hunters weigh them for the fattest and strike down with clubs those they wish to bring for eating, as many as a hundred in a night."

The men also continued to hunt the great green sea turtles, corralled many more wild hogs, dragged to shore fish of a size to equal two men, so that we lacked not basic nourishment. But our soldier cooks often turned good meat into tough, dry and tasteless pulp. And there was much discontent at our messes, some of our company disappearing into the woods from whence came the sweet smoke of roasting pig. Others found ways to disappear to the main island and sit a mess at our neighbors' table. Thomas Powell's trenchers, though not inspired, at least tasted like food.

I sometimes felt badly for the rude Mr. Powell. He did seem to try to please. But there being no flour, and so no bread, and no spices that weren't sullied by salt and damp rot, and no more sugar, he was unable to provide dishes as he and others were accustomed. Moreover, he seemed to lack natural ingenuity with food.

After one ill-fated meal of oysters in a watery stew, we heard of the governor's entire company falling sick and gravely incontinent all the night. No one died, but many swore they wished to. The governor blamed Mr. Powell and swore if he ever again poisoned his company, the cook would pay with his life.

And the governor was not a man accustomed to idle threat.

One morning, just before dawn, I was returning to our cottage, having relieved myself in the nearby glade designated as the lady's privy. The first streaks of new light shone apricot and plum over the eastern horizon as if painted by an artist's brush, and I looked up to see Mr. Strachey, sitting alone and absorbed in his journal.

"Girl!" he called to me, when I would rather have returned to my pallet for as long as Mistress might allow. "Come."

I approached warily, unsure of his mood. "Sir?"

He was still writing, eyes following the tip of his quill. "You never finished your story."

"Pardon, sir, but I told you there is none." None I wished to reveal. And anyway, why should a man who kept records of a sea journey be obsessed with a serving girl's life? Unless, I thought, his writing interests involved stories of another sort.

"You read. I've seen you."

"A few words."

"Servants are not taught to read at all. Therefore, you have, *or had*, another life before this one. I would have it." I said nothing. "Do you write also?"

I shook my head, growing more and more fearful at his inquisition. I knew how to make numbers and calculate them. It was one of the tasks my father gave me in keeping the accounts of the apothecary, for that had been his trade and our livelihood. The few words I easily recognized were those that appeared in his ledgers. Names of potions, of customers, or descriptions of ailments and soothing ingredients, and payments made by and for each.

"But you know how to hold a quill."

"Only to make my mark, sir." I felt a chill at each question. What did he intend to prove?

Spies. Beware of spies, Elizabeth.

Those loyal to my namesake, Her Majesty Queen Elizabeth, reported everything in the least suspicious to her court officers. And after her death—an event in which I secretly exulted!—we would be no less fearful of the evil gossips who brought rumors to King James's magistrates. But that was not the end of our worries. The Lord Mayor had his own spies, as did the Church.

Who had betrayed us? Which of our neighbors or customers or friends had seen my mother take her rosary from its silken purse and count off her beads? Even now the doubts gnawed at my stomach and made my chest tighten. She only ever brought out her rosary after dark and behind closed doors. But beads alone wouldn't have been enough to condemn my father. Someone had whispered to the Queen's ministers that they'd seen him give a few shillings to a frightened priest to help him flee London.

Conspirator! That's what they had called my gentle, loving father. *A threat to the Crown!*

He'd never harmed anyone—royal or beggar.

Mr. Strachey's blue eyes fixed on mine, as if waiting for the answer he wanted. I felt a chill. Held my breath. Did he wish to entrap me? Or were his intentions innocent?

"Tell me about your parents," he said leaning back against the powdery dune and closing his eyes. "You did have two?" Now he sounded playful, mischievous even.

I dared not let down my guard. "I wish not to speak of my family. Such talk brings back the pain of losing them."

"Then you would banish them from your heart forever? In not remembering, you forgo the joy of reliving their love." His mood ever changing, now he waxed gentle, caring. Did he act a part? One minute the jester, the next father confessor? "Tell me about them, girl."

It came down to this: to disobey a gentleman was unwise if not unlawful. Particularly since this one appeared a favorite of both Admiral Somers and our governor. Each seemed to welcome Mr. Strachey to his table; and he was free to move between islands at will, whereas others were not. A special privilege, but how earned?

I might create false details of my life to satisfy him. But never had I been clever or quick with a lie.

And if he went to Mistress, who knew the truth of my family's tragedy, she would tell him. The only reason, I supposed, she had kept my history to herself thus far was because she assigned no great importance to my life. She never spoke of my dead parents and siblings. Probably she assumed that nobody cared to hear my sad tale.

But there was another possible reason.

My story was no different than the miserable accounts of thousands of other Londoners, thus made ordinary by frequency. Not so much a tired tale as an unpleasant one. So many perished of the summer plagues or the cruel justice of the Tower, most people thought it poor luck to speak of either. Bad luck to speak of the awful Black Death. Worse to criticize Good Queen Bess's punishment of Catholics on the scaffold, a tradition her heir continued.

"Your parents, start there," Mr. Strachey persisted, his voice sounding lazy but nonetheless determined.

How little might I tell him without endangering myself?

Suddenly, the strangest of impulses came over me. Against all my mother's cautions and my own common sense, I wanted with an urgency close to desperation to speak of my lost family. Wanted to bring them back to life, as the historian had tempted me to do, if only in memory and words and feelings.

I closed my eyes, steadying my voice. "My parents are dead, sir."

"How?"

No, I dared not tell him. "I would go now, sir. My mistress—"

"—can well spare you, little pigeon. Come. Satisfy my curious nature. Unburden yourself."

If he was being cruel, forcing me to remember so that he might see my tears or hoping to entrap me, his calm eyes and softly compressed lips kept his intent secret.

I held my breath and whispered, "My mother died only last year of the plague."

"And you were spared?"

"I was, sir. I know not why."

"You lived in the same house and stayed with her as she suffered?"

My voice failed. I nodded.

"You weren't allowed to leave, is that the way it was? They nailed shut the door and windows until it had passed."

"Yes," I breathed. Quarantine kept the ravenous plague from spreading even faster through London's crowded neighborhoods. The Black Death was a most horrid, ugly way to die, feared above all other diseases.

"I tended to them . . . to *her* until she passed." I swallowed, or tried to, feeling as though a thorn had lodged in my throat. "May I go now, sir?"

His eyes had sharpened and focused on the tip of his quill, as if it were the past, the present, and all of the world to come. "Both your parents died then."

Should I at least attempt a lie? I sighed, looking away, burning tears filling, then brimming over my eyes. To lie about my father's death would be a dishonor to him.

But he didn't wait for my answer. "You had siblings."

"Two brothers, sir. And a baby sister."

"And they?"

"I alone lived."

"Not your father either?"

It would have been easy to tell him Father died by the hand of God. The plague. An accident. By the blade of a cutthroat in a dark alley. But it was by the command of a woman.

The same woman whose name I'd been given, no doubt in the hope of protecting us. A daughter christened, even if in the wrong church, after *her,* Elizabeth the queen, might be a talisman: *You see, we named our child after our beloved queen! Is this not proof enough of our loyalty?*

But I had failed them.

If Strachey were indeed a spy, I would eventually be found out anyway. He'd report me, and my life would end. But at least I should then join my sweet, gentle family in eternity.

"My father refused to renounce his faith." I stared down at my hands, feeling my damp cheeks flame then go cold, my hands tremble.

Renounce, renounce! warned my mother. *Say no more, girl!*

But it was the truth and I couldn't stop myself. "That was eight years ago. I was but ten years old then."

"He was Roman Catholic?" Strachey's voice sounded as tight as a lute string.

I had said too much. I was doomed.

"Sir, I beg of you. May I please be excused now?"

"The queen's guard took him to the Tower?"

"Yes, sir."

"For how long?"

"Three months, sir. They tried in many wicked ways to force him to admit he conspired against the queen."

"And?"

"He never did. He was a good man. An apothecary. He helped people when they ailed."

"Then, in the end, he was executed?"

I nodded.

I did not witness my father's end. My mother bade me stay

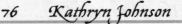

at home with my brothers and sister. But she went, wanting to be near him in his final moments.

I had seen other hangings. They were a part of our life in the city and, I suppose, in villages and towns in every other part of the world. The wicked were punished as their real or imagined crimes ordained—either lightly or more severely. Sometimes only a whipping or an ear lopped off in warning.

But there was no more serious crime than plotting against the Crown. One execution of a traitor differed little from the others, excepting that a gentleman might beg to be thoroughly, mercifully, hanged until dead or, if he were very lucky, shot. But those unable to move their sovereign to mercy suffered far worse deaths, their punishment drawn out into lengthy, complicated affairs before their souls were returned to God.

Dragged through the city behind a cart to the jeers of their fellow citizens, hung by the neck, but only partially so, the condemned often remained alive long enough to see their own bodies sliced open, bowels taken and burned before their eyes.

I watched one man live long enough to witness his own dismemberment. Only at the end was he beheaded. That was before I understood that not all judged for crimes were guilty, or evil.

My father's dear noggin rotted on a pike on London Bridge for over a year. Some days I could not bring myself to look at it, others I could not look away. I made silent prayer to him. My secret rosary.

My father. A good and fair man, who never spoke ill of another. He loved his family and thought a girl might learn numbers and even to write. He spent evenings with me and my sister, teaching us because the boys had school but we had none.

"My mother," the words burned my throat, "believed that my father was accused by neighbors jealous of his business. He was guilty of having the wrong faith, but never of deed or word against the queen." There, I'd said it. The truth.

For a long while I watched the angry orange sun burn its way up over the horizon as silent tears blurred its shape with the gray blue of the ocean. I thought Mr. Strachey might be satisfied now that he'd made me weep, dismiss me in disgust. But he did not.

"My cousin," he whispered.

I lifted my eyes to him and wiped away tears. "He was accused?" To be accused was almost certainly to be found guilty, of something.

"He sheltered two priests who had crossed from France."

I nodded, at last understanding. So we each had our secrets. The historian's family was Catholic also.

I wondered if the admiral knew that two Papists lived on his island. Did Mr. Strachey take precautions with his faith as I did? As my mother made me swear before she died?

"Show neither relic nor cross nor your rosary for them to suspect. Deny our faith, if you must. Stay alive, daughter!"

Until now, I'd done as she bade me. As she herself had done to protect us, her children. For with my father gone, if the queen's men found evidence of our faith in her house, all of us would be in peril.

But now, here on this island, the soot and filth and suspicion of London seemed far away. The air smelled clean, no

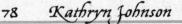

one pounding on our door, demanding entrance to search for evidence of real or imagined crimes. Sea terns and petrels screeched above us. A heron, tall and steel gray and elegant, waded in the shallows, slowly extending his long neck over the water's surface, pretending to be a tree limb and thereby tricking wary coney fish or fry to come within reach of his long beak. The lap of water against sand soothed. I dried my tears. There was much to love of this place, if only people opened their eyes to it.

"Come," Strachey said, standing and tucking his journal under his belt, "let us walk." He held out his hand and helped me to my feet. "So, after your father was gone, and years later your mother and siblings taken by plague, servitude became your only recourse." He spoke as if finally completing the riddle of me.

The sand was soft and molded my feet as I stepped along the tide's edge.

"Yes, sir. I might have tried to save my father's business, if I could, but after the plague did its work, the city commissioners ordered our building condemned. It was burned, along with all our possessions."

He sighed. "Yes."

The back of my throat flamed raw but, strangely, the tears had stopped and I felt a measure better. It had been a long time since my last confession. Ten Hail Marys for my past lies.

"I once had a son," William Strachey said, and I stared up at him. His eyes—such pain.

"He died?"

"He became ill. I wasn't there." A sound came from his

throat, not quite either cough or sob. "I was, in truth, not often *there*."

"You have a wife? Other children?"

He scratched his beard. He had stopped shaving and it was growing in a burnished copper. I thought a beard became him, and also, most strangely, made him seem more familiar, though why I couldn't say.

"I do. A wife and two daughters. They live in Stratford-upon-Avon, a little country village where I came from. Have you heard of it?" I shook my head. "It is in Warwickshire." He let out a long breath. "But my business is in London, and anyway, I prefer the city."

I was surprised, not by his choice of living arrangements, rather by his use of the word *business*. A true gentleman does not require work of any kind. He has funds at his disposal, an allowance or inheritance, lands and various properties furnished comfortably, with a staff to see to his needs and care for all he owns. Yet this historian carried himself as a gentleman of means while speaking of work that kept him in the city. Perhaps, I thought, his father, like mine, had been a merchant or craftsman, only richer and with property.

"What did your father do?" I boldly asked.

"He was a village glove maker, Elizabeth," he said.

I gave him a sour look.

"What?" he asked, laughing. "'Tis a respectable trade."

I frowned and kicked at the sand with my bare toes. I had long ago given up trying to mend my shredded stockings. "It's not that."

"What then?"

"Elizabeth. My name. I hate it."

"Because you were called after the queen, and it was *she* who took your father from you?" He was good at guessing what he wasn't told, but this was an easy riddle. "So you hate her, though Bess is now in the ground."

"Yes, I hate her." Hate seemed too simple, too tidy a little word for such dark, dark thoughts.

"You might change your name."

I laughed. "No one just changes their name."

"Some do, for a purpose." He sighed. "Change their name, their appearance, their entire life, if they wish."

I stopped walking, digging my bare toes into the sand, frowning at him. What nonsense was this? "People would accuse me of hiding something. They would ask questions." I cast him a challenging look. "As you have done."

And I still didn't know why. Why did he feel the need to examine me so? If he intended to report his discoveries to the governor or (at even greater jeopardy to me) directly to the king's minister in our company, I might yet find myself on a scaffold. Hadn't I just admitted to hating our "Good Queen Bess"? *They* might claim I now held equal contempt for His Majesty King James. Such thoughts and words had condemned hundreds before me. Traitors were regularly executed on far less proof.

"Now might be a perfect time for you to change your name, you see. We journey to a New World," he said. "Perhaps there you might become whomever you like, no more the serving girl."

I shook my head. Such a strange man. "Leave Mistress?"

"Why not? Leave the colony, if you wish."

Now *this* was madness. "And go off alone into the wilderness, to be at the mercy of savages and wild creatures yet undiscovered?" I shook my head. "That, sir, is a most foolish plan if ever I have heard one."

He tipped his head to one side and studied my face, looking a little shocked, as he had every right to be. A maidservant arguing with a gentleman! I shuddered at my audacity.

At last the hardness left his face; he sighed. "A fair point. Then with a husband to protect you."

I started walking again. "I will take no mate. No man is protection against plague, poverty, or human cruelty. And having once got him, grown to love him, his loss causes his woman all the more pain." Hadn't my poor mother mourned my father's murder with an agony equaled only by her own death throes?

Mr. Strachey kept pace with my lengthening strides, across the sand, his breathing coming louder for the exertion. "Why not choose a name you like? Make up another story for your family, if it makes you safe."

"That would be lying and a sin."

"Lying . . . telling a story . . . acting a role." He tilted his head, side to side to side, as if to say, are they not all the same? "Do you have another name? A middle or baptized?"

I rolled my eyes, a habit that usually resulted in a swat from Mistress. "I am Elizabeth Miranda Persons. Those are the only names I own or shall ever have."

"There you are!" He looked jubilant.

"Where, sir?"

"Miranda. You are Miranda! A perfectly suitable name. And when you marry—and you are close enough to marriageable age, I assume—you shall take your husband's family name and be a new woman yet again. Leave tragedy behind, Miranda, my child. Make for yourself a new life!" He looked entirely pleased with himself.

"It doesn't work that way," I said. "We may try to leave the past, but *it* never leaves *us*."

He knew. I could see it in the quick sorrow that flooded his eyes.

"No, it does not. Not the part that matters, those we've loved and lost."

I felt badly to have disappointed him, for selfishly, even greedily clinging to my sorrows when he would cheer me. I supposed it was just possible he wasn't a spy, only an old man trying to comfort an orphan, or to amuse himself.

I took a deep breath, willing my heart that had become a rock in my breast to beat again, loosening my clenched hands. *They are dead*, I told myself, *but I am alive*. To not feel blessed was an offense to God.

"Miranda was my grandmother's name. I loved her very much. It would please me to borrow her name."

"Miranda," he repeated then smiled. "I do fancy that."

"But how may I tell Mistress that I've changed names? She'll think I'm mad . . . or be suspicious."

"Ah yes." He stopped walking to stare out across the ocean, so blue it took the breath away and stole the brightness out of the sky, so unlike the iron-gray seas that lapped our dear old English shores. "That does require caution. We shall think upon it."

Ten

Speak what we feel,
not what we ought to say.
—from *King Lear*

Just as aboard ship, and with similar regularity, the admiral visited Mistress at her hut. He favored the soothing tea I brewed from mint leaves and chamomile blossoms I plucked from the edge of a freshwater pond. Sometimes he came alone, other days he brought Mr. Strachey or one of his officers. It was on one of those afternoons, in Mistress's rough abode, with the sea breeze whistling and whipping through the roof fronds over our heads, that Admiral Somers appeared unaccompanied and made the request that changed far more than my name.

"Good Mistress Horton," he began after I'd served my aromatic brew, "I've come to you on a mission today, for a purpose beyond our usual pleasant social conversation." She looked intrigued. "I'm sure you agree," he continued, "that our messes are now even less satisfactory than when Mr. Powell cooked for the entire assemblage."

She nodded her head, pursing her lips in dour contemplation of their shared problem. "Dear sir, have I not said so from the beginning? It is a miracle we survived the wreck at all, and another miracle that such poor victuals have sustained us. Why, I remember even the commonest of repasts in my home requiring no fewer than six courses, with no less than three meats, all prepared to perfection."

"Exactly," he said. "We cannot afford to continue as we have done, relying on soldiers, men who have no concept of the wholesomeness of food, to prepare meals for our company. They are as like to spoil as preserve it."

"Oysters." She winced in memory of her last illness, dabbing at her dry lips with her silk handkerchief. "And putrid turtle eggs. What shall be the next poison they serve us?" Every few days, some among us fell sick with stomach pains and runny stools; one could only assume it was the food.

The admiral gestured to me as I poured him a second cup. "Come and sit, Elizabeth. Take tea with us, won't you?"

Mistress's mouth snapped open, as if to object, only slowly closing as her expression took on a sly aspect. She said nothing.

"I have chores, sir."

Mistress looked from Sir Somers to me, back to him, to me again. "Oh, how you fib, Elizabeth." She let out a tittering laugh. "There is nothing that can't wait. Now, pull up a cushion here beside the admiral's barrel."

"Yes, madam." I didn't much like the calculating gleam in her eyes.

I dragged over a rescued flour sack stuffed with palm boughs, and sat between them—no tea for me as it was gone.

Clearing his throat, the admiral gave Mistress Horton an exasperated look. "I will come to the point, to avoid misunderstandings." He turned to face me. "Do you recall discovering clams and preparing a nourishing meal for your mistress the very day of our arrival on these islands?"

"She is a clever and practical girl," Mistress declared, although she had never before praised me.

"I can see that." He bit off his words in his impatience. "Miss Elizabeth, you also filled the shoes of our company's cook, Mr. Powell, for a few days when he was ill. Would you consider sharing your talents again but on a more permanent basis? I would have you prepare daily messes for our smaller company here on Somers' Island. What say you to that?"

Mistress's expression turned decidedly distressed. "Permanent basis? Become your cook, sir?"

The admiral gave her a tight smile. "For only a portion of each day, and not for my benefit alone, Mistress: for the good of our company. The men labor hard each day, building the ship that will carry us onward to Virginia. They need nourishing meals to keep up their strength." He looked to me. "What say you, girl? Are you up to the task?"

I didn't know how to respond. It seemed too important a duty. And anyway, one usually entrusted to a man.

"Mistress Horton?" he asked when no answer came from me.

Her lower lip quivered, her cheeks suddenly devoid of

what little color they ever had. "Providing for so many surely will require an entire day's labor. I would be lost without my dear girl in attendance."

"I might provide you with an alternate servant or companion," he suggested.

She coughed out a laugh. "From where, sir? You would pluck a maid from the sea as Diana rose upon her exquisite shell?"

He shrugged. "I have men little inclined to the hard labor of building a ship."

"A *man*servant? One of your filthy sailors in my cottage?" She huffed at the idea, handkerchief fluttering in agitated fingertips. "I think not, dear sir! I won't have them with their sticky fingers among my precious belongings, nor their . . . their *wandering* eyes and *obscene* thoughts in such intimate proximity to my person."

Now it was Somers's turn to look astonished. He flashed me a look.

I hid a smile behind my hand. The image of Mistress with her cracked old skin and gray hair eliciting passion, how delicious!

But he recovered quickly. "You are of course right. Too great a temptation there, dear lady." He smiled at her, peaking fingertips beneath his chin, narrowing his eyes in contemplation. "A compromise then. The company should have Elizabeth's services only for the middle meal of each day, that most critical to extending our laborers' energies."

"I—I don't know," she whimpered.

"Your girl will be free to tend to your morning toilet and

peaceful evening suppers. Does that not suit?" His voice, I noticed, had become firmer.

Mistress Horton sipped at her herb tea, no doubt gone cold by now, then rested the cup in her lap, for no tables had been rescued from our poor *Venture,* and our carpenters were too busy working on the new ship to make furniture. I could read confusion in her darting, worried eyes.

She had kept me to herself, enjoying the dishes I made for her without comment or compliment to me. But I wondered—had she boasted of my cooking to one of the officers' wives, declaring she simply would not eat the awful stuff provided at mess when her maidservant was oh-so-much-more clever with food? If so, she must now be regretting her loose words.

"I will release Elizabeth," she said with a sniff, "for three hours in the middle of each day while I take my nap." She pressed her thin lips tightly together, clearly unhappy with the arrangement but realizing she could cut no better deal. "That is all I can possibly spare of her."

The admiral nodded, glancing at me. "Is this enough time for you, Elizabeth, to provide hearty messes for our company between noon and two glasses past?"

I stared down at my hands. Another job. More and harder work. But it also meant a measure of freedom: time away from the dark little palm-frond hovel. Time away from Mistress's constant plaints and demands.

"I will try, sir."

"Good girl." He stood up to leave.

Mistress Horton waved a regal hand over their cups, now

sitting empty on the dirt floor, as if dismissing them to wander away under their own power. I picked them up and turned away to wipe them out with a rag while she walked the admiral to her doorway, a courtesy she rarely granted anyone, preferring all food, objects, and visitors come to her.

"If the girl requires more time to feed us," I heard the admiral say in a low voice as he passed her by, "you will give it her."

Eleven

And men sit down to that nourishment
which is called supper.
—from *Love's Labour's Lost*

*O*f course I wished to please the admiral and make him glad of having chosen me for such an important task. I would work hard at heartily feeding our Somers' Island inhabitants. But I confess the sin of conceit also inspired me. I yearned to better Mr. Thomas Powell.

Strangely, I wanted to show *him*, even more than the admiral, that I was no ordinary serving girl, and was at least as important and respectable as a ship's cook.

The little gifts my parents had left me—Father's remedies and herbal potions, Mother's lovely fragrant dishes—they lived with me, in heart and memory. Why should I not share them with others? Why remain the meek, invisible maidservant? Hadn't the admiral offered me a chance to be more?

Besides that, Thomas deserved to be put in his place. Sarah had told me that the first day in our islands he had spoken haughtily of my sweet little clams: "Any street wench," said he, "might scrape cockles from a pier."

Ha! He is not so clever himself! I thought. Mr. Powell still cooked for the governor's men on the main island and (so my friend Sarah again reported) would take no criticism of his receipts—many of which relied upon ingredients no longer in our larders—or their bland results. She complained that his gravies where thin for lack of flour to thicken them. He rarely offered any kind of vegetives. His stews were flavorless, devoid of the accustomed herbs and spices, all washed away in the storm.

I was determined to show him, and all of our company, food well cooked and of such delicious varieties as our islands provided. (So clever are the traps laid by Pride that I never saw the danger in my plot.)

In place of the one dish Thomas offered at each dinner, as our midday meals were called, I would provide three: a soup, a meat course, and vegitives. If possible, there would also be a sweet.

To thicken my broths and provide a substitute for our accustomed breads, I consulted our naturalist, Mr. Crispin. He had found on the main island a lovely clump of arrowroot, which he'd dug up for study and now gave to me. "And here, see I've noted it in my journal, the location of a goodly sized field of wild grain."

"Where?" I asked.

"Unfortunately, it's neither hard wheat nor rye." He sighed. "So Cook has no interest in it."

"But even a lesser grain might still produce a flour of sorts."

He nodded. "I do not see why not. But it must be milled. And how one might manage that here, without a proper millstone—" He shook his head. "I doubt the governor would relinquish any of his carpenters to build you a mill while the keel hasn't even been laid for our ship."

I decided to worry about millstones later. For my father I had ground minerals and chemicals harder than any grain using simple mortar and pestle. The limestone of our islands would provide ample grinding tools, even if the process might prove slower.

I found the field our naturalist had described. The grass sprouted tall and fine, delicate brown stalks topped with plump little heads waving in the wind. They appeared to be a variety of oats—sea oats? Whatever type of grain it was, it had not been at seed when we first arrived on our blessed islands. But now, after many fine days of sun and just enough rain to keep the stalks from withering, the strange grass offered a generous harvest.

I brought Sarah back with me, and we gathered as many of the seed heads as we could. "Bread," she sighed, "oh how I dream of a lovely fresh brown loaf! Promise I'll get at least a bit of crust?"

"You shall, as payment for your labor." I smiled at her.

Later, I worked alone through the night at freeing the chaff. By morning I had ground all of the delicate kernels between two flat, black rocks. I added fresh rainwater and kneaded a coarse but pliable dough; then, having no leavening, I cooked savory flat cakes until they crackled over the fire.

These I served to the admiral and his officers along with succulent spit-roasted wild pig. To accompany the meat I offered a compote of baygrapes I had found growing on a leathery-leafed tree overlooking the neighboring cove. Sweetened with wild honey I had discovered in a tree hive on one of my earlier treks into the wood and asked two sailors to harvest for me, the fruit was as delicious as any I'd ever tasted.

It was a simple meal, but the men devoured each course with relish. And the sight of bread on their table, although unrisen, was met with shouts of joy, for we'd had not a bite of bread of any kind for too many weeks to count.

"I am very well satisfied," the admiral told me, at the end of the meal, as I wrapped left-over meat in soft green palm leaves for Mistress Horton. "What do you propose for our evening meal, Miss Elizabeth?" Mischief twinkled in his eyes.

"You do recall my mistress releasing me for only the one meal each day, sir."

"I do."

"She won't allow me even a quarter more of a glass away from her, I'm sure."

"I know. It was only a wish, the meal was so fine." He sighed, looking almost a young man even with his white hair.

I thought it strange that he, an admiral in His Majesty's Navy, should be reluctant to order an old woman to release her servant to him. May be her wealth was that critical to the company's continued ventures.

He spoke again, his mind evidently still on food. "Cook has learnt preparation of turtle eggs and hogback. He has taught my men to fry up a passable batch for our breakfasts. But how I dream of fine, plump sausages, Elizabeth." He smiled, wistful.

My father had also loved a good sausage. I tucked away that thought. It stewed within me for weeks before I did anything with it.

Elizabeth's Baygrape Jelly

Pick both green and ripe Baygrapes, in equal amounts, and boyle until soft. Press out all Juice and strayne through coarse cloth, muslin or hair. Add a teacup of honey and boyle again, skimming away foam. Let set until jelled, covered to keepe away the bees.

Twelve

O tiger's heart wrapp'd in a woman's hide!
—from *King Henry VI, Part III*

An early November morning bloomed sunny and dry after five days straight of rain and winds that waged a war in my poor head, reminding me of our tempest at sea. I had not seen our historian during any of these fierce days and nights, except for a few brief glimpses at mealtimes when he came silently to fetch his food and take it away with him back to his shelter, to eat without companions. He appeared solemn, brooding, as apart from us as if he were the only soul on the island. I would not have known he was the same gentleman who had entrusted his secrets to me.

The elements stayed me from my accustomed searches for edibles. This dry, sunny day was my first chance in many to wander the island, looking for ingredients to add to my dishes. I sharpened my knife on a whetstone, took a pail, and went off to hunt for something new and tasty.

The first treasure I found was roots from a cassava plant, which I hoped, for its starchiness, would give me another substitute for bread than the pitifully small harvest of grain. It seemed unfair to serve our officers only and have nothing of even a crust for the rest of our people. Although as promised, I had saved a generous portion of that first flatbread for Sarah.

A fine crop of mushrooms sprouted along the forest edge. I was overjoyed to find them of a respectable size. They resembled a plump woodland variety from home. But it was difficult to know, with mushrooms, which were edible and which deadly. So many fungi here were unfamiliar to me.

I nicked a bit of one cap, held the sliver to my lips and waited. No warning tingle came. I placed it beneath my tongue and held it there. It tasted sweet and fine, of nuts and fern fronds. I cautiously chewed, waiting to swallow so that I might notice any ill effects. When none came, I swallowed it down.

No dizziness, gripe, or distress.

I harvested three more of only this one kind and noted their location in my mind.

If neither cramps nor other unpleasantness troubled me, I would eat a full mushroom the next day. Then wait three days. My father had taken me picking, and this was his means of eliminating an unfamiliar, poisonous breed.

I found and dug up more arrowroot for thickening my stews and puddings.

Although I'd easily learned to milk our domestic sows,

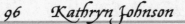

the wild breed of pig did not welcome this process. But with help from a few sturdy sailors to hold them down, I could express rich, creamy milk from our captured she-hogs. My stomach growled softly at the promise of a luscious custard.

Palmetto berries I added to my pail, small and seedy but ever so sweet. I thought to sod them up into a glistening, rosy jam for spreading on my next batch of flatbread, as a surprise for the admiral.

I turned toward what I'd come to think of as home after these few months on our little island. A rustle in the grasses behind me brought me up sharp.

I listened.

Wild hogs could be dangerous when angered, and I had been stealing their favorite berries. I turned slowly, a shiver of apprehension tickling between my shoulders.

It was not a hog but a man. Robert Waters.

He grinned awfully, showing yellow teeth, his filthy hair hanging in long, dark strings about his face. He smoothed it out of his eyes. "Ye'll be wantin' a hand there, Miss, with that heavy pail."

"No, sir." Neither master's mate nor boatswain, quarter-master, tradesman, or gentleman, he deserved no such courtesy. But I was alone with him, and that in itself, not to mention his handiness with a stick at my skirts, made me nervous. "I am well able."

"Then I'll 'company ye back to yer mistress," he said.

"I can find my own way. Thank you." I avoided his dark eyes and stepped past him.

"Pope's bitch!" he shouted after me. "Not good enough for us, are ye?"

My body went cold, shoulder to heel.

How had he heard of my faith?

Mistress knew of my family's link with the enemy faith. It was one way she sealed my loyalty. But she wouldn't have passed a word of any sort to a common sailor. Mister Strachey, he knew because I had let him wheedle it from me. But how could he not realize, after seeing his own family's tragedy, what damage such news could do if trusted to the wrong ears?

I gritted my teeth, moving a faster pace, daring neither to look back nor spare the breath to answer him.

The end of the woods came in sight. Blessed sunlight beckoning. Shallow breaths. *Faster, faster, Miranda!*

Footsteps crushed leaves behind me. His steps, now a run, as a cat springs just before it pounces on a mouse.

His hand clamped my shoulder, spinning me around, forcing me to a stop. My breaths, deep and whistling, nearly brought our breasts to touching and, though I tried to fall back and away, he held me fast.

"Ye think the admiral's pleasure with a little crust o' bread makes ye important?" he sneered.

"No, I—"

"Ye think he can protect ye?"

"The admiral will punish you"—I gasped, his face looming closer still—"most severely, if he knows you put hand to me."

He was shaking his head, looking amused. "Don't go choosin' yer master yet, dearie. Things may change."

I had no idea what he meant. I only wanted to be away from him. "My mistress. She expects me."

He laughed loud, spittle dribbling from his cracked lips.

"All over the islands ye roam while the old sow sleeps. I been watchin' ye. She won't miss her girl. Not fer a good while." His free hand slid behind my neck and squeezed, pressing forward.

The pail fell from my fingers. I raised a hand to slap him away, but he caught it in his hard, sun-blistered paw. His eyes, dull and black as mud, laughed at me.

I struggled.

But he was stronger. He fell on me, his weight dragging me down, down to the musky smelling ground. Straddling my waist he sat upon me.

I couldn't breathe for his heaviness on my chest. His hands played freely with my helpless body through my woolsy shift, squeezing, pinching, bruising.

He reached around and behind his hips, dragging up my skirts before spreading himself over me.

My screams seemed only to urge him on to his dirty task. Struggling felt futile, causing me more pain than him, I was certain. My efforts only managed to delay his attempts to pull his member from his britches. I braced one arm between our bodies, feeling it might splinter any moment under the force of his weight.

My free arm I flung wide, feeling frantically for my spilled pail, and what had been in it. Fingertips scattered berries, roots, mushrooms, herbs then, finally, brushed a familiar wooden handle.

He was still struggling with his britches, paying heed only to keeping me pinned, my hand beyond his vision.

"Leave me!" I screamed. "Or cut you, I will!"

His eyes skittered left, right, then above my head to my good, sharp knife.

"Oh my." His cunning gaze mocked. "'Tis a big one, ain't it?"

It's a game to him, I thought. *He thinks I'm playing, or incapable.*

Terror spun itself into fury, clawing its way out of me. I slashed at his ugly face.

He fell away, rolling off of me a gnat's breath ahead of the knife's arc. But the blade's tip ticked his cheek, drawing a bead of blood that clung, trembling between whiskers before trailing a thin red line down his sunburnt cheek. Kneeling in the grass, he watched as I scrambled to my feet and backed away.

I should have run but feared turning my back on him. He stood up, pressing a grimy hand to the tiny wound, his wicked smile gone. At least, I thought, he might take this as a warning. He might now leave me alone.

I held the knife straight out before me with both hands, sucking in raspy breaths, backing away a step. Two more. Still another.

He looked down at the ground, his eyelids lowering as if in defeat, and I thought I had won and might yet escape. But when his sooty eyes ever so slowly opened, the gaze that rose to meet mine was cruel, resolute.

There was no time to react. He dove at me, seeming not to take any steps at all, rather flying across the ground with the growl not even of an animal but of a demon from the very bowels of Hades.

Before I could run, he struck the knife from my hands, knocking me to earth.

No amount of howling, kicking, scratching, or spitting dissuaded him. I had all but given up hope when, as if conjured aloft by a magician's hand, his body rose above mine.

Brushing the web of tangled hair from my face, I saw we were no longer alone. Two men stood in the beaten-down grass of the clearing above me. Mr. Strachey and Thomas Powell.

Thomas's oak-trunk arms had hefted the sailor aloft. He tossed Waters, cursing and flailing, to the hard ground with no hint of gentleness. Mr. Strachey bent down beside me, reaching toward my naked shoulder.

I flinched, covering myself, for I knew not his intent.

Didn't animals steal each other's prey? Why should not a man, they being creatures driven by lust?

Mr. Strachey frowned as if offended by my reaction and stood away. Replacing the strap of my shift on my shoulder I tugged down the hem of my shift, then accepted the hand the historian held out to me. He eased me to my feet.

"Miss Elizabeth," Thomas asked, scowling darkly at Waters before turning back to me with a pained expression in his eyes, "are you . . . ? He didn't . . ." The big man fumbled for words, never finding them.

The heat of shame rushed into my face. Shoulders and limbs bared before three men! I had by now repaired myself, but still could not look him in the eyes.

"I am well enough, thank you." But I could not stop trembling, and my stomach threatened to heave up, so shaken was I by what had happened.

I made myself busy, retrieving my spilled pail, scooping berries, now dust covered but still firm and usable if washed, back into it on top of the mushrooms snuggled in its bottom.

Robert Waters tried to stand, but Thomas kicked his feet out from under him, sending him sprawling again. The way he landed might have broken his nose.

"You are missed from the yard," Thomas hissed at the sailor. "The admiral's men search for you."

"Whose right is it, I ask, to order us 'bout?" Waters coughed out dust, wiping blood and sweat from his face onto his sleeve. "Not a cook's, I'd say. As to yer darlin' admiral,'tis his fault we're wracked upon this rock, not mine. Let him build his own bloody ship."

"You, like every man on board, signed a contract with the Virginia Company," Thomas said.

"Them's papers is fer Virginia. Ye mightn't a noticed, this ain't no king's colony." He cackled but fast sobered. "Treat us worse'n slaves, they do, workin' us to death by day, keepin' us from our pleasures by night." He cast me a hungry eye. "We ain't never gettin' to their blessed colony." He spat in the dirt, eyes wild, mouth twisted and vicious as a tusked hog's. "Contract is broke. I'll do what pleases me with my time."

"Then you won't be eatin' with us," Thomas said, his face bright with anger. "See how long afore you starve, man!"

Waters exploded. "I have me rights to the ship's stores, like any man aboard *Venture!*"

"Not if you don't work for them."

Mr. Strachey stood silent and back from us, glancing first toward Waters, then at Thomas, finally at me—detached yet interested, as if he were enjoying a scene in a London play.

Waters spun and curled his lip at me. I stood even straighter and did not step away. His hands knotted and worked at his sides, as if gripping, kneading, tearing something. My flesh? Thomas's throat?

Then, with a snarl and shake of his head as if dismissing us all, he whirled and marched away.

Thirteen

My master through his art foresees the danger
That you, his friend, are in...
—from *The Tempest*

*M*y two saviors observed the sailor's retreating back while I tried to calm myself and regain my breath.

"I do not like this talk," Strachey said. "It is mutinous."

Thomas nodded solemnly. "Others talk too. I hear 'em at mess. Some think as he does. One Stephen Hopkins, I hear, gathers like-thinking men around him." He paused. "Some call him a Brownist, as he argues chapter and verse with our minister and would turn our folk away from the king's church. If enough break with our company, there will be too few men willing to finish the boats."

Boats? I thought. "Is it not just one?"

"Two smaller than our *Sea Venture*," Mr. Strachey murmured. "Our head carpenter thinks it will take too long and be too difficult to build another single craft large enough for all of us."

"Why would they not want to finish the boats?" I swept up the salvageable remains of my herbs, glad to be discussing anything other than my humiliation, though every part of my body ached from the struggle with the disgusting Robert Waters.

"The dissidents wish to remain here," Mr. Strachey explained. "They say the conditions and work in Virginia will be even harsher than here. Some crewed with Captain Newport on his voyage to Jamestown last year. They tell the others there is little to eat because the settlers sent there were not farmers but gentlemen with little practical sense of growing things. The hunting is difficult, the insects as large and ravenous as bats, the savages dangerous and unpredictable."

All of his watching, listening, and note taking evidently had paid off, for I had heard none of this disturbing talk. But then, why should I—closeted with Mistress day and night? Even my few hours of freedom to prepare noontime mess kept me separate from my fellow islanders, at work over my fire, scouring the fields, shore, or hills for little gifts from nature with which to impart satisfying flavors to my food.

"Come, Miranda, my girl, are you together enough to walk back to the stockade without help?"

Cook gave him a puzzled look, but it pleased me that the historian had used my new name. "I am fine now, as I have said, thanks to your and Mr. Powell's timely arrival."

Out of the corner of my eye I saw Thomas reach out a

hand, as if to offer a comforting pat on my shoulder. But he drew it back when I turned to face him and our eyes met.

Don't! my look told him.

"Good then," Strachey said. He started off across the field, Thomas beside him, glancing back at me now and again, as if to make sure I was still there.

"If mutiny is in the hearts of the likes of Waters," Thomas began again, "our officers have reason to worry about more than unfinished ships."

The historian nodded his graying head. "These are dangerous times, my boy."

But aren't they all dangerous, William Strachey, for people like you and me?

I trudged along behind them plucking a few chamomile blossoms as we went, trying to ignore the shaking in my limbs, weakened by my struggles. In truth, I had never been so terrified, and I still felt the fear cramping my body. But thinking about how terrible things might become for our company if the Brownist provoked many of our men to a rebellious cause took my mind a little off my discomfort. If they succeeded in thwarting the building of the ships, we might forever be stranded here on these islands, to me a fate not so detestable, for what else did I have in this world? However, such a plot would not be tolerated by the governor or our admiral. And failed mutineers faced but one fate—the same punishment as for conspiracy against the Crown.

How long, I wondered, before we saw a gallows erected in our Paradise?

Bermuda Cassava Root Bread

Scrub clean with water and cut away outside skin of a large root. Scrape the flesh with grater made from a board driven through with wide nails. Press out the shredded flesh into a bag of haircloth, as you do Verjuice, then spread the grated roots to dry in the sun.

Grind dried root in mortar until it resembles meal, neither kneading nor adding water as you do for dough. Strew on two or three flat stones and bake over a little fire for one half of a glass. Turn three or four times to bake through.

Serve with palmetto-berry jam or Baygrape Jelly.

Fourteen

An honest tale speeds best being plainly told.
—from *Richard III*

With the lusts, conspiracies, and the unpredictable nature of men casting a pall over the islands, I postponed my journeys out of the stockade for safer days. Even within camp, I kept close by Mistress and within sight of the admiral's guard for protection.

One would not have thought a shriveled old woman offered much surety, but the sailors and craftsmen appeared to fear her even more than our stout marines.

Sarah, who loved good gossip, said one day, "Don't you know, your Mistress Horton has great influence in His Majesty's court? I heard my master say so."

"But London is so far away," I reasoned. To communicate with our mother city was impossible and would remain so until a ship was built sturdy enough to carry word of our fate back to England or we met up with an England-bound vessel. "What power can His Highness have here in the middle of the ocean?"

Sarah considered this as she scaled fish for me. "Perhaps some of the sailors hope to find their way back to London. If they can make the journey, so could a letter from your mistress."

Yes, I thought. A letter of censure from Mistress Horton might be enough to cause a seaman's arrest, imprisonment, or even a tortured death. Less had caused my poor father's end.

And so, within the first months of our struggling ashore on the Isles of the Devil, I had learnt that treacherous thoughts, plots, secrets, and devilments lurked in the hearts of my fellow castaways.

Yet even had I foreseen the tragedies yet to come, I do not know that I could have stopped them.

After several weeks, snug within our little compound on Somers' Island, my restless nature drove me to again take risks. I dared venture along the beach and to the edge of the woods in search of new additions to our larder. However, I still avoided the men with hooded eyes, who pointed me out to their companions, their mocking laughter and rude, smacking lips setting my nerves to quivering.

It was on one such day, as I took a wide route around a small group of men hauling firewood, that I found William Strachey sitting on the next beach over from our encampment. I had a moment to observe him before he became aware of me.

He was a delicate man with thin wrists and long fingers, holding his quill as if it were an artist's brush, drawing swift, decisive strokes across the pages of his journal. More gray showed through the red-gold hairs in his beard than when we'd first arrived in the Bermudas. His eyes seemed to me sad, or perhaps just distant and thoughtful. As I approached, though, they shone as a young man's, alert and bright and blue as the azure water lapping the beach.

I wondered what he did with all his hours of solitude, for he was often out of the stockade and away on his own. Did he note the tides, the phases of the moon? Perhaps he listed each of the many orders given by our admiral, the governor's dictates, Master Bucke's daily admonishments that we turn our backs on the Devil's inducements toward sloth and palm wine and labor all the harder. As our historian, it was his job to keep a record of all we experienced.

Feeling bold and mischievous, I dared creep up and look over his shoulder at his recordings. But what I saw resembled nothing I had imagined.

The writing was short lines of poetry, shaped by his hand then scratched out and replaced, only to be blacked out again by a ruthless sweep of his quill. He had already printed his initials, WS, at the end of the last line, although the poem was incomplete with words missing.

As I'd told him that day on the *Venture* before we wrecked, I did not read, at least not as a schooled person. But some words were familiar to me from watching my father read to us in the evenings, and other words' shapes and positions among their slender black fellows on the page hinted at their meaning. What I recall of the unfinished verse, to which he was still adding, scratching out, muttering over in dissatisfaction, looked something like this:

> *As does the doe her fawn in safety keep*
> *So do I _____ o'r my _____ daughter*
> *And wait fair chance to reap a vengeance steep*
> *On he who usurps . . .*

He snapped shut his journal, looking up and out over the sea, his expression closed, eyes hardening.

I held my breath, my heart beating painfully in my breast. Caught!

I swallowed. "Beg pardon, sir, for intruding on your peace. I was curious and—"

"You don't intrude, Miranda."

I smiled. All these days, he had remembered the name I'd chosen. The name that made of me a new woman, and gave me hope.

"Have they sent for me?" he asked, sounding unhappy at being called away from his daydreams. For now I knew he was not about his work, only playing with words.

"No, sir." I felt suddenly foolish for the request I'd been about to make. "I've come on my own behalf."

"Well then?" He looked at me, not critically, but with some little impatience.

I plunged on. "I would like to venture out to the marshes,

then over to the main island in search of vegitives and herbs."
I hesitated, not wanting to remind him, or myself, of my
degradation at Waters's hands. "But I—"

"You wisely seek a companion."

"Yes, sir."

"You trust me?"

"I do, sir." I drew a breath. "But I see you are engaged
and—"

"It is no matter. Time here slips by at an easy pace.
And"—he yawned, stretched, and then smiled as he stood
up—"adventure is welcome and real in this place."

"Why would anything that happens not be real?" I asked
and turned back up the beach toward the wood.

"When it is of the mind, of the imagination." He fell into
step beside me, journal tucked under his arm. His boots
slid against the sand, losing half a pace for every two he
achieved. I walked barefooted, curling my toes into the sand
for traction.

"I have no time for imaginings." I sighed. "There is too
much work to be done."

"More the pity, girl."

We walked for a good mile up and over rough gorse,
through wood, then down into swamp and swill. Mr.
Strachey stood silently by while I filled my pail with this
and that. When I couldn't identify a plant, fruit, or root, he
sometimes supplied a name.

This reminded me: "You grew up in the country."

"Yes."

"But you said you chose to live in London?"

"That is where the work is . . . was."

I asked the question I'd thought of days before. "I did not know gentlemen ever worked."

Seeming distracted, or thinking hard on some issue, he did not answer.

"Oh, good," I said, stooping to pluck sprigs of lemon grass. "This I will use in today's meal."

He stopped and stared down at me. "Everything is work for you. Do you never stop to entertain yourself?"

"How should I, when I have Mistress to satisfy as well as the feeding of all of the admiral's men?"

"You must keep some moments to yourself."

I had no answer for that. In truth, I fell onto my pallet each night in utter and absolute exhaustion, without the strength to think of anything at all.

"Entertainment lightens the heart, replenishes the soul, makes one"—his eyes turned knowing—"forget the pain."

The way he studied me made me suddenly uneasy. "I told you, there is no time for anything but doing my chores." How irritating he was today.

I marched on. So did he.

"Before you went into service"—he fixed me with a gaze that let me know he was intentionally avoiding the mention of my parents' deaths—"what sort of life did you lead?"

"It seems very long ago. I do not remember."

"Only one year," he reminded me.

One year since the Crown burnt our house to the ground after the plague did its work, with all I had loved in it.

"I do not wish to talk about this."

"You were reading my journal back there on the beach. Therefore, you have been schooled, unusual for the daughter of a tradesman."

"My father, sir, he believed a woman should be able to read and write. My mother encouraged us to learn."

"Why?"

I was unnerved by his questions. Was he trying to trap me in some way I didn't yet understand? "I don't know."

"Those of the Roman church do not read the Bible. They are dependent upon their priests."

My nerves pricked, warning of danger. Talk of religion had killed my father, and many others besides. Mr. Strachey had hinted at his own ties with the old Church, but he might have lied to ease my tongue. It was as risky to speak of a faith other than His Majesty's as it was to praise our enemies, the Spanish, or to excite treachery against the Crown.

"My father was practical," I said at last. "In order for me to figure his accounts, I needed to read a little. My mother liked poems and stories, but mostly plays. She came from a landed family who taught their daughters as well as their sons." I hoped these details might satisfy him at last.

He went very still, as if listening to meanings heard between or beyond my words. "Which sorts of plays? Dramas? Comedies?"

"All, I think. Histories too. She saved up coins and bought a quarto of Marlowe's most popular play. She read it to me then took me to see it at the Rose."

"You saw Marlowe's *Tamburlaine*?"

"I did, sir."

"And do you recall how you found it?"

If this were a trap, I'd be wise to keep silent now.

"And how did you find it, Miranda?" His gaze hardened. "Have you no opinions of your own, dullard girl?"

I flinched. He had never before been intentionally unkind to me. I did not know what he wished to hear. Unable to guess, I had only the truth.

"I was very young, sir. It is difficult to . . ." I closed my eyes, hearing the voices of the actors from the stage, and again Tamburlaine's lines from my mother's lips as she recited them from her death bed. I whispered,

"With milk-white harts upon an ivory sled
Thou shalt be drawn amidst the frozen pools
And scale the icy mountains' lofty tops,
Which with thy beauty will be soon resolved."

Words suspended, like the wings of ivory herons on a warm breeze. Beautiful words.

Neither of us spoke.

"I loved the play," I said. "I think being among the groundlings in the Rose, watching the players, must have been the happiest moment of my life." He said nothing. I added, "Mr. Marlowe must have been a brilliant man. He died when I was but a babe, I think."

"He did."

"Did you know him?"

"Christopher? Ah, yes." He smiled, but only weakly, briefly. He gave me a curious look. "Brilliant, you say. By what standard does a serving girl measure the quality of a poet?"

"His play made my mother happy. It was the first time

since my father's death she smiled. And the last." I closed my eyes and breathed in, out, feeling the rhythm of my heart quicken in my breast. I could almost see her. Almost. "Remembering her pleasure makes me feel close to her once again." Maybe that was as near to my own happiness as I could ever again come.

"Marlowe," he muttered, and strode on, "the hothead. The fool! Would that he had never taken up sword or—" He swore, then said no more.

I remembered something my mother had said of the great Marlowe's death. A sword fight, or bar brawl, something violent resulting in his early demise.

As I'd witnessed before, Strachey's mood changed yet again, swinging from convivial to curious to brooding. Eyes narrowed, their blue shadowed but still powerful in their concentration, he muttered something I couldn't quite hear, then walked on so fast I could not keep up with him.

And so I let him and his suddenly soured mood go—while I found my own way back to the safety of our compound.

Fifteen

All torment, trouble, wonder, and amazement
Inhabits here.
—from *The Tempest*

*T*he next time I saw Mr. Strachey, his black mood seemed to have passed and he made no mention of our previous conversation.

He was again writing in his journal but no longer as casually. He behaved as a man possessed by fever, his hand's motions rapid, erratic, accompanied by wrinkled brow and soundless stirring of his lips. Dips of quill into inkpot came as often as grains of sand sifting through Mistress's hourglass. Pages filled and flipped and filled again.

I wondered what so captured his interest that required these many words and demanded such industry. After all, progress on the pinnace and her sister ship came slower and slower each chill winter day, as more of the men wearied and complained of the hard labor, some refusing to work at all. So long as the weather remained fair, both the governor and admiral had kept their men at task from dawn to dusk. At nightfall, torches lit throughout the shipyard enabled already weary carpenters, smiths, and their assistants to continue through the night. Such was their exhaustion that they welcomed a good heavy rain, making work impossible.

Even those commissioned to harvest cedar trees from the islands' woods, cutting and squaring and planking the logs to ready them for the shipwrights, grew less industrious in their duties. More than half of them quit their labors and wandered off to laze in the woods. Eventually, the carpenters lacked wood with which to continue construction. Then, nearly all work in the yard stopped.

I came to understand the reason for their sloth and fascination with the woods only after I began to notice their breaths, wreaking of a queer smell when they came to mess. When I mentioned it to Sarah, she laughed. "I seen some of 'em sneaking up into the forest, and it weren't after cedarwood, me girl." She flashed me a mysterious smile.

"What, then?" I asked.

"To tap the trees and drink of the natural palm wine, don't you know." Although Governor Gates had forbidden all liquor but for our officers, and even so there was precious little to be had. Or so I'd thought.

Thus with so little work being accomplished and only silly drunkenness to report, how many words did Mr. Strachey require for his daily journal?

"What do you suppose he writes now?" I asked Mistress one night.

Though I rarely confided in her, we shut ourselves in after dark each day, covering the doorway of our little hut with more palm boughs to ward off the frigid sea air that dug its fingers into flesh and bone. In these intimate confines, sheltered from the howling wind, warmed by a small glowing brazier, she sometimes became girlishly amenable to gossip. And I was, perhaps unwisely, too hungry for companionship.

"Write?" She gave me a look. "What business is it of yours what the man writes?"

"But does it not seem odd that he records prodigiously, even as nothing is happening in camp? And the only time he roams the island of late, is to accompany me."

It had slipped out.

Her flat black-button eyes slid toward me. "Accompany you where, girl?"

I closed my eyes. Why had I let loneliness drive me to take her into my confidence? Until this moment I had kept my investigations of the island's flora to myself, as I knew she would object. She believed, because I had led her to do so, that whenever I was away from her I was at the admiral's kitchen down on the beach.

"Only to find sweet and savory herbs."

"And you go with Mr. Strachey, alone?"

"He is not like the other men. I trust him." And I did, as to my virtue.

But I had come to believe his motives for being among us might have little to do with the work of an historian. He asked too many questions of a serving girl. And I had often seen him observing others as lowly in our company with an expression of zealous rapture, as if physically soaking up word and gesture and emotion.

Why? How did he conceive of ever using this information? For he seemed a man of industry, who didn't waste his time or energies in useless ways.

More than once I had considered the possibility of his being one of the king's agents. After all, I had only his word that the story of his cousin's arrest was true. It was not beyond reason that His Majesty King James might send one of his court to be his agent among us, to protect his interests in this New World venture, to defend his church from insidious Papists bent upon dethroning him.

"Not like other men?" She drew a deep, whistling old-lady breath through pinched nostrils. "One man is like every other," she muttered. "Don't be foolish, girl."

I rolled my eyes. "Yes, madam."

My lack of enthusiasm must have angered her. She rose up creakily from her cushion and stood in front of me, a wizened, stooped bundle of rage, shaking her finger in my face. "Stay away from Will! He pretends to be your friend, but he keeps secrets. Oh yes—I see your surprise and doubt, but the man is not who you think he is. And he has enemies you would not wish for your own."

Shocked, I stared at her. A deathly chill coursed through me. Enemies? Quiet, plain William Strachey? Did she know about his family's ties with the old church?

What had she found out about him that I had not? Or was she just trying to frighten me because it pleased her to do so?

"The gentleman is a good man," I said. "He saved me from Mr. Waters—"

"Yes, as did that useless cook who would poison us all. But there are issues you cannot comprehend. There are—" She struggled to find words to tell, I suspected, only what she wished me to hear and no more. "There are individuals who are dangerous. Whose displeasure William must evade. You imperil him by making his presence among us known."

"But of course he is known," I objected. "He is on *Sea Venture's* manifest, as are we all." And anyway, in a community of only one hundred fifty souls, by now everyone knew everyone else.

Mistress closed her eyes and dropped back down onto her cushion, as if so drained she could no longer keep to her feet. "Stubborn girl, I warn you. Whatever you observe or hear from Mr. Strachey, keep in confidence. And do not demand his company in your risky adventures. Should you draw attention to him, he shall be the one to suffer."

Sixteen

Love looks not with the eyes, but with the mind,
And therefore is wing'd Cupid painted blind.
—from *A Midsummer-Night's Dream*

What will you do when your journal is full?" I asked.

This is how curiosity nudges me toward trouble. Warned to avoid my friend, I could not stay away from him. In my defense, though, I decided it was prudent to discover all I could about Mr. William Strachey, henceforward to better protect myself. Mistress, despite further urging, refused to say more about him.

He sat in his usual posture, back pressed into a dune, the warm sun on his face, inkpot nestled in the fine pink grains of sand beside him, his little book resting on his thigh in lieu of a desk.

"You must not come up on me like that," he said without lifting his head.

A small movement of his right hand drew my eye. He slid a slim ivory-hilted blade beneath his leg, out of sight.

"Pardon, sir." This was not a fortuitous opening to my asking a favor, the second reason for my being here. "Will you come away with me for an hour or two? The admiral has given me permission to borrow his skiff to go to that island over there." I pointed to the south.

It was much smaller than Somers' Island. When the tide ran high it nearly disappeared. But I yearned to investigate the greens easily visible at its crest.

He let out a long, weary sigh. "I'm occupied, can't you see?"

"Yes, sir. But I thought you said you relished a good adventure now and then. There's not much adventure in sitting and writing all of the time."

He shook his head, eyes still fastened to the page, as if it were another world into which he peered, like a soothsayer into her crystal ball. "Take someone else."

"But there isn't—"

"I am occupied, girl!" And cranky, I thought. "Thomas!" he shouted.

I spun around at the heavy pad of footsteps on packed sand, coming toward us from behind the dune.

"Yes, sir?" Thomas Powell stopped short of us and looked past me toward the historian, his face an obedient blank.

He had discarded his usual grease- and gut-smudged apron, customarily worn at his cauldron and chopping block, and replaced it with what appeared to be a freshly laundered shirt. His hair was combed back from his forehead. His face and hands gleamed, suspiciously clean. To my surprise, I saw a man of pleasing looks with a warm smile and intelligent eyes.

I frowned at Mr. Strachey, then at Cook. To assume Thomas Powell's appearance—either its timeliness or its scrubbed condition—was by chance would be naïve. What were the two of them up to?

"Do me the favor of accompanying Miss Persons to scout out her weeds on which we are to dine today." The corner of the historian's lips twitched, but he kept his eyes on his words, flowing uninterrupted from the pen's nub.

"No," I said quickly. "I would rather go alone."

Thomas turned to face me, his expression shifting from nothing to grim. "He is abroad, Elizabeth."

"Who?" I asked. But I knew from the concern in his eyes.

"Waters with his lazy tagalongs. They have left the pinnace in Frobisher's shipyard, telling their master carpenter they mean to do no more work."

"Then I cannot go at all. I will get one of the guardsmen to kill us a boar." We would eat plain but well.

I started to step around Thomas. He moved as if to reach for me. My hand slipped into my skirt folds. Never was I anymore away from the compound without my good and true knife. But I did not yet bring it out.

Whether or not Thomas knew the blade was there, I cannot say, but he took a step back. "Do you fear me, Miss Elizabeth?" His eyes were a gray green, as rich in hue and as alive as the delicate lichen growing up the bark of a tree. I had never seen them gaze upon anything with such rapt interest, even to the finest fish.

"Do I have cause for fear?"

"No. Never."

I searched his eyes. They appeared as composed as a priest's. But it was their lingering warmth that troubled me.

I remembered my earlier worry of my rescuers seeing my nakedness the day of Waters's attack. Had Thomas belatedly been driven to lust?

How was it that men obsessed on the female form? The mere passing of a fully dressed woman set their bodies to stiffening. Drunk at the sight of her, even if not a swallow of ale had passed their lips, they'd titter and guffaw amongst themselves. Revolting behavior!

I didn't care if they chose to act like clowns and tell their ribald jokes. Let them. What I hated was the raw male energy, pressing upon me until I felt exhausted from fighting it off, demanding something I didn't wish to give.

Admittedly, I had lived a protected life, first with my parents, then with Mistress Horton. Although royals sometimes wed young, even as children, to seal political ambitions of their parents, young women of a merchant's household often waited for their twentieth year or later to marry and bear children. But I wanted no man. Ever. I had heard through thin walls the screams and groans of women being fiercely coupled by their mates. Dogs in the street were gentler.

That invisible male vigor, I felt it again now.

I felt it in the tension of Thomas's body, and trembled.

"Come with me," Thomas coaxed softly. "No harm will come to you, lass. Will here is my witness and bond. Tell her, sir."

Mr. Strachey kept on writing, head down. "You are safe with him," he murmured.

I felt dizzy and short of breath. I did not move. Could not move.

"Go! You interfere with my muse," the historian barked.

I moved slowly away from him. Why had he turned on me?

My heart tripped and floundered in my chest like a fish in a seine net. I gulped down air.

"Come," Thomas Powell said softly, "it will be well."

I turned and walked, prickling at the nearness of him as he followed.

We came to the skiff beached at the admiral's cove. Thomas shoved the little boat down the sandy bank, waving me into it before he pushed the bow into the lapping waves.

He rowed in silence toward the unnamed island. If I had known how to swim, I might have made it without boat or this borrowed, troublesome Charon. The island no longer looked so green or inviting.

I recalled a young girl who had been brought bleeding from between her limbs to my father's apothecary. He gave her aggrieved mother a poultice and potion to stanch the flow. When, in my innocence, I asked the girl the reason for her injuries, she had been so embarrassed she would not tell me. But my father seemed to know.

If her fate became mine, my father would not be here to heal me.

I remembered the rough force of Robert Waters's hands. I stared at Thomas's hands, dipping the oars with a sure rhythm, larger by half again than those of the awful sailor. Hands made strong, butchering hogs and lopping off fish heads the size of a man's. His wide shoulders hitched forward then back, forward then back with each stroke. His body sent out heat, even though he sat in the middle of the little craft and I perched in a lump as far forward in the bow as I could. He smelled not of palm wine or turtle grease but emitted a mild musky smell, vaguely pleasant.

Thomas brought the skiff into shallow water and gently beached her. Standing calf-deep in the shallows, he held out both hands as if to catch me by the waist and lift me, dry footed, to shore. I leaped off into the wavelets from the other side of the skiff, wetting my skirts but avoiding his big hands.

I pretended he wasn't there as I hunted for tasty additions to our menu, but felt his presence. He shadowed me, not too closely but always within sight. He said nothing.

In the center of the island sat a small pond. So sheltered was it from the sea, it captured only fresh, sweet rainwater. Growing in the rich, coffee-colored mud at its lip I discovered a delicate leafy plant not unlike our English watercress.

I nibbled a leaf. It was delicious, with a peppery bite. Most healthful, I thought. I gathered tender bunches.

Without a word, Thomas bent and began pulling up fistfuls of the herb, roots and all. As his big hands passed mine to drop them into the pail, his rough fingers brushed against my wrist. I tensed but did not draw away. In little time my pail was full, and we returned to the skiff.

He did not offer his hand to help me in. Did he guess I would refuse it?

I sat in the bow holding my pail atop tightly locked knees. Thomas started to row.

"You bruised half of the plants," I said. "They won't do for the admiral's plate."

His eyes met mine. "I will be more patient next time," he promised.

Savory Cahow Purses

Take a little breste meat from the Byrds and grind well in Morter with small Raysons or Courrants, Dates, wilde Rosemary, Ginger roote, Sinemon (if you have), Nutmeg and Honey. Put in a fine puffe paste and frie in good turtle Oile until dun.

To Make a Puffe Paste

Take Flower of wilde grain and enough yolkes of Eggs from tern, cahow, or plover with a little colde sweet Water suffice to make a nice paste. Drive it abroade with a wooden dowele or staek (if no rouling pin), putting downe lumps of goate Butter, folding over, driving againe, then again adding more butter, folding and driving eache tyme. Convey between two sheets of paste anie forced dishe, savory or prettie. Bake or frie.

Seventeen

Now is the winter of our discontent
Made glorious summer by this sun of York.
—from *Richard III*

Mr. Edward Samuel, *Sea Venture*'s coxswain, stood at Mistress's door, cap clutched in hands, head bowed, eyes averted. "Pardon, Mistress Horton," he said when I had let him pass inside the hut. "I bring a message from our most honorable gov'nor."

"I shall choose to pardon you or not after I have learnt how important this message might be," she snapped. "You have disturbed my nap." In truth she had been dozing in the rough-hewn cedarwood chair one of our carpenters had knocked together for her.

It was now late November, and after weeks of listening to her plaints of aching joints and sore limbs on rising in the morning from her pallet, the admiral—in desperation, I'm sure—ordered one of our men to satisfy her with a simple chair, thus raising her off the cold ground.

I felt certain she next would persuade from him a full bed with posts for canopy, though it might fill our entire hut.

The coxswain twisted his wool cap between knobby fingers, glanced at me sitting on my pallet sharpening my best knife, and went on. "The honorable Gov'nor Gates, he asks Mistress Persons to attend to me. No." His weatherbeaten face screwed up in frustration, as if he were a player who had muddled his much-practiced lines. "What I means to say is—for me to attend her." Another grimace. Still not right. "That is, I should fetch her, if you please, Mistress, fetch her back to the big island. If you please," he repeated.

It was an unfortunate choice of words.

"I am *not* pleased. First the admiral spirits the girl away, leaving me helpless and unattended for hours. Then the governor beckons and—"

"I's so very sorry-ful, Mistress, but he says 'tis of great import. Them's his words." He stood his ground, a stooped little man in rags, silhouetted in her doorway against the pale morning sun. "His lordship is waitin'."

She lifted her gaze to the heavens, threw up her hands and shifted her glare, and all blame, toward me. "What have you done now, Elizabeth?"

I set aside whetstone and blade. "Nothing, madam. I have been—"

"Oh, never mind. Go with the man. See the governor." She sulked in her chair. "But return quickly."

Mr. Samuel led me not to the little dory or the raft we

employed for island hopping but to the governor's longboat, parrot green with a bright red bootstripe, waiting in our cove. I climbed in, and he began to row across the narrow band of azure water between islands, calmed of waves by its sheltered position. His smooth, long strokes brought us around the point and into the harbor, where the larger of our new ships was being constructed. I could see its skeleton, supported by broad beams, holding the hull in an immense wooden cradle as men scurried about, as industrious as ants, pegging and hammering and shaving smooth the wood. To one side, and under a shelter, planks were being sweated for bending to fit the curve, I imagined, of the bow. At another time I might have wished to watch them work, but my mind was elsewhere.

Mistress's words had set me to worrying. Had I unwittingly offended the governor or done something to deserve punishment? Why else should the governor summon me except for the purpose of discipline?

In the four months since we'd come to our islands, discontent and arguments had resulted in civil misbehavior by some of our party. Drunkenness, thievery, disobedience, and, of course, mutinous talk. Stocks had been erected and sentences passed, but none yet more severe than public rebuke and a few days latched, ankles and wrists, into the stocks, or a public dunking.

Just a week earlier, two sailors, drunk to their gills, had come to my mess and started a row.

"You have the larger portion," one claimed, observing his friend's trencher.

"Piss off! I do not," returned his mate.

"You do, and I being the bigger man deserve more." And he snatched the other man's food away.

Before I knew it, they were at each other, fists flying, knives flashing. I shouted out to the nearby guardsmen, who soon had the two knaves by their collars and off to the governor.

They spent two days in the stocks, with only water for sustenance, sobering up and pleading to be let loose.

Others had been punished for leaving their assigned duties. Perhaps Governor Gates had heard of my ramblings and meant to end my freedom. But why, when the admiral seemed so pleased with my services to his company?

My ferryman rowed up to the newly built pier. When I looked up, to my surprise there stood Thomas, looking as if he'd been waiting for me. He reached down and took my hand to help me out of the swaying, bobbing boat, up onto the pungent fresh-cut planks. This time I let him.

"Good day to you, Elizabeth," he said. "I hope you are well."

"I am," I said, then to be polite, "and you?"

"I miss our walks."

"Our walks?" I gave him a look.

"The little island. I . . ." He hesitated. "I found more of those pretty herbs and tried them in a sallet."

"Did you now?"

"I did." He walked alongside me down the wharf, shortening his long strides to match mine. "They were most delectable."

I nodded, and nearly smiled.

"I be waitin' here for you, miss, to take you home," the coxswain called, and then he pointed up the beach. "There *he* be, at his charts."

"Do you know why the governor summoned me?" I asked Thomas.

"No, lass." He looked curiously at me. "You don't?"

"No," I said.

He nodded. "Ah well, can't be anything you did wrong, if that's what yer thinking. You do nothing but bring pleasure to this world."

I wished he wouldn't be so nice to me. He made it harder for me not to smile at him. And I did not wish to encourage his attentions.

"I will go on alone now, Thomas," I said.

"Ah well, I should be getting back to my galley now anyway." He doffed his cap, gave me a shy smile, and walked off across the sand. I watched him for a moment, thinking I know not what, then remembered the governor waited for me.

Beneath a canvas canopy, above the tide line, rested a rough wooden table. With cramping stomach and moist brow, I trudged across the sand, still damp and packed hard from the receding tide. Seabirds wheeled overhead, mocking me. Hogs in their pen at the far end of the beach squealed and shrieked in terror. (Thomas selecting his meat for mess later that day?) The sun shone brilliant and white-hot, though the air was chill. I squinted against its glare on the coral sand, trying to quiet my mind.

Governor Gates looked up at my approach, rolling the

chart he had been studying. Higher up on the land, among a stand of elegant cedars, stood a goodly sized cabin the men had constructed for him. It overlooked the belly of a harbor at the east end of the island that had been our salvation.

How fortunate we have been, I thought, that God brought us here in our time of need. We might be cast away by the storm, but surely He hasn't abandoned us. How else might we have found such a bountiful Paradise?

We had taken to calling the settlement here St. George's. The few light cannon salvaged from our ship were erected at the mouth of the bay and sentries posted, armed to defend us should unfriendly ships appear. The Spanish were most dreaded, of course, but our sailors and marines spoke of privateers of many flags roaming these seas. If the tales of prisoners taken or left to drown were true, few of these captains were as honorable as our good Sir Somers who, before serving His Majesty, had sailed as a British privateer.

But in the months we'd been in the Bermudas, not a single ship had come into sight, friendly or otherwise. Captain Newport claimed it unlikely we'd see any vessels passing close enough to the Devil's Isles to notice and rescue us, as navigators were more likely to go to lengths to avoid this place. Even if their crew did not believe in witches, monsters, black magic, and evil enchantment, the islands' reputation for fierce winds and treacherous reefs was enough to warn away the wise mariner.

"Ah good, Elizabeth," said the governor. "I hope you are well."

"Yes, sir, I am." Did my voice tremble?

He gave his charts one final look then straightened up and studied me for a moment before saying, "I have a favor to ask of you."

"Sir?"

"We are to have a feast soon."

"Holy days approach, sir, yes." Christmas was still weeks away, but I had already begun gathering and trying out ingredients with which to stuff fat seabirds, some growing as plump and delectable as English partridges.

"Before Christmas, two of our company are to be wed."

"A wedding on our islands?" I smiled, feeling immediate relief. No punishment today! "What a joyous occasion, sir." Names of possible grooms rushed through my mind; we had a surfeit of men. But it didn't take long to realize who the lady must be, as only three females remained unmarried, not counting Mistress Horton: Sarah, myself, and—"Mistress Anna?"

"Yes, and Master Arthur Brody. Our good minister will announce bans this coming Sunday. The couple wish to marry quickly, ten days after bans. I would ask that you prepare the wedding feast."

I stared at him, blinking in surprise, overcome by a wave of uncertainty. "Why not Cook?"

He didn't remark on the impertinence of my question. "Thomas will not do for this meal."

"But he will be offended not to be asked." A greasy queasiness crept into my belly. "He will expect, and naturally so, to be asked, as he is officially our company cook and I am just—"

The governor waved a hand. "Thomas is a good man and

works hard, but has neither your clever touch with food nor your sensitive palate. I want this celebration to warm the spirits of our community, to cheer the discontent. To bring all together in celebration. Do you understand, Elizabeth?"

"I do, sir." But I feared that by agreeing I would most definitely injure Thomas's feelings.

When I looked back at him, his eyes were sharp, focused, determined. "So you will make for us this wedding feast, Miss Elizabeth?"

Though I wished to ask again what was to be done about Thomas, I did not. "I will."

"Good girl. Commence preparing your menu. I would like to hear your choices within two days. Is that sufficient?"

"It is, sir." How else might I answer?

"Whatever you require from the general larder will be at your disposal. If you have need of men to hunt for game or fish, I will supply them." He turned a worried gaze across the harbor toward the skeletal pinnace. "I hate to lose men from the loyal few still laboring, but we must restore morale, one way or another."

With a satisfied nod, he turned back to his charts, unrolling a water-stained scroll and smoothing it flat on his bench, leaving me to retrace my steps back across the beach to the naval pier.

The coxswain was waiting for me, as promised, at the longboat, surrounded by a handful of Captain Newport's men, begging news from our little island. Or perhaps only eager for a rare glimpse of a female.

I brushed past them, keeping my eyes low, not wanting to encourage conversation by look or gesture. I felt their stares

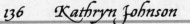

heavy on me but none molested me or muttered a coarse word. In fact, two assisted me in a most gentlemanly manner down into the longboat. I felt badly for only thinking the worst of them.

We rowed back into the silken waters of the harbor and around the rocky point to the admiral's island. The beach was as empty as when we had left it. Mr. Samuel drove the pretty green bow up onto the sand.

"Thank you," I said, stepping out and away. He immediately shoved off, back into the lazy waves.

Perhaps because my mind was occupied as I strolled up the beach, spinning out anxious thoughts of Thomas's soon-to-be disappointment, then skipping off like a flat stone cast across wavelets to cheerful visions of wedding toasts, music, dancing, and a feast—oh, yes, a glorious feast of my own creation!—I failed to hear him come up behind me.

"Why so hurried, Miss Elizabeth?"

Eighteen

Thou poisonous slave, got by the devil himself
Upon thy wicked dam, come forth!
—from *The Tempest*

I turned my head to look at Robert Waters but slowed not my pace even a little. His sallow eyes, bleary and red-rimmed with drink, squinted at me as he scurried crab-like, sidling up the beach as he tried to put himself in front of me.

I widened my strides and did not answer him.

"Mistress Elizabeth, are you well enough now?" my ferryman called, already away and cresting the surf, taking the governor's boat back to him.

"Yes!" I shouted back, more hope than assurance in my heart.

Waters took a long, sinister stride, rounding on me, blocking my way. He carried a burlap sack and shovel. For clams, I thought. He must be among those fellows who had absented themselves from work on the pinnace.

My fingertips slid into the rough folds of my skirt. "Let me pass," I said.

"Nay. We have unfinished business, you and I. Don't we now, girl?" He grinned nastily, bloodshot eyes menacing, and to my surprise lunged forward, throwing the burlap sack up as if to bag my head.

I ducked out from under the scratchy cloth, my breath coming sharp, heart thrumming like a captured dove's. I ran, feeling for the protection of my knife's bone grip. The knife I never left behind.

It wasn't there.

In a moment of horror I saw it lying where I'd left it when the coxswain arrived—beside my pallet, half sharpened.

And now Waters was gaining on me.

I changed course as swiftly as a mariner pulling on his tiller, throwing myself down the gentle slope of the beach, back toward the water, toward the departing longboat.

The coxswain must have seen the sailor's intention and was already rowing back to meet me. "Get in!" he shouted.

I leaped through waves, skirt soaking up cool seawater, weighing and slowing me down. But I reached the bow and hauled myself over the gunwhales and in. The boat bucked, riding the swells, and I toppled into the bottom, breathing so hard my ribs ached.

I expected the old sailor to speed us away with his long strokes. Instead, he shipped oars and jumped into the waist-deep water. "You leave the scurvy bastard to me, Miss," he growled. "I be teachin' 'im a lesson."

"No!" I cried, terrified, for Waters far outweighed the older man. "Don't! Please come back." I watched, helpless, as Mr. Samuel waded toward the beach.

The oars lay in the bottom of the boat. I slid them through their oarlocks and clambered onto the center bench. Should I row out to where Waters couldn't reach me? Take the boat around the point to the neighboring cove where our compound lay, guarded by our marines? Whatever the coxswain had in mind to say or do to Waters, I was ready to row us away to safety as soon as he returned.

I tried to maneuver the boat back toward the beach, so as not to float too far away from my defender. But the surge and drag of the surf gripped the oars, and the narrow hull spun, heading further out into the current despite my best efforts. I kept the two men in my sight as they marched toward each other across the sand. A rogue wave caught boat's bow, whipped her toward shore, sending her skittering sideways into shallow water, and nearly beached her.

Waters and the coxswain stood face-to-face, shouting at each other. Suddenly and with great force, Waters shoved the old sailor aside and, shovel slung over his shoulder, stalked toward the ocean's edge, and me.

"Leave the girl!" the coxswain shouted. "You hear me, you bloody bastard, I say leave her be."

Waters ignored him. His rheumy eyes gleaming and evil, he marched into the water's edge and seized the bow of the longboat.

My ferryman rushed in after him, leaped on Water's back, and down the two went. Churning up mud. Scuffling and rolling in the surf. Waters pushed the coxswain under and held him there. I swung an oar but missed the devil's head, the flat wooden blade splashing harmlessly and digging into the sandy bottom.

Coming up for air, the coxswain shouted, "Row, girl!" But Waters sat on him and down he went again.

I swung again, this time clipping the sailor's shoulder, knocking him off the older man. The ferryman bobbed to the surface, gasping for air.

Their blasphemies and my screams must have alerted our guardsmen. They came running down the beach, more excited to observe a good fight, it appeared to me, than anxious to break it up.

I looked back just in time to see Waters staggering to his feet, lifting his shovel high over his head. He brought it down in a vicious arc, its blade striking the other man above his right ear.

"No!" I screamed. "Stop them. Stop!"

My defender went down with a splash. Waters stood ready with his weapon to deliver another blow soon as his victim recovered his feet, the marines still too far away to stop him.

But Mr. Samuel lay in the water, unmoving, tendrils of crimson snaking through the sea foam.

My breath caught in my throat.

Before anyone in the approaching throng could react, Waters dropped his shovel and ran. He disappeared into the woods just as fast and noisily as a wild hog, squealing triumphantly at his victory.

Nineteen

*W*ord of the coxswain's murder reached Admiral Somers within minutes and Governor Gates not long after.

The governor summoned all who had been present at the tragic combat to the main island to give testimony. Waters had gone off with his mutinous companions, I imagined, to celebrate his defeat of the poor coxswain with another draught of palm wine.

Each of us witnesses gave testament to Waters's cruel and unnecessary violence and drunkenness.

It didn't take the governor long to come to a decision. He turned to his guard. "Captain, take three good men with you and capture Mr. Waters. Bring him to me."

Sick at heart, I returned to Mistress Horton's cottage. Seeing that I had been weeping, she demanded to know the reason. What was I to do but tell her everything? In time she would hear it from others.

If I had hoped for sympathy, I did not receive it.

"You see what your silly flirtatious ways have come to?" she scolded.

"I did nothing to encourage the man!" I objected, the tears starting all over again. "I never have."

She laughed, wagging her finger at me. "Of that I'm not convinced. Why else would men want anything to do with a pitiful, plain serving girl, but that she made herself available to them?"

Why else indeed . . . except for man's natural warped nature? For I'd learned one true thing in my short years. People needed no encouragement to do evil. Be it torturing and killing on a cross or a scaffold a man whose only sin was to see God in a different way, or plowing a woman until she bled, or beating in the head of a good soul who tried to protect a fellow human.

The evil were simply evil.

"I hate you!" I screamed at her.

I would have said more but the look she gave me, brimming with malice, sealed my lips as surely as hot tar.

"Yes-s-s," she hissed. "Think hard about what you say, girl. I took you off the street when no one else would, did I not?" She narrowed her eyes at me. "You may have a patron in the admiral, but he knows better than to cross me." She looked pleased that I found no response.

I closed my eyes tight, but burning tears squeezed between them. *Witch!* I thought. *Witch, witch, witch!* But to say it out loud, that was dangerous talk. I'd seen the damage of rumors and accusations and fear warping people's minds. I could not be the cause of such wickedness, even if she deserved as good as she gave.

I choked back the words and, sobbing, covered my face with my hands.

"I see you are penitent," she said, her voice softer now that she believed me duly chastised. "Go away from me until you've dried your useless tears and made peace with God for your sins." She looked around her. "Then the floor needs sweeping."

I found Mr. Strachey sitting on his favorite beach, despite the cold wind off the sea. He must have heard me slipping and sliding over the sand as I scurried down the dunes, for I caught a surprised look from him before I threw myself into his arms and buried my tear-drenched face against his chest.

"Dear girl," he said softly, stroking my back, "I heard. Did he injure you?"

"No. The coxswain prevented him." I could not stop weeping. "And paid for his kindness."

It was some minutes before I could utter another word. Stepping out of his comforting arms I looked up at him, my head throbbing, eyes aflame, embarrassed to have appealed to him with no less intimacy than a daughter to her father. "Mistress says it is my fault."

His laugh sounded bitter. "Yours? For tempting the man?" He considered this. "Ah well, yes . . . *she* would think that."

"But I never—"

"Of course not." He waved the thought away. "But that isn't to say sex can't be a useful tool, on certain occasions." He looked at me, as though to determine if I might be horrified by the suggestion. And truly I was, though I tried not to show it. "Did I ever tell you how I came to be wed as a young man?" He smiled, looking amused and as if he'd quite forgotten a killing had happened on our little island and a murderous fiend roamed free. "My clever Ann. Ah, but who could blame her? A child needs a father."

I waited for him to tell me more. Instead, he led me back to his place in the sand, where we sat sheltered by the rolling grass-covered hillocks from the wind, warmed by a yellow sun and facing the sea that separated us from the rest of humanity—beloved England, the colonies, and all of the rest of the world, civilized or heathen. So alone were we here, our little group.

It was some moments before he spoke again.

"Can you think why Mistress Horton might accuse you as she did?"

"I gave Waters no encouragement," I said firmly.

"That's not what I meant, Miranda."

My new name again. Soothing. Taking away the old life, the pain. I did indeed feel different when I thought of myself as Miranda, survivor of storm and wreck, cook to the admiral's men.

"An old woman, her beauty gone," he continued. "With few if any friends. She brings a young woman into service who is intelligent, sweet and clever . . . as well as pretty."

His gaze in my direction made me blush. No one but my father had ever described me thus. Was he saying she was jealous of me? Impossible.

"But she is powerful in court, and rich!"

"Her only weapons. Thus she uses them. She's feared, dear Miranda, not loved. Do you not see?"

I thought for a moment then looked up at him.

He gave a quick nod. "Don't take her waspish temper to heart. You are an enigma to her and a torment, but all she has. She needs to be served. How else might she present herself as a lady of exalted station in our extreme situation? But every time she looks on you, she is reminded of all she has lost and will never again have. Beauty, suitors, the power to influence in court."

"But how can any of that matter on these islands in the middle of this vast ocean?" I said. "We are all as one, trapped here. There is no court for which to primp. No seamstress to visit for the fittings of her gowns. We eat the same food, use the same privies."

"Indeed. It truly is a New World, though not the one your mistress nor any of us expected." He sighed. "You see, Waters gives her an excuse for hating you. She needs that. It is all she has, her bitterness, for she will probably die here. If not here then in Virginia, if we ever reach that place. This was not her plan, Miranda."

I would give his words more serious thought later. But now I had another question, one that would not wait, and no one else to ask.

"You are kind to say I am pretty, though I know it isn't

true." I held up a hand when he seemed ready to argue, for I knew myself well enough. My mother had been pretty, perhaps beautiful. My little sister, had she lived, would have taken after her. "I have my father's strong jaw, too-widely spaced eyes and his high, proud forehead. Even so, men stare at me, saying rude things under their breaths. Why?"

He shrugged. "You are female and scarce here; that is enough. Do not make it more complicated than it is."

"But you do not behave like that."

"My interests, in this time of my life, lie in another di-rection." His gaze rested on the horizon. He let out a long breath. "Now tell me, what is to become of this Mr. Waters?"

"The governor has ordered him caught and brought to him."

He nodded. "Then the man will hang and that will be the end of your troubles."

If ever a man deserved the gallows, it was Robert Waters. Even so, another death among us did not sit comfortably with me. We were down to 149, by this man's evil act. With his execution we would number 148 souls.

I feared the dreaded counting down of our company. How swiftly would the rest of us leave this earth, by God's hand or our own?

Although the governor's guard eventually found and de-tained a drunken, cursing Robert Waters and tied him to a stake outside the governor's quarters, his friends came during that same night, cut him loose and stole him away. Together they again ran off into the woods and hid.

The next day when I told Mr. Strachey of their daring

escape he seemed not at all surprised. In fact, he was more interested in whatever he was rapidly noting in his journal. "Did you hear me? The devil, he ranges free. What am I to do? What are any of us to do?"

"I don't see that bringing the man to justice is any concern of yours," he mumbled.

"But he truly is a concern," I insisted, reaching for his pen to stop it, then thinking better of it. He was most protective of his writing tools, another strange thing about him that made me remember Mistress's warning. If William Strachey wasn't who he claimed to be . . . who then was he? I blinked away the riddle for now, to concentrate on more important issues. "Until these men are caught, I can't roam my islands."

"Then I will pluck your magical herbs for you, Miranda." A twinkle lit his eyes as he finally lifted quill from page. "No, better yet, I will give you an enchanted cloak to make you invisible. Then you may roam protected."

I laughed. "If such a cloak existed, I would wear it always, never taking it off."

"You would deprive this world of your beauty, dear Miranda?" He was toying with me now, I could see that.

"I am not fair. Do not say so."

"But I did not claim you fair, for you are not."

"No?" Despite my objections to his flattery, I was disappointed.

"For the sun has turned your face golden, and goddesslike, daughter."

I looked up at him and saw a father's eyes. The humor was gone. "You miss your children."

"I do. If ever I return to Warwickshire, I would live with my eldest daughter and her husband."

"Not with your wife?" Somehow, I knew the answer.

"With Ann?" He shook his head. "We've spent too many years apart. It would seem strange."

I stretched out on the sand and lifted my face to the sun. Soon I should have to return to the grim little shack and try to please my unplease-able mistress. The day was warm for winter, the sky fair and a silken blue with fairy clouds wisping across it like goose down. I wished to soak up all the glorious sunlight I could before returning to my duties.

I glanced down at his journal, resting half open in his hands now. I longed to ask him to read to me something of what he wrote. Maybe I was in there.

"What do I do, having no magic cape to protect me?"

He drew a long breath and shrugged. "Take advantage of the one defense a woman has against the corruption of men."

"And that is?"

"Marriage," he said.

I shook my head violently. "No."

"Not to a Waters. Choose a good man, one you do not fear. One who lightens your heart."

I narrowed my eyes in suspicion.

"No, not me." His lips pinched in an almost smile.

"There is no man as you describe here," I insisted.

"What of Thomas?" And somehow I knew he had been waiting for this moment.

Yet I hadn't expected the hint of warmth that stole over me at the mention of Cook's name. I thought of Thomas's words after our herbing trip. "I will be more patient . . ." But was patience a sign of kindness? Or was it just a clever way of hiding a man's lust?

"He wants what the others want. I see it in his eyes."

He shrugged. "But Thomas would keep you safe. Use him for that purpose, and for the purpose he would use you, for comfort and for pleasure." He turned back to his journal and began anew his writing. "Tit for tat, Miss Miranda."

Twenty

I am tied to the stake,
and I must stand the course.
—from *King Lear*

*F*or another fifteen days, Waters remained free. Sarah, whose master, Seth Erwin, was among the searchers, came into my beach kitchen as often as she could escape her duties to bring the latest gossip.

"Mr. Erwin, he do say, the old devil's friends smuggle food and clothes to him in the woods where he's secreted himself," she said, plucking a bit of roast pork from my cutting board and popping it into her mouth.

"If the guard knows he's there, why don't they just follow his fellow sailors and snatch him out of his hiding place?" I tossed another log on my fire and poked it into the middle of the glowing coals beneath my bubbling cauldron. The flames leaped, blue and amber, crackling. On a cold, rainy day nothing felt better than a good fire.

"Tweren't that easy. They be shiftin' him from one hidey spot to another, don't you know? Eludin' both the gov'n'r's guard and yer admiral's men. Ain't you mortally ascared, Lizzy?" I had not yet convinced her to use my new name. "I fear he'll be comin' after you again."

"I keep to the compound, as do you." I shrugged. "It's as well. My mistress seems better tempered for the extra care I give her." Besides, if anyone could frighten off a man good or evil, I thought with a wicked smile, it would be Mistress Horton.

Sarah shook her head. "I should slice either my own throat or hers, had I to live with such a sour old rag as that." Her eyes brightened with mischief. "Oh, did y'hear the weddin's been postponed? Our bride, she threw such a ter'ble fit."

I had already heard. If Anna was already with child she would be anxious to make fast her marriage before she grew a belly. I might have felt more sympathy for her had she been of a sweeter nature.

"I overheard the admiral," I said, "telling Mr. Strachey that he and the governor decided order and discipline must be restored before there are celebrations of any kind."

And so the days of confinement to our own stockades on each island continued while the hunt for Waters went on. I saw nothing of Thomas during that time, but the thought came to me more than once—no doubt inspired by our good historian's unasked-for advice—that had the brawny cook been allowed to accompany me into the fields, I might gather my good vegitives and herbs without danger.

And so, until the beast was captured, I was forced to prepare only the simplest of meals for the admiral and his men, drawing from our shrinking larder, depending upon our loyal guardsmen for fresh-killed pigs or netted fish. And every day came rumors of the murderous Robert Waters spitting out venomous and deadly threats against those who would take from him his freedom.

The weather had become less pleasant, although nowhere near as cold as our London winters. While the governor and admiral conspired by ever more ingenious means to capture Waters, the renegade created more discontent among Somers's men, sending word back through his friends that they were being made slaves by the admiral and Governor Gates. Then he, or some one of his cohorts, started a tale that all anyone had to do was steal a longboat and row a day or less to the west and there come upon New Britannia's shores. In the wilderness, so they claimed, they could make their own life, take as much land as they pleased, be free of harsh labor and orders from others.

Many more of our men then stopped working or went off on their own to hunt and make palm wine and drink it as fast as sap came from the trees. They returned drunken, begging for food, promising good work the next day, then went missing again as soon as they were fed. In time, there were too few working in the shipyards to make any progress at all. With discipline destroyed, true mutiny seemed a breath away.

At last came Admiral Somers to visit Mistress one afternoon. He looked haggard with worry, his eyes sunken with lack of sleep—the worst I'd seen him since our storm-tossed days and nights aboard dear old *Venture*.

"I am most distressed by these events," he told her.

"And well we all should be!" she crowed. "I can't understand the difficulty in locating one idiot sailor on an island. It isn't as if he could have gone far!"

"I agree, madam, and so does Governor Gates, who tells me he can tolerate no more. Desperate measures must be taken to restore order. Desperate!"

And so two guardsmen, tipped off by one of Waters's own comrades under inducement of a reward, found and dragged Robert Waters out of the woods and into the governor's stockade.

Our carpenters erected a gallows on a hill overlooking the site of our wreck. I would not have attended the hanging but had no choice. Every man and every woman was ordered by the governor to stand watch over Robert Waters's punishment for the vile and heartless murder of his shipmate.

As the governor was in desperate need for strong men to keep at work on our ships, Waters might have been spared if he'd agreed to labor in earnest with his mates. But it was, ultimately, his traitorous talk, tempting the other men from their loyalty to the Virginia Company, that sealed his fate.

His punishment would serve as a lesson to others to stay true to their contracts for the voyage.

Waters was dragged, weeping and pleading, to the foot of the gallows, whereupon the governor read his decree of death by hanging. I had never seen Mistress look so pleased with a day's events, her cloudy eyes seeming to clear in the day's brilliant sunlight, pursed lips ticking up at the corners in delight.

But I found no joy in the death of another, even so wicked a man as this.

I stood beside Sarah and her family, with Mistress on my other side. Across the yard I could see Thomas standing next to Mr. Strachey, both looking solemn as priests at confession. Thomas glanced past the gallows to me, and I held his gaze for a moment, imagining I saw concern in it. For me? I wondered why.

As Waters was brought past the admiral and governor and their parties, my attention turned to our officers. I noticed a sudden tension among his escort as Waters spoke rapidly, his voice drowned out by the raucous cries of foolish seabirds come to perch on the gallows' head.

"What is happening?" I asked.

Mistress Horton looked disappointed. "He is pleading status as a gentleman. How wearisome."

"He, a gentleman?" Sarah cried.

"Please God!" I gasped. "He would then be freed?"

Dazed, I bit my lip, held my breath. Sarah reached out to lay a hand on my shoulder but said nothing. My insides churned as though I were tossed in the tempest again. To consider this evil man living amongst us again! My stomach seized.

"Gentleman by birth, not deed. Simple girl," Mistress spat. "He begs a gentleman's right to be executed by firearm. A less painful end, so they say."

Some discussion among our officers ensued but, at last, the governor nodded. Two of our guard tied Waters to the foot of the gallows then stood away. One took up arms. And my tormentor was shot once in the heart.

A quicker, kinder death than the devil deserved, I thought as I turned away. Would that my poor, dear father had been treated as compassionately.

Twenty-one

Give me an ounce of civet, good apothecary,
to sweeten my imagination.
—from *King Lear*

*T*he days that followed were noticeably more peaceful. Most of the men returned from the woods. They worked harder at their tasks, with less grumbling. Even Waters's scraggly band of co-conspirators seemed penitent, his execution a powerful enticement to goodness.

The few who remained lazing in the wood continued to brew their tipple in secret and stash it away amongst the trees. We heard rumors of plans to petition the governor to allow some of the party to remain behind on the island when our ships were finished and the rest of us sailed away.

"Why would they want to stay?" I asked Mr. Strachey.

We sat on his beach, he scribbling as madly as ever in his

journal, me peeking over his shoulder to steal a word or two when he wasn't paying attention. Another poem, from the shape of the lines, I thought. He seemed dissatisfied with every tenth word. Cross outs and corrections swirled across the page, giving it the look of a labyrinth of letters— overlapping, twisting back and forth in confusing patterns.

If this was another sonnet, as he had explained to me the other poem was, whose praises did he sing? For whose eyes were these adoring words intended? How sad that his lover would never see them. For certainly the object of Mr. Strachey's affections could not be among us.

Affection.

I sat back on my heels and brooded on the word.

Was that what Thomas Powell felt for me? It wasn't the word I would use, were I writing a sonnet. I saw the hunger in his eyes whenever we met. Indeed, as the days passed and the memory of Waters's execution faded and men grew braver again, I felt their eyes wandering toward me during my chores among them. So troubling.

Mistress noticed too. Simple personal cleanliness seemed to her preening. Courtesy was taken as brazenness. "Keep your hair covered. Avert your eyes, Elizabeth. Dear Lord, don't *speak* to them!"

"I do not encourage them," I protested.

She puckered her face at me, as if she'd bitten into one of the wild persimmons I'd found growing on the south side of the main island.

Now I sighed and turned my thoughts back to Mr. Strachey. I watched his words form, yet another page growing beneath his pen, and a thought came to me. The shape and length of the lines, the number of pages and people's names showing here and there—this was no poem.

"You are writing a play!" I said, delighted at my discovery.

He snapped the journal shut and glared at me. "Why do you say that, Miranda?"

I knew he could not be truly angry with me if he used that name.

"My mother's quarto of Marlowe. It appeared the same, with characters' names written separate and lines for each player to speak."

He looked hard at me. "It would be best," he said slowly, his words weighted as if held down with my father's brass tally weights, "if you did not share your observations."

"Why?"

"You do not need to know why. Just, please, keep your tongue in check, girl."

"But if I understand your reason, I might be more inclined not to let the wrong words slip." I felt so clever.

"I have enemies!" he barked, his gaze going cold. So Mistress had told the truth. He was in some sort of trouble. "As do you. We have discussed such things."

"But enemies here?"

"None that I can name, yet." He paused, as if giving this some consideration. "Back in London though, yes."

"I don't understand. How can they harm you here, when they are so far away?"

"Go," he growled. "You ask too many questions for either of our good."

But unanswered questions haunted me for the rest of that

day and for many more to come. What dangers had my old friend brought with him to Paradise?

Sadly, our population decreased again.

Under orders from Governor Gates, five of our men departed the Bermudas in a small, sailed bark fashioned from native cedarwood, their mission to reach and inform the settlement in Virginia of our survival. They would tell the colonists of our men building the pinnace, which was to be christened *Deliverance*, and a second smaller ship. They would discover which among the other eight ships in our fleet had made it safely to Jamestown and those that had been lost during the tempest. Then they would return to us here in our refuge to report their findings or, if it were possible, lead one of the fleet's ships back to us.

That, at least, had been our officers' plan.

A week passed, and we felt a great surge of hope. Captain Newport told us he judged our brave emissaries were just then setting foot in the colony, no doubt joyously greeted by our countrymen. As we had agreed before their departure, we lit bonfires along the beach so that they might find us even in the night. We waited . . . and waited.

They did not come.

A third and fourth week passed without word of them. We spent a cheerless Christmas. Anna and Arthur's wedding was put off, as celebration of any kind seemed inappropriate while the fate of our brave men was unknown. With the dead of winter wrapped around us, we could do nothing but mourn their loss.

Our Master Bucke spoke at services of salvation and offered special thanks for our intrepid messengers' sacrifice. I read fear in every face, fear of such I had not seen since our wreck in July. If that sturdy little bark had indeed floundered and all aboard drowned, would the same happen to the rest of us when we set sail in *Deliverance*?

Dark times haunted us. One of our men drowned. We buried him beside Waters's grave, well up the hillside, with Christian solemnity, even though it was commonly known that he'd stumbled into the pond, drunk and stupid with palm wine, and was to blame for his own death. Two other men died of unknown illnesses, though some claimed it was from the severity of their labor.

Our minister preached every day, and twice on Sundays, on the evil of drink. It did no good. If men could not have their favorite vices—whoring, gambling, or thieving—they would have another. In the Bermudas the choices were few.

Twenty-two

I would have thee gone;
And yet no further than a wanton's bird,
Who lets it hop a little from her hand . . .
And with a silken thread plucks it back again.
—from *Romeo and Juliet*

*B*est take 'em off, they be gettin' too dark."

I had been standing at the fire, daydreaming as I turned my spits—around and around—remembering my dear mother's glowing hearth. If I had a favorite dream, it was to return to London, become a victualer and rent myself a modest little shop with its own oven, and there sell nourishing dishes such as those I prepared for our company.

But dreams, in my experience, are no more substantial than sea foam or sunset, impossible to either grasp or hold, and so I satisfied myself with visiting them in my imagination, until too tired to think or interrupted by a meddlesome cook.

I scowled at Thomas. "Wild birds require slow roasting and patience. They will not burn while I attend them."

He tipped his head to one side and observed the dark, crackling skin. "The tasting will tell."

"I shall remove them when they and I are ready," I said, cranking the iron spit still slower to spite him.

I had not expected to see Thomas that day or any other, as now I only crossed to Gates' Island to gather wild mint and other herbs once every few days and, of course, to attend the king's services with Mistress, as all were required. Although I knew he occasionally visited Mr. Strachey on our island, I stayed away when they were together, fearing the historian would further encourage Cook's attentions toward me.

Most of the time, though, I was too busy laboring over my messes to worry or even think about Thomas. Our sly admiral had increased my duties threefold by now. A breakfast begged from me one desperately cold day—"for the benefit of the men," he implored, "who must labor in the bitter wind all day"—had soon enough become an everyday expectation. A supper to celebrate Christmas Day turned into an evening meal three days a week, then five, then all seven.

All of January, Mistress fumed and cursed, but only behind the admiral's back. She seemed to lose both spit and spirit in the early months of the year, as if she realized she had lost control of her life. Something the rest of us already knew.

I looked at the plump, breasty birds sizzling and fragrant over the flames. Perfect, I thought, not burnt. They will be delicious.

I felt Thomas's gaze, warm and constant on me. My heart quickened, its beat rising into my ears. I didn't turn to look at him. I willed him away.

"Why do you fear me?" he asked.

"I don't—"

"You do," he insisted, his voice husky-soft.

I felt him step up closer behind me.

"I do," I said and swallowed. "Please go away. I don't want to be touched."

"Why?"

Why? Wasn't that so very obvious? "Because it is unpleasant!"

"You don't know that my touch isn't to your liking, lass. You have never let—"

"Stop," I said, moving away to the other side of the fire. I gripped the spit handle with both hands, turning the birds faster, faster.

He looked across the flames that flared in the dripping juices. "Elizabeth."

"Call me Miranda," I said.

He frowned. "But your name is Elizabeth."

I glared at him.

"Elizabeth." He sighed. "I won't hurt you."

I shook my head.

"I can show you the pleasure of—"

I stared at him in horror. "No!" I deserted my birds. "No! Don't talk to me this way."

"Stay," he said, holding both of his big hands up as if I were one of his boars, a wild creature to be prevented from bolting back into the woods. "Please stay. Listen."

"Go away now. I'm busy."

"I won't. You need me."

I laughed. "I do not, sir! Look, I do well. The admiral's men all are fed and healthy. Mistress Horton is satisfied with my service." A lie, but then why should it matter to him?

"And you will be hounded by sailors, tradesmen, and ship's officers alike for as long as we are on this island, which may be forever, unless you—"

"The pinnace will be complete in another month, no more than six weeks," I objected. "So says the admiral himself."

"But we dare not sail until spring, when the ocean settles."

I stared at him. So long must we wait? My eyes fell to his big, hard hands, hanging loose at his sides. My stomach churned as if I were on a spit along with my birds—starting to char on one side, no doubt, for I had stopped turning them to move farther away from Thomas.

"Winter storms will keep us here, lass. The governor has no intention of leaving 'til April, possibly May. Later if the winds do not abate."

My heart withered, a blossom in frost.

He continued. "*Deliverance* is not large enough for all. We must either complete the other ship, or leave behind some of our company, and the men have let its building lag behind, putting all their efforts into the larger ship."

Staying in this paradise would suit me, if I were alone. I might live out my life contented, feasting on fat little birds, feeding the pretty angelfish and their rainbow of sisters, counting turtle eggs and watching the hatchlings scramble down the sand into the surf, chasing comic lizards. But the governor would never allow me to leave Mistress, and she would never agree to stay here, such was her hatred for the Bermudas. I supposed, after a time, even I would grow lonely.

I blinked away tears. When my gaze cleared, Thomas was beside me. I flinched when his hands rested on my shoulders. An unfamiliar sensation settled low in my body.

"Steady," he whispered from down in his throat.

"Leave me."

"No."

"Go."

"I stay." His breath tickled the side of my neck beneath the edge of my cap.

I looked around us, hoping to catch the eye of one of our armed marines. The beach was deserted, every man off working. Or had Thomas warned the stragglers away?

I held myself stiff as a deck plank as his arms came around me. Heart thrashing in my chest, I closed my eyes. If I struggled, he, so much stronger and a good two heads taller than I, would win. If I pretended indifference, perchance he'd decide that taking me was poor sport, and he would go away.

"You're cold," he breathed in my ear.

"The cooking fire keeps me warm enough."

"A woman has her own fires within, if she fuels them."

"Do not talk foolishness."

He gave a soft laugh, and—here was a surprise—I thought it not an entirely unpleasant sound. There certainly was no meanness in it. "You have a lot to learn, Elizabeth Persons."

"I will learn as I please, when I please." I took care not to rest my head against his conveniently positioned chest. Even so, the low, steady thrum of his heart reached out to me. The heat of his body warmed my cheek.

He rested his wide chin on top of my cap, a solid weight.

"If you were mine, *they* would leave you in peace."

A curse on the historian! The two of them had been conspiring. "You would fight off all of them?" I taunted him.

"Even men with dark souls usually respect a woman protected in marriage."

"And those who do not respect her or her husband?"

"I would kill a man soon as a hog, does he come near my wife." He said it so plain and simple I believed him.

But what price to pay for security?

Wives vowed obedience to their husbands. *In all ways!* What of those shrieks and wails of women being poked?

I had asked my mother, once, if no one heard their pain and made the men stop, but by then my father had died and she refused to speak of life as a wife. It was all she could do to instruct me as to my monthly bleedings when they started.

Thus I knew little of what a man sought from a woman except that it lay between her thighs and his doing his filthy business there gave her great anguish.

How foolish would I be to give my flesh over to a man's bestial lust, with no recourse but to submit whenever he fell upon me? Even Master Bucke, in his sermons, called it "a wifely duty!" Never would I marry. Never.

"You have no response to my offer, Elizabeth?"

I lifted my chin, stared at the horizon. Out there, somewhere in the distance, was Virginia. Mistress could not live forever. Maybe Mr. Strachey was right after all. In New Britannia I might have a chance of a life of my own. Savages could be no worse neighbors than ours of London.

"Leave me," I choked out. Closing my eyes, I waited for him to curse me. Strike me. Beat me into submission. Why I hadn't seized my knife when I'd had the chance, I shall never know.

Thomas stood very still, holding me. I was aware of his member, through our clothing, hard and terrifyingly large against my back. I kept my eyes shut tight. Neither of us spoke, nor breathed.

Weak-kneed, head spinning, I trembled at the vision of his big fists knocking me to the sand.

But they didn't. He didn't.

Leave me, leave me, leave me, I repeated silently.

At last he said, "For the moment." Muscled arms relaxed and unclasped from around me. He stepped away.

When I turned to look, he was gone.

Twenty-three

Sit then and talk with her.
She is thine own.
—from *The Tempest*

*T*he familiar leather volume and writing tools lay on the sand beside my cauldron when I came to cook our evening meal. I looked up and down the beach, but the historian was nowhere in sight. Should I bring his things to him?

He might have taken himself off to the privy or for a stroll to stretch his legs before returning to his labor of writing. I looked down. A mercurial breeze riffled journal pages. Black ink swirled and spiked across creamy vellum. How many words might I recognize, if I attempted . . . if I *dared* read a whole line?

The sea breeze selected another page for me. I looked

around. No one stood within sight except two guardsmen standing at opposite ends of the crescent beach. My toes inched across the sand to hold the page open. I read as many words as I could, skipping over the two that puzzled me, surprised that so many came easy to me:

> *My mistress' eyes are nothing like the sun;*
> *Coral is far more red than her lips' red;*
> *If snow be white, why then her breasts are dun;*
> *If hairs be wires, black wires grow from her head.*
> *I have seen roses _____, red and white,*
> *But no such roses see I in her cheeks;*
> *And in some perfumes is there more delight*
> *Than in the breath that from my mistress reeks.*
> *I love to hear her speak; yet well I know*
> *That music hath a far more pleasing sound;*
> *I grant I never saw a goddess go;*
> *My mistress, when she walks, _____ on the*
>   *ground.*
> *And yet, by heaven, I think my love as rare*
> *As any she belied with false compare.*

Releasing my toe from its duty, I let the pages fan shut, then turned back to my cauldron, lest he catch me at my mischief. I had much to consider.

Our two shipbuilding yards, Mr. Frobisher's on Gates' Island, the other on Admiral Somers's smaller island, began again to make good progress as the days warmed. Our lumber supply doubled, finally keeping up with the carpenters' demands for beams and boards. Sailor, soldier, gentleman, and scholar worked shoulder to shoulder, dawn to dusk.

But cedar, the wood most plentiful on the islands, made poor shipbuilding material. The reddish timber splintered woefully, and although it weathered the salty air well, making it ideal for our cottages and furnishings, the pungent boards warped and the timbers twisted. Thus our carpenters fashioned the vital hulls of our new ships from salvaged wood from dear *Sea Venture*, her sad remains still ensnared in the coral shoals.

The problem in either ship, I heard the men complaining at mess, was a keel. For we had neither iron works nor a source of any metal beyond that rescued from *Venture*, and her iron keel was of such weight and so jammed between sharp coral spurs there was no moving it. So with great ingenuity our governor ordered the heaviest rescued woods to be laid at the bottom of the ships as their keels, saving the lighter cedar for decks and other portions above the water line.

Our men worked to exhaustion, and I felt satisfaction preparing good, hearty messes in my outdoor kitchen, for they ate with great vigor, giving me many words of praise.

Admiral Somers frequently voiced his favorites. "I would you might serve your savory turtle soup with every evening meal, Miss Persons. It settles my stomach and nourishes my soul."

I blushed at his compliment. "I will, sir." And I learned to grind and season scraps from slaughtered hogs to make delectable sausages, which he ate with relish at any time of day I chose to serve them.

I worked no less vigorously than the men, only stopping to see to Mistress's necessities—empty her chamber pot, bring her warmed pond water with which to bathe her, combing out her long, gray hair as thin and delicate as a spider's web. Once each week I washed our clothing and hung it to dry. I chose a shaded place at the edge of the woods so that the colors, already fading in the brilliant sunlight—so unlike our gray, filtered light of London—might last.

My pot, around which I arranged my kitchen, I asked to be moved to the leeward side of the island as protection from the fickle winds. The men built a sturdy and thick roof of palms over it, so that I might cook in comfort even in a steady rain. Woven reeds provided shutters I lowered over the sides to keep out blowing rain or glaring sun. But, mostly, I liked to leave them open and enjoy the clear, sapphire waters and watch the terns, gulls, and cormorants wheel above and dive into the waves after fish.

Mr. Strachey came every day to eat with us, ask of my health, and deliver news of the governor's colony, for he rode back and forth in the ferry skiff between the islands whenever he was not recording his histories.

"The wedding comes soon," he remarked the second day of February, puffing on his clay pipe. He sometimes accompanied me on my excursions over the islands and, much to his delight, we found tobacco growing wild along one hillside. He had taken to cutting and drying it then shared his product with the officers. "What will you prepare for the festivities, Miranda?"

The wedding. It had been so long delayed because of one trouble or another. But at last bride and groom implored the governor to grant them a date, and he agreed they might proceed.

A wedding—so much more work! My stomach roiled at his question. Though satisfied with my duties as cook to the admiral's company, my body and spirit were as thoroughly worn as my single pair of stockings, which I had long-ago discarded. Even with the governor's promise of help from his men, and the assistance of the few other women in our company, my share of the preparations would require many days' labor. But it wasn't the food that worried me so much.

Palm wine, which had been banned in theory since Robert Waters's execution, would pour forth at the wedding feast with the governor's blessing. The men missed their beer, considered by all sailors and laborers as part of their usual pay. Governor Gates had decided they deserved a bit of cheer for all their hard work. But I feared they would drink until crazed and dangerous to themselves and others.

"Your dishes, dear girl, have you decided upon them?" Mr. Strachey prodded.

"I keep changing my mind," I told him.

He observed me in his quiet way, over the bowl of his pipe. "Do you not think they make a fine couple?" There was a playful twinkle in his eyes. He was testing me, as he seemed inclined to do when in a good mood.

"I think Mr. Brody had few choices for a mate, stranded here on this mostly male island. And Mistress Anna fewer still by now, since she is quite clearly already with child." For indeed I had noticed a change in her shape.

He cracked a laugh. "You are learning, girl."

"I know more than enough."

"You know then that Thomas dotes on you."

I had been prepared for the conversation to turn in this direction, sooner or later. In defense, I took it off in another.

"As you dote on your dark lady?"

His face paled whiter than the chalky cuttle-fish shells I plucked from the beach and used to scour my pans. He looked away and blinked.

It wasn't often I got the better of him in our conversations. Now it pleased me, though I felt a little cruel. "Does she truly have wires for hair?"

"You speak madness, girl," he snapped.

"But in your journal—"

He turned terrible eyes on me. "And do you pry into others' private affairs so readily as mine?"

"You left it by my fire. The wind blew pages open. I merely looked down at my feet. Am I to blame for what my eyes perceive?"

"You told me you did not read," he accused.

"I read but poorly, sir. I said so. But your words were plain." How had I become so bold, to be arguing with a gentleman poet?

"Plain?" His eyes widened. "You should not have . . . should not—" He sputtered to silence, staring down at his soft, long-fingered hands, calloused only where his quills rubbed. Berry ink etched the pores of his thumb and second finger. "Wicked wench."

Strangely, his anger encouraged rather than dissuaded me. For it hinted at secrets Mistress still refused to disclose. Secrets I had decided to uncover, were I able, if only to protect myself. "It seems to me, sir, it is your poem that is wicked. You say vile things about your beloved."

"Not vile, honest. Far better truth than the flowery drivel spilling from the pens of young Masters Webster and Middleton." He stopped and shook his head. "Aside from that, she is not mine, as you call her."

I shrugged. "You would have her though, if she stayed true." I paused, feeling naughty for teasing him, but attracted by a romantic thought. "Is that why you are journeying so far from London? To escape the sadness of losing your love?"

"You have no idea what you're saying, stupid girl." His words were harsh, but his eyes less so. "Love, 'less you experience it, is as much a mystery as anything in life." He seemed unsettled by my words, not enjoying the game as much as I.

"You are right," I admitted. "I don't understand love. So tell me, sir. Tell me about love."

"I am beginning to think I should never have given you a new name," he snarled. "For in so doing I have created a woman of a different and less agreeable nature." He gave a weary sigh. "The submissive Elizabeth was far easier to tolerate. What is't you would know now, Miss Miranda?"

I thought for a moment. I had so many questions. "Why do men marry if they have no intent of faithfulness?"

He sat down on the small barrel where I kept the precious flour I'd ground from wild grasses, tipping his head to one side, laying his journal upon his lap, hands folded across it as if in tender protection. "To other men, I cannot speak. To my circumstances—"

"Yes?"

"It is difficult not to fight the trap."

"Trap?" I asked.

"A babe out of wedlock, Miranda. We spoke of this before."

"I remember." I hoped this time he'd tell me all of his story.

"She was older than I, my Ann. Well experienced in the ways of catching a husband, I suppose. And I, of decent family but young and foolish, did lust for her. She took me to her bed with all apparent joy. And I did love her then, as I am sure she loved me."

"She was with child and you arranged for the license in haste, just as our couple here in the Bermudas?"

"Exactly so. But I had no trade other than my father's. Glove making. No house for us, and so we lived with my parents. I could not support her and the babe otherwise. Before long, another two came. Twins!" A flash of joy came into his eyes.

"So you worked with your father in the glove trade?"

His gaze lifted to the distant horizon. "I might have done. Yes. Except there was a small matter of my poaching from a powerful man's woods." He winced. "But more dangerous still, the queen's spies watched us close."

"You were Catholic like us," in a whisper now. He'd more than hinted at this months before, his cousin being accused and executed.

"Rumors, dangerous gossip was spreading. I had to leave and find work elsewhere."

"Where?"

"With a noble benefactor and his company. His players offered me labor, and he a form of protection for my family."

I gaped at him, my heart racing with excitement. "That is how you came to write poems and dramas, for players to recite?" I had seen traveling troupes two times in my life. Both before my father was taken from us. Then there was the one glorious day when Mother took me to *The Rose* to see Marlowe's play.

"The poems were *private*, for a friend," he explained, giving me a chastising look, "as was the poem you read here." He pressed his hand over his journal. "But the plays, we all in the company wrote them, some adding more than others, being better at it and finding the task more agreeable. We wrote them, played them, moved from town to town, keeping ahead of our enemies. Some claimed we were an evil influence, encouraging adultery and plotting against queen and country. Happily, we became the Lord Chamberlain's Players and fell under his formidable protection."

Elated by my discovery, I threw myself down beside him on the sand. "*You* wrote plays just like the dashing Christopher Marlowe?"

He made a face. "Vile hack."

"He was not! I loved *Tamburlaine*."

"Did you ever see a play called *Richard III*?"

"No."

"That one is better than anything Marlowe or even Ben Jonson ever could write." His eyes lit with sudden delight.

"A play about a dead king? And a bad one at that." I remembered my history. "The king, that is, not the play, I should hope. And who wrote that one?"

"William Shakespeare."

"Of course I have heard of him." I shrugged, not wanting

to sound stupid. "And you admire him so much more than the great Jonson and Marlowe?" For even peddlers on the street knew of them.

He laughed and shook his head. "Admire Mr. Shakespeare? Not exactly that. I had just hoped one day . . ." He closed his eyes for a moment and breathed deeply. "Never mind." Reaching down to pat my hand, he stood up with energy, as if to be on his way. "There is little use speaking of plays and such. London is as distant to us as the moon. We may none of us ever see her or her playhouses again."

I nodded. It was true.

"But that should not stop you from seeking love," he added.

"There is only one thing I wish for myself here and now."

He looked down at me. "Yes?"

"I would learn to read better. Maybe even write a little, like you."

"Why?" he asked.

"Because," I said, "I see that it is a pleasant and interesting thing to do when one is alone. I see how you enjoy it."

He planted his feet, as if he had made up his mind now to stay. His voice went soft to match his eyes. "And you truly would prefer to be alone all of your life?"

"I told you my story. My family is gone to queen and plague. And as to friends . . . they were the ones who betrayed us." For uncovering Papists our good neighbors each would have collected a reward.

I stared at my hands, knotted in my lap. When he said nothing in response, I continued. "If I must be with people, then I would wish to be a victualer, cooking as I do here.

That is as happy as ever I could be in the shadow of my family's loss."

I didn't look up, but I felt his smile on me. "Have you never longed for a young man to love and to love you?"

Here he was, back to that nonsense again. I swallowed and bit my lip, struggling against memory's pain. My aching heart had no answer for him.

"Never?" he persisted.

"As a foolish girl I dreamt of marriage. But that was before I understood what men did to women in the name of love."

"What is that, Miranda?"

Tears filled my eyes. I had sworn to never speak of that time. It was unthinkable to do so now, saying these words to a man. Yet if I did not, never would he cease his pestering.

"My uncle . . . two months after my father died. One day when my brothers were away he came." I swallowed. Yes, more than sounds through walls, this was the memory that haunted me. "He took my mother, roughly, though she begged him to cease."

I had tried to stop him, though I was still a child. But she bade me leave her and later told me she feared he would have taken it into his head to fancy me as well, the filthy devil, had I stayed. He was in no way a mirror of his brother, my father.

Without looking at my friend's face, I sensed his rage. He spent a long while before speaking, as though he were writing and rewriting the words in his head until satisfied. "Rape is not love," he said.

"Men know not love as women do!" I cried. "They poke a woman for the pleasure of causing her pain and grief. They call it love, but it is a trick to get what they want. To satisfy their disgusting urges."

"A man who would abuse a woman is not a good man."

"There are no good men!"

"Am I not good in your eyes?"

"You are not—" I stopped myself. "You are different. Your passion comes through your words." I pointed to the journal.

"Before passion flows to pages, it must travel through the heart. The hands. The body. I have loved in my day."

I stood up abruptly and walked back to my cauldron to give it a good stir. He was telling me he was like other men. I did not want to hear it.

"Here." He opened his journal to a particular page and held it out to me. "Tell me if this answers some of your questions."

"You know I cannot read all of the words," I objected. "These appear harder than the others."

"Then I will read them to you." And he began,

"A woman's face, with Nature's own hand painted,
Hast thou, the master-mistress of my passion;
A woman's gentle heart, but not acquainted
With shifting change as is false women's fashion;
And eye more bright than theirs, less false in rolling,
Gilding the object whereupon it gazeth;
A man in hue, all hues in his controlling,
Which steals men's eyes and women's souls amazeth.
And for a woman wert thou first created,
Till Nature as she wrought thee fell-a-doting,
And by addition me of thee defeated,

By adding one thing, to my purpose nothing.
But since she pricked thee out for women's pleasure,
Mine be thy love, and thy love's use their treasure."

I swallowed. "I do not follow all of the words nor all of their meaning. But is this not about the love of the writer for another man? He wishes for this young gentleman with womanly attributes . . . to be a woman."

My friend tilted his head to one side and looked at me. "Love by any other name, my dear. With no less passion, pleasure, nor pain than any other."

I stared at him. Had he written this, or simply copied another's work? Did it matter? He presented it as a lesson, but how could I benefit when all it did was to confirm the very reasons I had vowed never to love?

"Love only brings sadness. Your poetry proves my case." I looked away.

He let out a breath of frustration. "Perhaps you are the wiser of the two of us." He tucked his journal into the leather satchel he sometimes carried about with him. As if in afterthought, he took from its folds a smaller book with a worn cloth cover.

"Since you would improve yourself, practice reading on this." He tossed the slim volume to me.

I looked at the cover as he walked away. *Metamorphoses.*

If this were a love story, I'd return it to him, unread, on the morrow.

Twenty-four

But love is blind, and lovers cannot see
The pretty follies that themselves commit.
—from *The Merchant of Venice*

*I*n devising a suitable menu for the wedding feast, I made the mistake of asking the bride for her opinion. Anna, the daughter of a tradesman, treated me with disdain because I was a serving girl. Yet the attention she received from our company as her nuptials approached made her worse, silly girl.

"I will have no common food served at my wedding feast," she proclaimed. "No turtle soup, for I am sick of it. No tiresome roasted seabirds."

I thought for a moment, wishing to give her only the plainest of foods while still needing to please the governor. "Two whole wild hogs roasted, then?"

She rolled her eyes and simpered. "They will have to do. But you must baste them in luxurious sauces and glaze them over until the skins crisp and ripen and shine. And I would have fresh fruits in a delicious compote. And sweet sallets of greens, such as rumor says you obtain for the admiral's table."

Being on the main island, she did not know that all of the admiral's men dined on such fare or better three times a week. Admiral Somers kept my talents to himself, no doubt fearing the governor might snatch me away for his own kitchen.

I held back a smile and pretended meekness. What to her seemed elaborate, to me was as simple as eggs and fatback. "I shall follow your wishes," I said. "What will you wear for your wedding gown?"

Her eyes brightened, and she seemed for a moment to forget I was beneath her and therefore an unworthy companion for casual conversation. "Oh, it is perfect. I shall be the most beautiful bride." She giggled. "In a Paris-made gown, do you believe it?"

In truth, I did not. The girl was delusional! We had no means of communication with the Continent. No way of even getting word to the Virginia Company that we were safe and in good health after surviving the storm. If any of the other ships in our flotilla had returned to their home port with word of the tempest, all of London must assume us drowned.

"I don't understand," I said.

Her eyes gleamed. "Mistress Horton has promised to lend me her frock of silk and fine lace."

A little pinch of pain made me gasp. Had I been the one marrying, Mistress never would have offered to lend me so much as a glove.

But of course I wasn't marrying.

A vision of Thomas came to me unbidden. His full-moon face, teasing green eyes, tousled hair growing longer by the day, and his body . . . as tall and strong as the lordly cedar tree. When he stood near, he towered over me. He had to bend to fold his muscled arms around me. Remembering that moment in my kitchen sent a shiver through my body. To my surprise in its wake came an agreeable sensation. Annoyed at my rebellious imagination, I chased out of my mind all thoughts of eyes, arms, lips, and any other part of the man.

The morning of the wedding came, clear and bright and beautiful. Never had the sky appeared so richly blue, nor the ocean that surrounded us so vivid a turquoise, with nary a whitecap in sight. The sun soon baked the sand, leaving it warm beneath my feet as I crossed it to my kitchen. New flowers bloomed where they had not been before, and I grieved for not knowing their names.

Had I a chance not to be present at the wedding ceremony, had I escaped the task of preparing and serving the marriage banquet, I would have spent the day with Mr. Ovid's little book, cozied in a sunny spot, sheltered from the still-chill wind and away from the raucous affair. I had discovered a liking for the old Roman's tales and wondered if, like Daphne, I might change into a bay laurel and thereby escape my pursuing Apollo.

However, as with all services of worship on the island, the governor ordered every man, woman, and child to attend.

The only souls missing were those same handful of sailors who remained apart and in their woods, lazing about in their foolishness—useless, drunk, and scoffing at the rest of us.

However, these days the governor was more concerned with another form of insubordination. Stephen Hopkins, a learned man who often read from the Bible with his friend, the troublesome Mr. Want, debated with our minister on matters of theology, and was growing bolder of late. Hopkins had gathered around him a group of men who met to debate issues of importance, challenging the governor's authority, making seditious suggestions to others that they might break with the company entirely. They stood as one at the ceremony, bearing sour witness to the proceedings. I hoped for Anna's sake they would cause no disturbance.

Anna's mother had adjusted Mistress Horton's dress to suit the younger, plumper, figure of the bride. Anna was right; she did look beautiful, though I hated to admit it.

I tried to imagine myself wrapped within yards of silver foil and creamy silk, shimmering in the sunlight, my face alight with joy and flushed with love. But the last time I had peered into Mistress's looking glass, the creature gazing back at me had been an ordinary woman with sunburnt cheeks and common brown hair. What man could love this?

Anna's betrothed, Arthur Brody, wore a leather doublet and a borrowed waistcoat only a little too big on him. The couple held hands and gazed, most rapturously, into each other's eyes. I wondered at the girl's foolishness. Did she truly believe she could trust this young man and he would never hurt her?

I tried to remember what I could of my dear father. He

had been a good and kind man. He had never struck us, his children, nor his wife. The only pain he'd caused my mother was the unavoidable agony of bearing his four children. How rare a man was he?

Thomas.

Thomas Powell was unlike my father in physique and mind and temperament. I had seen him drinking with our guardsmen before our beer ran out, although he disdained palm wine. There seemed nothing special about him, despite what Mr. Strachey said.

Forget him, I thought.

The wedding service was held in the small chapel the governor had his men build of palm fronds, reeds, and grass mats within the main island's stockade. There were no pews, for the wood could not be wasted when we needed it for the ships, so all stood at worship. The service seemed to stretch on interminably. I kept my eyes lowered, as if in prayer. The only time I had prayed, since the day they took away my father, was over my mother's bed. There was little else to do for her or my siblings.

Sometimes, though, as now during this celebration of marriage, my fingers strayed from habit toward my mother's rosary beads, sewn into my hem. To clasp them between my fingers and whisper my Hail Marys would be a comfort. But even as I imagined the cool strands looping my fingers, I felt a warning tingle at the back of my neck, such as when one senses watching eyes.

I looked up and around. Mistress, seated beside me on her chair, carried there by two sailors from her hut, had closed her eyes and appeared to have dozed off. All other faces were turned earnestly toward the bride and groom, standing before Master Bucke. But I saw Thomas only a row behind me, and though his attention seemed on the couple, his gaze flickered quickly toward me then away, and I felt sure it had been his eyes I'd sensed on me.

I kept my hands tightly clasped to prevent them from trembling at the thought of him.

At last, with a "Hurrah!" from the congregation for bride and groom, the ceremony was over and time for feasting had come. I rushed down to my kitchen and found the meat sizzling and perfect to my pinch, three soldiers having been left to keep the spits turning.

In addition to two glorious hogs, I served up kickshaws of hog-liver pâté, fat crabs with pine nuts, mustard greens, wedges of palm heart, immense raw oysters in their shells, herb tart with mint and wild basil, steamed prawns, and my version of hot codlings using roasted beach plums. For although I'd vowed to keep the feast simple, when it came time to prepare it, I could not contain my muse.

When all were served, I took a bark trencher and perched on a dune away from the company, glad to be separate from the noisy merriment.

Mr. Strachey, I saw, sat with Governor Gates, Admiral Somers, and Captain Newport. The bride and groom as well were given a place of honor at their table. There was, in fact, only one table, that for the bridal couple and our officers. All other guests had spread blankets, cloaks, or palm fronds upon the sand and sat there to eat.

To my embarrassment, but apparently to no one else's, the bride and groom were unable to keep their hands off of each other, exchanging caresses and greasy kisses between bites of my succulent pork.

I turned away.

When I glanced back at my plate, a familiar hand reached over my shoulder and dropped a rosy beach plum on it. As it withdrew, the fingers brushed the side of my neck. I closed my eyes on the lovely little quiver as they departed.

"You need to eat more," Thomas said. "You work hard. You are getting too thin."

"I eat enough." Remembering his embrace, feeling again the warmth and strength in him these many weeks later, I flushed.

His mossy green eyes roamed my features. "Your food is delicious because you cherish it as you would a child."

I laughed. "I think it is just good food."

"No one else cooks like you, Elizabeth. I can't cook like you do."

I shrugged, looking away, but it was true. His dishes lacked flavor or delicate texture. "I cook what is here. The fowl, the hog, the fish."

He shook his head. "No." Reaching down, he wiped away juice clinging to my lips from my last nibble of sweet meat. "It is a gift. Your love of food makes it delicious."

I did not know what to say.

He sat down beside me. "Will you teach me, Elizabeth?"

I scowled at him, shocked. "I have nothing to teach you. I have less experience than you about foods."

"You have secret ways. You gather spices, herbs, weeds, berries—I've followed you sometimes on your expeditions, did you know that?" He spoke on quickly, seeing the panic in my eyes. "Because I worry about you, not to bother you. Your natural treasures become magic in your hands. Teach me, Elizabeth. Please."

I looked into his eyes, expecting to see evidence of teasing. But he seemed as serious as our minister on a Sunday morn.

"If you wish." But I did not like the idea.

He smiled. "Tomorrow. I will come to you after my noon mess."

I nodded and ate his plum as I watched him go. It was sweet and juicy and good. But the tightness in my stomach remained.

Twenty-five

This is as strange a maze as e'er men trod,
And there is in this business more than nature
Was ever conduct of.
—from *The Tempest*

I have another favor to ask," I said.

Mr. Strachey looked around at me from where he stood, tapping his foot, clapping to the music of the two sailors playing flute and whistle while another beat a tattoo on a barrel top—the wedding orchestra. Bride, groom, and friends laughed and danced on the sand, while others wandered up and down the beach, glad for the sun on their shoulders and a closed shipyard. I had waited until my friend was alone to speak to him.

"Does this have anything to do with the conversation I witnessed between you and young Thomas an hour ago?" His old-man blue eyes were bright with mischief.

"And you scold me for minding others' business?" I shook my finger at him playfully.

"Out with it then." He tugged on the gold earring in his left lobe, a nervous habit I had noticed more often these days.

"I need you to put to writing receipts for my cooking."

He frowned. "Why? You never have trouble remembering your ingredients."

"To give to Thomas."

"Ah." A small smile.

"He wants me to be his teacher," I explained. "I would avoid his interference in my kitchen, if possible. It is all I can do to prepare three messes a day without him peering over my shoulder." I sighed, trying to sound as if this made sense. "Besides, my writing is so poor he should never understand it even if I did figure out the right words."

"I see." He stroked his beard, which had grown in full and resplendent. Indeed, most of the men had tired of shaving. The reddish hue of his made the gold earring shine the brighter.

"If I give him receipts, he will follow them in his own kitchen and won't need to . . ." I pictured his massive hands gripping my stirring sticks, gripping me, and shivered. "He won't need to spend so much time away from the main island and his duties."

"Of course. A practical solution—but then, you are a

practical young woman. And how many receipts do you wish written for him?"

I breathed out in relief. He would do this for me. Praise Mary! "Ten . . . is that too many?"

"One is too many," he grumbled. "I am a busy man."

"Yes," I agreed. Sitting on this island, writing plays that no one would ever perform. "Maybe only five or six would satisfy him?"

"So you intend that I become your secretary." Now I was certain he was teasing me.

"Only for this one task, please, sir."

He laughed. "That's what they all say. Just one more. Write us one more."

"One more what?" I asked.

He waved me off. "More important is the question, does Thomas read?"

My hopes fell. "I don't know. I hadn't thought." He was clever enough to, but he had never mentioned schooling. He was not a gentleman like the governor or Mr. Strachey. Why should I think he either read or wrote?

Then I remembered. "He keeps a log of his supplies. I have seen him checking off used items, noting down ingredients found. He must read and write a little."

"Good then. Where do we start? With your magical herbs?"

I nodded. "Yes. Thank you, Mr. Strachey."

"If I am to be your secretary, you should call me Will."

I laughed. "I couldn't." He was mocking me, making me feel foolish for asking such a boon.

"It is my name. But do as you like." He sounded suddenly irritated with me.

"If you continue to call me Miranda, I shall call you Will," I agreed. And somehow this pledging of names made my new life all the more real, and hopeful, to me.

The weather was vile without respite for the next fortnight. The rain never stopped, and bitter-cold sea air chilled the body to the bone. My hands were chapped raw, my lips cracked like weathered parchment, so that I must salve them with turtle oil morning, noon, and night. I felt I should never be warm again.

Piss pots waited to be full to the brim before emptying. Our huts stank of us. All work on the ships stopped, to the annoyance of our officers. Few ventured out from their shelters unless ordered to sentry duty.

But my cooking fire had to remain on the beach, apart from the compound and our palm-bough huts, for fear of a spark catching the leaves and burning us out, although I thought that unlikely in this weather. Nevertheless, there I stayed at my beach kitchen, forced to brave the elements for most of every day to make my preparations. Volunteers braved the fierce, whistling winds and drowning rains to bring the cooked food back to the compound where it was distributed before it cooled.

Although our carpenters had provided for me a sturdy roof of palm fronds and woven reed blinds, rain still blew in from the sides. It was all I could do to keep my fire from dying in the wicked blasts. I was cold all day and only dried myself at night in order to sleep, wrapping myself in a quilt and hanging my clothing to dry. Even so, every morning my shift still felt damp. I put it on and shivered all the day long. Nothing felt dry to the touch, and a sinister gray-green mold began to grow over everything.

On the fourteenth day Our Lord returned the sun to us, and spirits lifted. During the rain Mr. Strachey, Will, twice visited me in my cooking hut and, despite stormy conditions, dutifully took note of my cooking. I made a stew of oysters, boiled a turtle soup, and prepared a lovely sallet of wild carrots and greens.

While he watched me work, he recorded my instructions for Thomas.

"Have you written more poems?" I asked.

"No."

"You should write another play," I said.

"Like your favorite, Mr. Marlowe?" he snapped, in one of his moods.

"Or as Ben Jonson or Mr. Shakespeare, whosoever you prefer." I looked at him to see his reaction.

He .did not seem pleased with my suggestions. "Why should I write a play when we have here neither players nor theater, nor even a town square in which to perform?" My earlier thoughts exactly.

"You might write a play just for us," I suggested. "We could have a grand revel and each take a part. Make certain to mark down the lemon grass," I added, pointing to the paper he protected with his cloak from the blowing rain.

"I might," he said thoughtfully. "But if I took on such a foolish task, what should be my theme?"

"You ask me?" After all, he was the learned gentleman. "Something about magic."

"Magic?"

"Because the sailors told us this was a land wicked and enchanted."

"Well, yes, everyone loves magic . . . dark and dangerous."

"Or good and sweet, delivering innocents, such as we are, from peril." I thrilled at the ideas suddenly swimming in my head.

He looked out across the cove, the horizon invisible beneath the gray cloak of driving rain. "Perhaps we should begin with a storm like the one that landed us here."

"I don't want to think about storms again." I shook my head. "'Tis bad luck. We don't want it to follow us to Virginia."

He laughed. "You speak of the tempest as if it were a creature, stalking us."

"Sometimes I fear it will come back and sweep us off our island. No storms please."

He smiled to himself. "I rather like storms. They are useful and very exciting to an audience." He thought for a moment. "Will you settle for a magical storm, Miranda?"

"If it is gentle in the end, as ours seems to have been to us."

"Good then. A forgiving storm. We will need characters." He gave me a long look.

"Don't forget the roots," I reminded him when I saw he'd stopped copying my additions to the pot.

He looked away over the water again, and even as he did I saw a promising slice of blue sky show through the clouds.

"A wizard," he whispered.

I sighed. "Roots!"

"A dark intrigue and hidden identities," he mused.

There would be no receipt worth using this day, I thought grimly. Every third item would be missing.

Already I had put off Thomas three times when he asked if he might come and learn my methods. And I had caught him trailing after me twice, when I crossed to the main island to search out my ingredients.

"Why do you do this?" I'd asked. "You will be accused of shirking your duties."

"I wish to see no harm comes to you." He winked. "Consider me an older brother, looking out for his dear little sister."

"Then come walk with me instead skulking behind trees." I shook my head in frustration. If I could have accepted him as a companion, as I had Will, all would have been well. But the need and heat I felt from his body whenever he was near, and the long looks he gave me when he thought I wasn't aware, were in no way those proper to a friend or brother.

I could see that his impatience would soon drive him to my kitchen, with or without Will's notes. Bother!

"What say you to royals as characters?" Will persisted.

I gave up and joined in. "Every play has them, so I suppose you must. But make them special. And add a fairy creature or monster or avenging goddess!" Another idea. "Oh, and cannibals, but not too frightening ones, and a beautiful princess and a kingdom to be saved and—"

"No more!" Laughing, he held up a hand. "Like your receipts, too many ingredients or the wrong mix and the stew will be spoilt."

"Too few make for a boring, tasteless porridge. Ask your friend Thomas."

He did not have a response to that.

When I turned from my cauldron to look at him, his eyes had clouded over as if he had left this world for another. He stood up and strode away into the rain, and somehow I knew I wouldn't see him for the rest of the day.

Twenty-six

She is a woman, therefore may be woo'd;
She is a woman, therefore may be won.
—from *Titus Andronicus*

*P*utting off Thomas any longer became hopeless. He sent messages by way of the new ferryman every day, asking if I was ready to teach him. Each day I sent word back that I was too busy, promising to accommodate him soon.

At the end of another week, Will returned to me with three complete receipts. He read them to me slowly, while I watched the words. I remembered many more of them from my father's schooling than I had thought I would. Others, unfamiliar at first, started to take shape in my mind after I begged the historian for a second, then a third reading.

I sent the receipts off to Thomas in the hands of our ferryman. Less than two glasses later came his reply in a brief letter:

Will study your notes to prepare for my first lesson. I come for my first on the morrow. Thomas.

I groaned. Was there no way around the man?

The day he came to me, the March winds beat out of the north, as cold as any our previous winter. Fortunately, the rains had stopped, and I was lucky to have the land at my back, blocking the worst of the gusts. The palms rattled angrily overhead. Terns, swallows, and gray seabirds hunched in the brush, their feathers fluffed to provide warmth. It felt almost a true English winter gale, though not one flake of snow did we see and our admiral told us we should expect none.

Thomas arrived immediately after noon mess, ducking beneath the canopy, immediately filling up my kitchen with his big body so that I felt crowded. "Don't touch anything," I said. Tucked under his right arm was a bundle of canvas. I watched as he untied three hemp laces that bound it, then shook out the coarse fabric with a sharp *flap*, revealing another layer of cloth inside.

"What is that?" I asked, warily.

"A quilt."

"It looks more like a lot of horrid old rags all patched together."

"Naw." He grinned. "'Tis good Scottish wool for keepin' a body warm."

I examined the ugly thing. It appeared to be pieced together with no apparent pattern, the stitches of random length, showing themselves in loops and puckers. "Did you sew these scraps together yourself?"

"I did." He grinned with pride.

I thought the thing pitiful—the colors faded and mismatched, the edges all around frayed.

"Why did you bring it?"

He looked at me as if I were simple. "To keep us warm while you teach me."

"The fire will keep us warm." I fixed on him a hard look.

"Our fronts, yay, but what of our shoulders and backsides while the wind whistles 'round us? Come here, lass, I'll show you."

I pretended not to hear him and kept busy at my cauldron, but he was patient, standing there, his ugly quilt suspended in outstretched hands while I feigned hustling about with great urgency—stirring, chopping, tasting, mincing herbs, scattering them over the surface of the stew. Soon, however, there was nothing left to do but let the pot simmer and allow Thomas to prove himself right. In that way he was as stubborn as my brothers had been. Bless them.

I walked over to him. "Very well, then, you may show me."

He draped his rags across my back, then across his. The blanket was wide enough to encompass us both.

"There," he said with satisfaction, "you see how comfortable we are now, lass?"

"I see," I said warily.

He reached in front of me and tugged my end of the quilt around in front of us to meet his end. And now we were wrapped together as if two caterpillars within a single cozy cocoon.

He was right. It was warm. His body standing beside mine made a good deal of heat even without the fire.

"Fine," I said, pushing against the cloth. "Let me out. I need my hands free if I am to do any cooking."

He didn't release the ends, and I remained trapped there with him.

"I can see 'twill be a while before you need to do anythin' more. And I have your receipts here." He drew out the rolled pages from inside his shirt. "'Tis fortunate I can read. We will discuss each of these now to make sure I understand your instruction, which will save time later."

This wasn't working the way I had planned.

I studied his face for signs of deception. He observed me solemnly with eyes that reminded me of winter ale—open, trusting, eager.

I groaned. "All right then."

The warmth of the fire on my face, the sweetly seductive smell of wood smoke, the sound of the ocean's liquid pulse and my own bone weariness made me lazy enough to object no further. I hadn't been this blessedly warm in over a month.

"Let us sit," he suggested, easing me down with him onto the big driftwood stump from which I often watched my pot.

I settled beside him, our hips touching. I would have moved aside, but he seemed unaware of the intimacy of our bodies as he unrolled Will's recordings of my cooking. "I shall read these one more time aloud," he said, "so that you can hear them and make comment."

I nodded to urge him on. The quicker he was done, the sooner I could chase him from my kitchen and return to my work.

He read one receipt after another, nodding now and then

with understanding, sometimes murmuring an "Ah yes," or, "I see, of course."

I said nothing.

Already drowsy, under the spell of his deep voice, I knew I should stand up or fall asleep. I wished he would finish with his reading and leave me but wanted not to lose the warmth of his quilt. Would it be as warm without him in it?

Letting my eyes drift closed, I felt somehow lighter, no longer attached to earth, almost floating. My head dropped forward, too heavy to lift again. Then . . .

I sensed that time had passed, though how much I could not say. When I raised my eyelids, I saw that the sun had descended toward the western horizon, pulling the earlier storm clouds with it to reveal a calm lapis sky, except in the west, which was starting to take on the hues of gemstones— amethyst, ruby, topaz. The ocean reached into the distance in a seamless blue expanse, rippled by only the softest of swells.

My cheek rested on a warm, firm cushion. I cringed, re- membering my circumstance. Thomas's shoulder, that was my pillow. His arm encircled my body, bracing me against him.

I shifted, and he turned his head to look down at me.

"Awake now?"

"I was sleeping?" I was horrified.

"Very soundly, lass."

I wiped a dribble of spittle from the corner of my lips, hoping he hadn't noticed. When I turned to tell him I would now arise and finish preparing supper, as he must return to do for his own men, he bent and brushed his lips over my cheek.

I stiffened.

"Do you not think if I wanted to hurt you, lass, I might ha' taken advantage of your slumber?" he whispered.

"I—" I shook my head, confused, because this made sense. Then why hadn't he? "My stew will burn."

"I've been watching it. The fire burns low." He brushed my lips with his. His hand, around my shoulders slid down as if to leave me, but stopped around my waist. "It needs a while more for the meat t' be tender, accordin' to your instructions." He nodded at the receipt, weighed down by a seashell on the ground in front of him.

"Any longer and the pot will boil dry. Then it will taste like your stews." If I offended him, so much the better. He'd then release me.

Instead, he laughed loud and long, tears springing up in his eyes. "What does it take to woo you, Elizabeth?" He opened the quilt, stood up, and then rewrapped me alone within it.

I stared up at him. *Woo me?* Sweet Virgin Mary, Mother of God, please no!

He looked down at me. "I shall take your receipts to study more. You keep the quilt for when I come again, or if you are cold before then."

I blinked up at him, unable to speak for shortness of breath and tightness in my throat and a dizziness that made me think it unwise to stand up.

Do not come back, I thought as he walked away. *Do not.*

Twenty-seven

A little pot and soon hot.
—from *The Taming of the Shrew*

A week passed and Thomas did not return to Somers' Island. The first two of these days, I felt fretful and nervous, terrified of his appearing at my fire. The next two, fear turned to anger for his having teased me so. Surely he must think I was simple, to believe he was sincere, plying me with such sweet murmurings and kisses. Wooing me? More like making of me, the fool! Then three long, long days dragged past with still not a glimpse of him, and each seeming bleaker, sadder, colder than the one before.

At night, as soon as Mistress slept, I took Thomas's quilt from beneath the straw of my pallet where I'd hid it, wrapped it around my shoulders and lay warm within its fleecy, ragged folds. If I let my mind drift, I could feel his strong arm still around my shoulders. The memory of his wind-chafed lips against mine sent shivers down to the very soles of my feet. But when I dreamt of his wide fingers with their flat, square nails touching me—here, there, and in secret places—I woke in alarm, trembling.

And yet I wondered, was he still watching over me in secret, as he had told me he had done before? A concerned friend might do such a thing. What would be the harm in that?

After ten days, I felt like screaming back at the gulls that wheeled over my kitchen, begging fish heads. Such is the perversion of the heart, I thought. You wish him away, Elizabeth Miranda Persons, but when he stays gone you curse him.

And then, one bright and dry March morn, there he was again. I had removed my shoes, knotted the hems of my skirts above my knees to keep them dry, and bent down to scour a skillet with sand in the salty surf. When I turned my back to the ocean and stood up, he was above me on the sand, fists planted on his hips, feet placed wide and as naked as mine, a roguish smile on his lips.

"Well?" I did not smile back. "How did they work?"

He looked puzzled.

I rolled my eyes. "The receipts. You used them?"

"Ah." He tipped his head one way, then the other. "The gov'nor was pleased well enough."

"So you've come for more?"

"Yes, I've come for more." His tone worried me, as did his grin.

I scowled at him. "I have no more written. You will need to return after Mr. Strachey has a chance to record others."

He was shaking his head. "Not more receipts." His gaze, so full of desire, weakened my knees. "I told you my intent, Elizabeth."

To woo me.

I saw the muscles in his thighs tense and bulge, as if in preparation to take a step forward. Before I could retreat into the sea, three enormous strides brought him straight to me. His arms latched around my ribs.

I shook my head in firm denial, pulling my arms up between us to buy breathing space. "I have told you and your friend Will—I want none of your or any man's wooing."

"How do you know if a dish is well seasoned?"

I stared up at him, confused. One moment he looked as if he might devour me, the next he had forgotten his lust and was talking like a ship's cook again.

"What do you—"

"Is it too salty, too sweet? Does it call out for pepper or basil or gingerroot? How do you know?" he repeated.

"I taste it, of course."

"Then how do you know a man isn't to your taste when you have not tried him?" There was devilment in his eyes.

"I know what men want," I said, "and what they will do to get what they want."

"Not me, Elizabeth."

"You don't want me?"

"Oh, I do." He stole a quick kiss, then another when I opened my mouth to screech at him in protest. "I do, lass."

"Stop that!" I cried.

Laughing, he kissed me again, his arms tightening around me but not fiercely or to hurt, just enough to contain me, as he had done beside my fire those many, too many days ago.

"Thomas, please."

His hands smoothed upward over my back then down again. Large and strong as flatirons, they nevertheless sent a message of restraint and willingness to please.

I had imagined unpleasant, intolerable sensations in answer to a man's touch: Pain, humiliation, disgust, shame.

But Thomas's hands brought none of these.

His right hand smoothed around from behind me, beneath my arm and across the side of my breast before whisking away. His eyes studied my reaction. I held my breath as a pleasant tremble resolved itself somewhere within my private places.

Closing my eyes, I willed the feeling to linger. Held my breath. Savored the delicate fluttering thrill.

Suddenly, cool air replaced Thomas's arms.

My eyes sprang open and he was halfway up the slope of beach toward the trees.

"You are leaving?" I shouted after him.

He turned and held up a hand in parting salute. "When you are ready to taste our stew, Elizabeth, come tell me."

Twenty-eight

No epilogue, I pray you, for your
play needs no excuse. Never excuse.
—from *A Midsummer-Night's Dream*

To celebrate the sacrifice of Our Lord Jesus, the governor's men played out the passion of Christ. Our new bride, Anna, wished to portray Mary, but Governor Gates would not allow it as the player's trade is reserved for men and boys. Peter Greeley, a sailor of small stature, accepted the role of Our Lady with great solemnity.

Mr. Strachey, though asked to take a part, excused himself. At the players' rehearsal, he stood watching the awkward pantomime supervised by our minister, and I beside him.

"These are no Lord Chamberlain's Men," I whispered.

"No indeed." He frowned, looking sorely troubled.

"But they aren't so very bad for never before having per-formed."

He was shaking his head. "It is a predictable story, acted badly. They need lines, properly written and committed to memory."

"You might write a play for them, Will."

"No."

"What about the one you were working on so feverishly a month ago? Seeing a real play would bring much comfort and merriment to our company, so far from our homeland this Easter season."

He grunted. "Impossible."

"You spend all of your days writing anyway," I argued. "Why not labor at something all can enjoy?"

And, I thought, his moods might improve if he had such a task to take up his time, and an audience to applaud his efforts. Some days he seemed at peace, others restless and angry, or guarded and fearful.

However, in the days just following the Holy Season in our brave New World, Will changed his mind for apparently no reason and announced he would produce a little drama for us, as soon as he completed the writing of it.

Just three days before the date he had chosen for our enter-tainment, he picked his players and passed to each a quarter sheet torn from his precious journal, across which raced tiny, spidery letters in black ink. Those who were unable to read he partnered with those who could, then dispatched his play-ers with an imperious wave of his arm to study their words.

"What is your play about?" I asked.

"You will see," he said. "Here is your part."

I snatched my hand back from the sun-yellowed sheet, as if it were a serpent that might bite me. "It is not allowed. I cannot be a player."

He snorted. "We all are."

"What does that mean?"

He let loose a weary moan. "If you do not know . . ." He sat down with his back to a massive cedar on Somers' Hill, overlooking the lush woods of the main island and the robin's-egg-blue harbor, where our stodgy bark, heavy with timber bulwarks and forecastle was beginning to look like a real ship, though a bit top-heavy, like a busty old woman, if anyone were to ask me.

No masts or rigging yet, to be sure, but her hull looked solid, sitting proudly up on land in spider-leg struts of ce-darwood. When our new ship was set in the water, along with her dainty pinnace, their boards would swell, so Mr. Frobisher had told me, further sealing them against the sea. But, he admitted, it was a worry to him that we had only one small barrel of pitch and one of tar with which to make tight the bilge of the larger ship.

Nevertheless, my heart raced at the sight of our new boat. Did I long for rescue as the others of our company? I had often thought of the pleasure of staying on our gentle islands. In truth, little did my desires matter. I would have no choice in this as in any of my life, my fate always being decided by others.

"Take your part," Will demanded, thrusting it at me with his usual impatience. "I have obtained special permission from the governor to let you be a player for one night." I glared at it. "Go on. Read it!"

If I were as stubborn as Mistress accused me, he was ten times worse. From the narrowing of his eyes and pleating of his brow, I could see there was little chance of my wiggling out of this. My gaze dropped to the page.

"Miranda! It says Miranda here."

"That is your name in the play." He did not smile, but I had no doubt he was teasing me. "Do you not approve? Or would you rather it be E-liz-a-beth."

"No, Miranda is excellent." This might give others in the company a reason to call me by my new name, a means of gentling them into the change. I was pleased. "But the other characters, are they named for themselves . . . the people who play them?"

"No," he said, "only you are you."

I flushed with pleasure. "Good. Is there also a monster?"

"As you desired, yes." So this was the same play he had begun weeks ago.

"This monster comes from the sea or the land or the sky?"

"Too many questions." He waved a hand at me. "Put your part to memory, girl."

I flipped the page over. All of the lines, Miranda's. "But how am I to know the story? There is only this much showing my words and no others."

He leaned back, yawning, and closed his eyes as if to shut me out with a nap. "The company will learn the story as they perform. It will be the more entertaining."

Twenty-nine

The brain may devise laws for the blood,
But a hot temper leaps o'er a cold decree.
—from *The Merchant of Venice*

 A s it turned out, there were no cannibals, which I remember specifically requesting. However, one of the characters, a wretched thing by the name of Caliban, came close
enough to cannibal for me, for all Will did was to jumble
the letters. This devilish and deformed creature, though he
didn't eat human flesh, was said to be born of a witch.

For the role of this monster, Will enlisted Mr. Stephen
Hopkins, our most troublesome gentleman. Fat and ugly
enough to be monstrous in his role, he had persisted in recent
months claiming to all who would listen that our allegiance
to the Virginia Company ended at the wreck, thus releasing

us from obedience to Governor Gates. In short, he all but urged the men to rebellion.

The execution of Robert Waters, which had also caused many of Mr. Hopkins's admirers to leave him, quieted him for a time. But if the gossip were true in these recent spring days, he had taken up his preaching again and was gathering support from those who would remove themselves from the governor's and admiral's people to form their own community.

Other characters, I learned at our first rehearsal, were just as interesting, though less terrifying than Caliban. I was to be Miranda, daughter of Prospero, who had once been the duke of Milan and had educated himself to be a wizard. They lived in exile on an island where, years before, they had been cast ashore after Prospero's brother, Antonio, and Alonso, the king of Naples, had conspired to seize Prospero's dukedom, setting him and his tiny daughter adrift in hopes they'd perish at sea. Now, years later, Prospero would use his magic powers to create a tempest and cause the duke's ship to wreck, bringing all aboard her, including his brother and the king, onto this island—to punish the guilty and set things right.

"Ooooh, lookie," Sarah said, pointing to the cluster of men standing near the water's edge, comparing and laughing over their roles and lines. "That strapping young officer, taller by a head than the others, will be your Ferdinand, prince of Naples." She giggled, sticking me with her sharp elbow "Your *lover!*"

I felt sorry now I had asked her to help me learn my lines.

"He is, I suppose, good enough looking to pass as a prince."

"Ah, Lizzy, he be glorious! Look what an elegant fellow he is, how broad his shoulders, and how sweet a dimple in his chin he has and his eyes—"

"Stop," I said. "If you will keep distracting me from learning my part, I shall send you back to your mistress."

She sniffed and blinked at me. "Fine then. If you don't wish to encourage his attentions—"

"I do not."

"Then I will catch his eye over your shoulder as he woos you."

I rolled my eyes. "Do so, but first my lines. I wish to not embarrass myself before the governor."

A mischievous spark lit her eyes. "Then the two of you must rehearse together, giving words back and forth. That is the way it is done, I hear." With no more warning than that, she grabbed my hand and dragged me straight down the beach to my Ferdinand.

"G'day, to ye, sir," she sang out gaily. "I've brought your Miranda, who wishes to practice her speeches against yours."

I shook her loose, blushing fiercely, unable to bring out a word of denial from my pinched throat.

"By all means, Mistress Miranda," he said with a bow, then consulted his slip of paper. "Here is a pretty scene for us. As Mr. Strachey has explained it to me, it comes after your father, Prospero, has set me to hauling lumber to earn your affections and I have announced myself a prince." He seemed very pleased with his assigned role.

I found my voice. "That is a clever trick, getting a prince

to work when our governor has trouble keeping a sailor at his labors."

He laughed. "Very true!" Smiling, he cleared his throat, then, to my horror, bent on one knee in the sand before me, took my hand in his and recited his lines:

> *"Hear my soul speak!*
> *The very instant that I saw you, did*
> *My heart fly to your service; there resides,*
> *To make me slave to it; and for your sake*
> *Am I this patient log-man."*

I looked down at the words on my paper then up again, only at that moment seeing we had gathered about us an audience. Standing back from the others, watching intently, was Thomas.

"Go on, Lizzy," Sarah coaxed. "You got to give a line for every one he gives you."

I nodded my head, swallowed, and read my words just as Mr. Strachey had written them: "'Do you love me?'" I could look at neither Ferdinand nor Thomas.

Ferdinand brought my fingertips to his lips and crowed dramatically,

> *"O heaven, O earth, bear witness to this sound,*
> *And crown what I profess with kind event*
> *If I speak true! if hollowly, invert*
> *What best is boded me to mischief! I,*
> *Beyond all limit of what else i' th' world,*
> *Do love, prize, honor you."*

I wasn't sure I understood all the lines but I stayed true to mine:

> *"I am a fool*
> *To weep at what I am glad of."*

Glad to be loved, honored, prized. What must that feel like?

But when I looked up for Thomas, I saw him cast me a sad eye and disappear through the crowd.

"Wait, stop." I pulled my hand free of Ferdinand's. "I think it best I practice my lines alone."

He frowned, looking disappointed and stood up. "Am I not performing like a prince?"

"Truly, you are," I said. "But we should not give away the play before its performance, and too many people have gathered curious around us."

"Ah, yes," he said, nodding in agreement. "Better to keep the drama a surprise."

I turned and walked away after Thomas, wanting to talk to him.

Sarah frolicked along at my side, laughing and chattering. "Oh, did you see how Ferdinand kissed your fingers so very tenderly? Chills it gave me!" I wished I could have shared her joy, but the desolate look on Thomas's face stayed with me.

Then an idea struck. "Sarah, why don't you go rehearse for me with the prince? You know my lines better than I."

Her face lit up. "Oh, should I really?"

"You should. I am certain he will appreciate having someone to practice with. But you must find a secluded cove to go to with him, so that others will not see and the spectacle will not be discovered before our performance."

"Oh, I will!" she called, even as she was running away.

I turned, searching the beach for Thomas. At last I saw him, along with two other men already in the little dory, being ferried across to the other island.

The play was done beneath the stars, with torches blazing gold and orange, shooting up brilliant sparks and lighting our stage of rock, tree, and sand. The flames produced fearsome shadows across the beachhead, making the scenes of our production the more mystical and terrifying—to the delight of all. Our musical accompaniment: the surf, a seaman's whistle, and drums fashioned from barrels and kegs. Our only spotlight: a silvery moon, full and bright, its round face beaming down on us in appreciation of our entertainment.

Our audience sat above upon the surrounding dunes, viewing us players, costumed and disguised as best could be managed with our limited resources. The night was clear, mild, and still—so different from our damp, bone-chilling London springs. In the glow of flickering flames, the faces of the players appeared as if from another world.

The wizard, Prospero, was played by Mr. William Strachey himself. An appropriate choice, as he had conjured the drama out of his own imagination. He wore a magic cloak, or so he pronounced it, as he created an imaginary tempest that drove a ship to ground near an enchanted island, the drama modeled after our own *Sea Venture's* plight.

All of the governor's and admiral's men were amused and convivial, although a little stupid with palm wine smuggled out of the woods. Only Mr. Hopkins was dissatisfied with his lines and role.

"I will not play this heathen, this monstrosity!" he shouted, throwing down his page at Mr. Strachey's feet after the second act.

I could not blame him for taking offense, for the audience hissed and jibed at him mercilessly whenever he entered, although this was appropriate to his villainous character.

"What will we do now for a Caliban?" I asked.

Will seemed not in the least concerned and immediately called up from the audience one of our sailors who, being drunker than most, played the monster's part with great relish, drooling and cursing and inserting his own words wherever he chose.

Governor Gates laughed and clapped throughout the acting, though a bit nervously I thought, when the mutinous noblemen plotted to kill their island-stranded duke and take his kingdom for themselves.

As I played out my scenes with a most passionate Ferdinand, I was all the time scanning the audience for Thomas, but I could find him nowhere. Yet I had a feeling he was watching, from somewhere I wouldn't be able to see him.

After all of our players had taken their bows, Admiral Somers, with a mischievous twinkle in his eyes, told Mr. Strachey he was nearly as good a playwright as Mr. Marlowe or Mr. Jonson, his comment throwing our historian into the blackest of moods.

After our audience had departed for their beds, I brought Will a sweet, made from hog's milk and honey, thickened to a luscious creamy texture with cassava root.

"You say my pride stands in *my* way," I chided him. "Yet you compare yourself with the great bards and find them lacking?"

He shot me a dark, brooding look, saying nothing.

I sat beside him, silent for a time while he ate his sweet porridge. "The governor was wrong," I murmured at last.

"What are you talking about?" he grumbled.

"Your play. It wasn't *nearly* as good as one of Ben Jonson's."

I could see his rage mounting as his eyes clamped shut and cheeks shot through with crimson and purple veins. His hands trembled as they gripped his cup. "Leave me in peace, wench!"

I smiled at my ruse. "One can't call it nearly as good as any other, when it was so much *better*," I said. "Truly, I liked your play more than anything ever I have seen or read or heard about. You made me laugh and feel apart from this hard life, Will." Tears tickled my eyes. And, I thought, he had given me the part of his daughter. I felt honored.

"O heaven, O earth, bear witness to this sound." He neither smiled nor looked at me now, but I saw his pleasure in the slowly relaxing slope of his shoulders.

I stood up, feeling braver than ever I had felt. "Who are you, Will?" For days, maybe even for months, I had been working myself up to asking this question.

His right eye twitched. Finished with his sweet, he laid aside pewter cup and wooden spoon, took out his pipe, packed it tight with pungent, sun-dried tobacco leaves and lit it. "I am William Strachey—gentleman poet, historian, adventurer—nothing more nor less."

"I do not think so." I shook my head at this strange old man. Now, at last, I thought I knew his secret.

"Prospero then?" he snapped in annoyance. "Who would you have me be, girl?"

"I am not sure it matters. But curiosity pesters me. You know every one of my secrets, sir; I do not know yours."

"I am an old man who has made many foolish mistakes," he whispered. His eyes, far darker a blue than the ocean at night, seemed fiercely troubled. "If my name does not matter, then leave me be."

"Not so many mistakes, I think, to outweigh your goodness, my friend." I touched his arm.

Gazing out across the moonlit water, he puffed on his clay pipe. His face shaped itself to that of a man weighed down by difficult, perhaps impossible decisions.

But how many choices does a man have, I wondered, marooned on an island?

Thirty

If you remember'st not the slightest folly
That ever love did make thee run into,
Thou hast not lov'd.
—from *As You Like It*

The following day was proclaimed by the governor one to be spent in festivities to celebrate our survival these many months so far from civilization. We were freed from all work except for prayer, two services to be preached by Master Bucke, followed by a feast. Sir Gates's good humor even extended to pardoning those sailors too drunk to attend church. I wondered if I might have been wise to sup from their brew until I too was silly with drink, thereby winning an excuse from the king's services, which had never been my own.

But I did not take even a sip of palm wine, and so, of

course Mistress Horton insisted I attend church with her, despite my complaints of exhaustion—having so little sleep due to the play and my preparations for the company's grand feast.

Most of the gentlemen were present, though some held their heads in agony when our minister raised his voice above a whisper, which he frequently did to admonish us as to our loyalty to the Virginia Company and devotion to the king's faith. I suspected the gentlemen presented their pained selves to the assemblage with the knowledge that their absence would be noted by the governor, who might then judge them lacking when he made important appointments for positions in the new Virginia government.

I was excused early from service to see to the food, which was to satisfy all of both islands. Thomas was given the day off from cooking.

Now, as I flew around my beach kitchen, with so much left to do, he arrived, all grumbles and black looks. "I come to *ass-ist*." He gave the final word a Calibanish hiss.

I looked out of the corners of my eyes at him and sniffed, catching a whiff of sap breath. "You have been off drinking with the sailors."

He shrugged. "Not enough to do any good. Palm wine turns my stomach."

"Then stir the pot while I chop." I nodded at the cauldron, already bubbling with the early makings of a fish stew that still lacked its fish and seasonings.

He leaned over it and drew a breath as he moved the spoon lazily about in the pot but said nothing.

"Are you angry that Will gave you no role in the play?"

"Plays are for fops and boys."

"Ah," I said.

We worked in silence for a time, but I felt his anger and did not like it. "If you are going to be miserable and no good company, leave me. You will taint the food with bad spirits."

"I will *taint*—" Groaning, he shook his head and looked out across the ocean, so pale and lucid a turquoise today that it outshone the sky. "I am not the one who casts ill on food or moods or the day's festivities."

I scooped up chopped roots and greens in both hands, dropping them into the steaming broth. "Who then?"

"Who then?" he mimicked. "Who then, she asks."

"Thomas."

"Mir-an-da!" In three parts, spite. He nearly spit out my name.

I spun on him. "Well, what of it? That is my name. Mi-randa!"

"Your name is Elizabeth."

"No! That is the name of the murderess who killed my father."

"She was Our Majesty the Queen. And your father was a Papist who refused the faith of his sovereign."

"He was a good man and no threat to her!" I screamed. Tears streamed down my face as I spun away from him. "I hate you!"

He called out, "Eliza—"

But I was halfway up the dunes and into the gorse and wood. I ran until I had no breath left in me. I ran until my weary legs would carry me no further. I had neither heart nor will to return to my kitchen, whether Thomas remained there or not.

"You can every one of you go hungry for all I care!" I shouted into the wind.

I flung myself on the ground and wept.

Wept for my father's poor dismembered and dishonored body and for his lost soul. Wept for my mother's rape and her plague-swollen body. And, selfishly, for myself. Here on this island with no hope of peace in my life. No hope of love, if it even existed in our vicious world filled with Calibans.

I expected the governor to order punishment no less than the stocks for my desertion of duties. Perhaps the dunking pool, which I feared the more of the two. Nearly every week, one or another of our sailors or craftsmen found his way to punishment for a crime against the community. Drunkenness, thieving, speaking mutinous words, or arousing discontent.

But in honor of this sacred day, good Governor Gates had granted reprieve to all. Therefore, the cedar jaws and drowning chair remained available for my use on the morrow.

It came as a shock when the guardsmen didn't immediately come searching for me. I looked out from my hiding place on the wooded hillside, feeling sick at heart as I watched clusters of people begin to drift, laughing and singing after service's end, down to the beach, trenchers in hand.

There would be nothing for them to eat but unbaked root bread dough and watery broth, as I had left my dishes unfinished. My heart sank. It was too late to mend my mistake. The entire company would go hungry. Thomas would never forgive my angry words. And I would never forget his.

I lay back in the bracken, closed my eyes, and in utter misery wished myself dead.

Some time later, I became aware of jovial shouts and singing rising up from the beach. Curious, I sat up then crawled to the edge of the trees to peer down upon the cove. Canvas sails had been erected as awnings and wind breaks to shelter the food from seabird droppings and the diners from a freshening breeze. Blankets and capes were spread across the sand in a colorful patchwork. In large and small groups people sat or reclined, sopping up stew with chunks of bread that seemed to have appeared from nowhere.

Prospero's magic?

Thomas, I thought. And breathed again.

Thirty-one

Time's glory is to calm contending kings,
To unmask falsehood, and bring truth to light.
—from *The Rape of Lucrece*

*T*he next day, while searching for a new source for cassava roots on the far side of the island, I came upon Will.

His temperament had altered yet again, this time to deep melancholy. When first I greeted him, he responded not at all, so that I wasn't even sure he had heard me.

His journal lay open, and in it I saw that he had been writing a letter. It was signed at the bottom, WS.

I squatted down beside him and held out a palmful of sweet, dried gooseberries I had saved over from autumn's bounty. He looked at them for a moment before taking two, placing them on his tongue and savoring their flavor for a moment before swallowing.

"Your play was very good," I said. "Truly. Everyone liked it." I would make but a poor court fool, if all my teasing ever did was sadden my audience.

He nodded.

"Will you write another?"

"I did not believe I would write that one."

Only a few weeks ago, I would have thought, *Well, why should he have?* But I was beginning to understand, both him and perhaps other things as well. I stared at the initials in his journal.

"Will," I said.

"Yes."

"You are Will . . . William."

"I am."

"But not William Strachey. You are another William." It must have occurred to me long before this, but only now did I dare to approach him with such an outrageous notion. "You write plays. That is what you do for a living."

He sighed as if our dear *Venture*'s anchor had been sitting on his chest and I'd relieved him of its weight.

I swallowed, waiting for him to speak, understanding without his saying that he did not wish me to announce his name—his real name—out loud.

"Why?" I asked. "Why are you hiding among us?"

He didn't answer at first, but turned his head slowly and studied my face. "Think, Miranda."

I stared at him. "But I—"

"Do we not fear the same monsters?" He stood with effort, as if weariness had seeped into every bone, stealing away his strength, and slowly, ever slowly walked away from me.

I dwelt on his words for days after. What monsters had I faced? The plague. The queen's spies. Cruelty and death. Which of these haunted him now?

After a while I quit puzzling over this question, and the truth of his identity began to burn inside of me. I yearned to tell someone of my discovery. Mr. William Strachey was not the man he pretended to be. He was Mr. William Shakespeare—a poet and playwright nearly as famous as the esteemed Ben Jonson. How incredible!

Or could it be that I was naïve and falling for an old man's addled fantasy? He might be mad, my friend Will—an ordinary man imagining himself a great personage, just as other poor souls imagine themselves kings and queens and great lords.

That might certainly be the case. Hadn't we all gone a little mad, surviving the tempest?

And those of us who had kept our sanity, through these many months of abandonment in the Bermudas, might still become fodder for Bedlam. With each passing day, we came to realize the unlikelihood of rescue, for not a single passing ship had been observed by our sentries and seamen.

And now when I looked at *Deliverance*, as all had begun with great hope to call the larger of the two ships under construction, I remembered Sarah saying one day, "She do look pitiful small, don't you think, Lizzy, for traveling the sea?"

"With luck we will not encounter the swells we suffered last summer," I said. But dare we trust ourselves to luck?

But there was another concern, for the building of the little pinnace lagged behind. If this second, even smaller, ship could not be finished in time for spring launch, *Deliver-*

ance might need sail alone, as many as a third of us remaining marooned here.

Whether that was blessing or death sentence, none could say.

Would that they all went away and left me here alone, I thought, not for the first time. Here with my cahows, heron-shaws, teals, goshawks, cormorants, snipes, and moorhens. With our wild hogs of the woods and angelfish of the crystal blue waters and the lovely palmettos and lofty cedar trees. My paradise.

But what of Will? If he really was Mr. Shakespeare, what would happen to him so far away from his Globe Theatre in London? To either continue on to Virginia or to remain on these islands meant he never again would see his family or stand on a stage or give to London another play.

And if he was either imposter or mad, then revealing his identity to our officers could only bring my friend suffering. If Will were found to be lying about who he was, Governor Gates would punish him grievously. And what had become of the real Mr. Strachey, if ever there was such a man? Had this player-poet murdered him and taken his place? Was that the dark deed that inspired the plotters who would murder the duke in Will's play?

No, I decided, I cannot imagine this gentle old man as murderer. And so I kept my thoughts to myself, for as long as I could.

Thirty-two

'Tis an ill cook that cannot lick
his own fingers.
—from *Romeo and Juliet*

*A*pril arrived, her days warmer but still blustery, the winds whipping up whitecaps across an iron-gray sea, driving waves into our coves and depositing clumps of tar, which we gathered and brought to Mr. Frobisher, who welcomed them as if they were bouquets of roses. Of all the building materials we lacked, good tar with which to seal our new ships' boards was the most direly missed.

Despite the welcome warmth of spring, our good Captain Newport cautioned us in assembly during Sunday service. "It is not yet safe for continuing our journey. Calmer seas, I promise you in May and June." We trusted him, for he had experience sailing this part of the world.

However, even the hope of our soon sailing lightened many hearts. Sarah could talk of nothing else. "I shall have me own family's house to care for—made more sturdy than palm boughs, don't you know?" She giggled. "A rambling big thing of stone or brick, with a little room for my own self, as Mistress promises me, and a garden as pretty as any in England."

I sighed. "I can think of no garden lovelier than the one we have here."

"This wild place?" She laughed. "You can have it, dearie! I will be happy to see the famous Jamestown. We shall be welcomed with such joy. Life will be so much easier there."

Even Mistress Horton seemed newly anxious to be away, urging the admiral with ever more energy to set a date for launching our ships.

However, I anticipated our departure not with their joy but instead counted off the days since Thomas had somehow saved my feast from disaster. For he had not visited Somers' Island, or me, since that awful day of our bitter argument. Although I hadn't meant to, hadn't wished to, I began to look for him.

At first I wasn't sure why I should long for his presence. Was it because I had come to think of him as a friend? Then I admitted to myself, though surely to no one else, not even to Sarah, that I pined for Thomas Powell's physical closeness. His words had been cruel indeed, but they had been honest. And although he had not approached me with sweet apologies, I supposed his generous deed had been meant as such. By completing my feast, he had saved me much grief.

Besides, I missed sitting beneath his quilt and feeling his

big body warm the air around us. I longed for his wide, strong hand that moved across my back and found a place to curve around my hip, as though it were meant to be there. I missed the terrifying, delicious chills that came with wondering at his intent.

"I am going to the governor's island," at last I told Mistress Horton one mild morning that felt of an English spring.

I had hauled pond water across half the island, because all of the men were busy at the ships, and heated it to her satisfaction over the fire. I had perfumed it with petals plucked from a shrub that seemed as happy to bloom in the colder months as in the hot. I had bathed her withered body, dried and dressed her, and served her a cup of tea brewed from herbs I had collected and dried in heavy bunches, hanging inside our hut and giving off their sweet, woodsy aroma.

"You are not done with your chores here," she stated, giving me her witch's eye. "The firewood is low. I shall freeze before you return." We were allowed but one small brazier to warm us in our shelters, for even glowing coals could send up sparks and ignite a palm hut to an inferno in a single pulse of the heart.

"I will bring wood with me. I won't be gone long."

"You are consorting with sailors in the field," she accused.

"I am not."

Her voice turned sly, her eyes glinting with evil mischief. "You are meeting your lover, Thomas Powell."

I looked away from her and laughed.

"You are. You are!" She cackled. "Wicked, wicked girl, your sins will be discovered and Admiral Somers will ban you from his island."

I kept my tongue and did not remind her, though I was tempted, that she would then have no serving girl at all. "I am not Thomas's lover. I am no man's lover." A few months ago, I would have added, *I will never be anyone's lover.*

"You increase your sins by deception!" she screeched as I slipped out the door. Her cries faded as I marched out from the compound and down the grassy dunes to the beach.

Our ferryman slept in the bottom of the skiff left to transport us between the two islands. If he was on the opposite shore when one of the admiral's people needed a ride, we summoned him with a shout and a wave. But today he was handy.

I shook him awake.

He opened an eye and breathed out sour vapors of palm wine. "Miss?"

"Jack, I need to go to the governor's island." As if this were not evident by my standing there.

He tottered to his feet. "Yes, Miss."

Our Jack had been given the job of ferryman after his predecessor's murder, as he was not under the influence of Mr. Hopkins, and therefore less inclined than some to mutiny. Palm wine seemed his only vice.

He rowed the calm, sheltered blue water between islands without speaking, now and then pausing to hold his head for a moment, as if to keep it attached to his neck, and squinting as though the brilliant sunlight pained his eyes. I minded neither his silence nor the slow pace. I was just happy to be on my way to where I needed to be, without having to answer questions about my going there.

"Gov'nor Gates were at Frobisher's yard, inspectin' new

lumber last I seen him," he said when I stepped off into the sand.

"Thank you." But I did not turn toward Frobisher's.

Not since the early days of Our Lord's deliverance of us to this blessed haven had I visited Thomas's kitchen. That seemed years ago now, though it was less than nine months. I expected he had fewer mouths to feed these days, as did I. The Brownists, led by Hopkins, having grown brave again, had gathered new members and taken to meeting in the wooded hills. There they captured and slaughtered their own hogs and roasted them on cedarwood. We could smell the pungent smoke and see the glow of their fires from our stockade at night.

The sight of Thomas's broad back as he leaned over a hog carcass, swinging his heavy blade down on it, cracking bone and severing flesh, seemed strangely welcome today. A huge pot of stew bubbled over his fire. It smelt of good pork drippings and woodsy herbs. I stopped well behind him and coughed twice, to announce myself.

He froze, his cleaver in upswing, then slowly laid it down on his chopping block, which was no more than the trunk of a huge, felled tree.

He said nothing and didn't turn to greet me, but I was certain he knew it was me standing there.

"Are you too busy to speak with me?" I asked.

"Aye."

"I wish to thank you for taking my place as cook on feast day. It was a fine thing you did, feeding the assemblage." *And saving my hide.*

He said nothing. The back of his neck, sunburnt and peeling, called to me. I imagined shaping my hand around it, the way his had closed so warm and tender around mine. I recalled his lips upon mine. I felt again, in memory, his warmth, as we feel the sun's radiance even at such a great distance.

"Many, I have heard, said the meal was good," I whispered.

"Ah well."

"I don't think they know you prepared most of it."

He shrugged, his shoulder blades flexing under his shirt.

"You didn't tell them."

"Naw."

How frustrating! I longed to talk to him about so many things. I yearned to tell him about Will, about my own secrets too. But more than that, I wished to look on his big, round face. And his smile. And hear his broad, boisterous laugh.

"Thank you," I whispered. "I fear the governor would have ordered harsh punishment for abandoning my post."

He nodded, his back still turned against me.

"Thomas?"

"Yes." A cold, dead word.

"I suppose you have no more need of my cooking lessons?"

"No more'n you have need o' my company," he said.

It was such a bitter thing to say. I felt lost. I opened my mouth to object, but nothing came out. And in the end, I left him to his stews—that in the pot, and that in his heart.

Thirty-three

For slander lives upon succession,
For ever housed where it gets possession.
—from *The Comedy of Errors*

*D*ays passed. I saw Thomas not at all. The weather warmed, then turned cold again. The winds came so icy they felt of snow—though I doubted we'd see a single white flake. Rain lashed my face whenever I ventured out from our shelter, which I had to do to find wild herbs or pluck those I had planted near the compound for ease of harvesting.

I sat with Thomas's raggedy quilt about my shoulders and watched the sea turn from azure to charcoal, frothy with spume. My head pounded and raged, as it had before the tempest beset us. More storms, I thought. Oh, no!

And all this time there had been no word of our brave

messengers sent forward in what the admiral had called a *bark of aviso* to Virginia. After weeks of keeping fires burning along the beach as a signal to our messengers that they might find us in the middle of this vast ocean, the governor had finally given orders that the flames be extinguished and no more wood wasted. Although we had long ago given them up for lost at sea, in service Master Bucke still prayed for them. I secretly fingered my rosary, still safe in the fabric of my cloak, and wondered—should we ever know their fate? Indeed, should we ever learn of the demise or the rescue of the other eight ships in our fleet?

It was then I started praying again for the first time since my mother's death. I cannot say why, or whether I thought God was even listening. It just seemed the right time. Besides, I knew of nowhere else to turn for help or comfort.

I fashioned a candle of beeswax to resemble the long, thin tapers my mother had made for us when I was a child. Since attending mass in a real church was far too dangerous, we had made for ourselves a small private chapel at one end of my parents' bedroom. Behind the false back in a cupboard we secreted a small cross with Our Lord suffering upon it, candles, and other sacred objects.

Just as in those days, I only lit the wick long enough to say my prayers, then blew out the flame and hid all evidence of my faith away. I dared tell no one, not even Sarah, for she too much loved her gossip. Here on Somers' Island, I placed my candle into a burrow I had dug beneath a log, high up on the bank, then ripped open the hem of my cloak and took out my rosary, adding it to my secret hiding place.

As careful as I had been, I believed Mistress Horton suspected me of keeping my faith with the old church, or at least, of a casualness toward her faith. If she knew I remained Catholic at heart, and she continued to find displeasure in my service, she might one day turn me in to the governor, even if doing so meant losing her slave.

It was while I was still down on my knees, saying a final Hail Mary as I buried my treasures, that I was discovered. My heart leaped into my throat at the sound of footsteps behind me.

"Don't stop," a quiet voice said. "You remind me of my daughter."

I turned to see Will. What mood would dictate the role he played today?

"Are you Prospero again?"

"No, I mean my own daughter, Suzanne. She still keeps the old faith."

"It is dangerous for her," I said, crossing myself and, still down on my knees, covering the moist new dirt with leaves and twigs.

"She lives in Warwickshire, out in the country and away from London intrigues." He lowered himself onto the other end of the log. "Many more of us are there. She tells me they look after each other and keep silent faith."

I rose up to sit beside him. "I have seen little of you," I said.

His beard had grown in fuller, a deep burnished red with strands of silver through it. "I needed to be away from people, to think."

It was a desire I often shared. When I could slip away, I spent my time longing for Thomas—a craving, apparently, not to be satisfied. "And now?"

"I am done thinking."

"About?" How so bold, Miranda? If I had known who he was when we first came to this place, I never would have had the nerve to address him so, nearly as an equal.

"I will not be staying in Virginia," he said, "if we ever get there."

I stared at him. "Why not?"

"I was trying to escape from something . . . someone, when I arranged to sail with *Sea Venture*. I am no longer running away."

I wished for the courage to ask him why he had left London. Why a great playwright who had so many admirers, who must have been rich and owned land and maybe even a share of the great Globe Theatre, would leave it all behind.

He seemed to sense my unspoken questions. "I want to return to London to face the man who would destroy me."

I stared at him, unable to imagine anyone who would set out to harm the bard. "Who is this person?"

"A fellow whom I unwisely befriended." He considered this, his gaze fixing on a thicker, darker part of the woods, where shadows shifted and took ominous forms. A perfect dwelling for Caliban. "Or maybe it was less friendship than fear that welded our relationship. However it came about, I gave him what he wanted, which was a mistake."

I waited for him to go on, and after a while he did.

"George Wilkins keeps a tavern on Cow Cross Street, at the edge of Clerkenwell." He gave me a look, as if to determine whether I recognized the place for what it was. Anyone from London, of course, would.

No good lady ever walked the streets of Clerkenwell, so notorious was it as a district of the roughest brothels. I gave him a blink of acknowledgment and he continued.

"I stopped in at his tavern some days. The food was only passable, but the clients were"—he smiled in a cunning way—"interesting."

"You used them for your plays?"

He gave a weighted nod. "As an artist would his models. Wilkens dabbled with writing poems and simple dramas. He envisioned himself a future playwright and asked if I would collaborate with him."

"You said no, of course."

"I should have done, but he could be a charming fellow when he wished. And he was a good enough host, providing in many ways for his customers."

I knew the *ways* of these sorts of taverns only by reputation—their private rooms where a gentleman might entertain or be entertained. I made no comment.

"After a time, we became quite friendly. I read a poem he'd written and got published, and I decided the fellow held promise despite his coarse nature and questionable reputation. I agreed we might work together on a play. After all, that is how it is done in the theater. Many spoons stir the pot."

"And was the play a good one?"

"Good enough. *Pericles* was performed and met with fair

applause." I watched his face change, harden, the light leave his eyes, as if he were reliving a disappointment. "Then things went sour as three-day milk."

"What happened to spoil the friendship?"

"I learnt what kind of a man he was. His pimping was not of the gentle sort. I watched him beat a woman, one of his girls, near to death. I saw him as he was that night, vicious and mean-spirited. Had I not pulled him off the woman, he might have caved in her skull with his kicks.

"Although he pretended repentance before a judge, his violence and cruelty began to come through his writing. I grew wary of him. When I said I would go home to War-wickshire for a few months while the theatres were closed during the summer plague, he suggested he come with me so that we might work together on new plays."

"But you did not want him near your family," I guessed.

He nodded. "I discovered he'd been hauled to the bench many times before. Eventually, as I made plans to leave on my own for the country, he threatened to spread a rumor that I was a Papist, involved in a bloody plot against the Crown."

This was my family's fate, replayed with my friend as the hapless victim. My heart raced with terror at the thought of it. "But why would anyone believe such a criminal?"

"Despite all who would come to my defense and swear otherwise, His Majesty's ministers and the Lord Mayor have so long been set against players and our company that they might eagerly take advantage of this 'plaint and drag me off to the Tower."

A terrible chill threaded through my body. "And he would

do this out of simple spite? Or for the few coins he might receive in payment for bringing the king's agents his lies?" I stared at him, sick with fear for my friend, this gentlest of men.

He shook his head. "His motive may be darker still. If I am found guilty of treason, my properties will certainly be seized. What doesn't go to the Crown will go to my accuser."

"And that is why you left England?"

"A good part of the reason."

"And the rest?"

"Always the questions, my girl?" He sighed, taking out his pipe, but did not light it. "I suppose I dreamt of faraway lands, such as those about which I have always written but never seen with my own eyes."

Frowning, I studied his face.

He gave me a lopsided smile. "Until you are triple the age you are now, Miranda, you will not understand. We old men hunger for a last great adventure."

"You are not old." Although I had called him that in my mind often enough. "You are hale and hearty. You will write many more exciting plays and—"

"Is that not the point?" His voice rose, tight with emotion. "I have always written about great moments, in history or imagination. I have provided for my audience grand and daring adventures, *but I have never lived them!* Do you not understand the difference, child? I have never ventured beyond Britain's shores. Until now."

His gaze wandered off beyond the trees, across the sea to mysterious unknown lands.

A queer thought suddenly struck me. "How is it no one

has recognized you? Surely, some of the officers among our company must have met you at theater or tavern."

"The admiral and governor, yes. And your mistress, she knows. But as long as they think I am just a crazy old playwright chasing a whim, they will not reveal me to others. At least I think not." He tipped his head to one side and stroked his beard. "I believed it possible to remain undiscovered by the king's agents, but I worry as they are everywhere."

"Even among us?" I was horrified.

He lifted his hands in a helpless gesture. "Of course. Do you not think a man like Stephen Hopkins would enjoy distracting from his own notorious reputation among us by accusing another man of a crime worse than his own? Is not treachery against the Crown a higher treason than mutiny against a naval captain? Our good Somers and Gates surely would act on His Majesty's behalf if they suspected me or any other man a plotter against James."

Even as he said the words, I knew they were as true as the ocean was deep. But something else about what he had told me was puzzling.

"You said you would not stay in Virginia. Where then will you go?"

His eyes twinkled as if he found humor in what I had said, or in what he planned to announce. "Back to England, as I said."

"But your enemy!"

"Yes, there is he. But I have learned to love and live life in a new way, a braver way, taught by this voyage. And I miss my boys at the Globe. I must find a way back to London."

"You will be in grave danger, sir!"

"Perhaps. But I wish to write more plays. Just a few. The young playwrights, they are already trying to edge this old man out. But I am London, and it is me. Life in Southwark is in my blood, from the bear-baiting pits of Paris Gardens to the six-penny drabs and their pricey sister courtesans. I long for my cozy chamber on Silver Street and the costume wardrobes behind stage at the Globe. London is mine, and I must reclaim her—danger or not. I will return to face my foes."

"But *how* will you return?" Although our new ships might carry us the short distance on to the Virginia colony, I doubted they were sturdy enough to make the dangerous and much longer trip all the way back to England.

"At least one of our fleet must have got through the storm," he reasoned, running his fingertips thoughtfully over his pipe. "Their captains had planned to return to England with whatever cargo Virginia has to offer, and with whatever stories are to be told of our adventures. I think it a good chance that at least one, if not more, will have held over for calmer waters. If so, I will sail with one of them."

My heart sank. How much worse for me! Trapped in a strange land without my friend.

I wished away tears, swallowing over the burr in my throat. "You will show His Majesty the play of our *Tempest*?"

"Perhaps. There is another I am writing. We shall see how it turns out." He tipped up his lips in a weak smile and laid a hand on mine. "You have not been with Thomas of late," he said, startling me by the sudden change of conversation.

"No."

"You should go to him. He has a good soul."

"He will not have me now." I felt the pain of his rejection as a dagger thrust between my ribs. "I have tried."

"Truly?"

I nodded.

"Then you have what you wished for, to be left alone."

"Yes." But wishes change. "He is not a bad man, I guess. As men are concerned."

Will smiled, his eyes crinkling at the corners, making him young again. His mouth puckered for an instant, not quite laughing. "You are certain he will not come to you?"

My chest tightened and sorrow bit into me. "He is too angry."

"You will go to him then."

"I have. He barely spoke to me."

He tilted his head to one side in thought. "The boy will heal. Then he will come or you will go, and it will be as it should." His eyes held a collection of emotions, of which I could only guess—longing and loss, sadness or resignation. Poems without words. "Love is elusive, Miranda. Catch it if you can, for even a short while, and you will be fortunate indeed."

To Make a Gooseberry Foole
(to cheer the soul)

Pricke two good handfuls of greene Gooseberries. Scalde these until soft then poure off water. Mash with forke to make small and sweeten with Rose water and sugar (or honey, if there bee none). To a quart of Creame add Mace and set this over fire to boyle then take out the Mace and poure Creame atop Gooseberries, stirring all about. Stand till cool. Eate.

Thirty-four

Let me take you a buttonhole lower.
—from *Love's Labour's Lost*

*B*ut Thomas did not come. And going to him, only to be turned away again—my heart could not bear it!

I was alone in spirit, but for my creature companions—the gray-and-white seabirds, Bermuda's clever and quick little lizards, dainty yellow tree frogs, and of course the immense gentle green sea turtles. My excursions to replenish ingredients for my receipts took me to other islands, Sarah brought me her gossip occasionally, and my cooking for our company on Somers' Island filled every other hour.

It will be enough, I thought. I can be content with my work.

But what would become of me once I was forced to leave my paradise? What then? I could only think that, despite

Sarah's continuing fantasies of a grand life in Virginia, our days might grow harsher. Although . . . hadn't we believed these Isles of the Devils would be cursed, bewitched, the abode of cannibals? Perhaps I was wrong and Sarah right about the colony.

I cooked, cleaned, and kept my mistress as best I could, while trying to ignore her petulant moods and constant cawing like a great, shriveled seabird.

Another week passed, and I saw Thomas Powell only at church and for a few moments when he came to our island on a visit to the admiral, bringing a gift of wild asparagus from the governor. If he was aware of my presence, he gave no sign. Each time as he disappeared from sight, I felt my heart rend in two. If you had not been so foolish, Elizabeth Miranda, I thought, you might have kept him as a friend.

Sarah came with news that distracted me a little. "Anna's babe is born on Gates' Island!"

"So soon after her wedding?" I lifted a brow and we smiled at each other.

But no one seemed terribly shocked. After all, it was the governor's decision to put off their nuptials, and once the couple had been pledged, their intimacy was all but assumed.

"Ah, Lizzy, such celebration we'll be havin' over this first new life to come to our islands!" Sarah predicted, her eyes shining. "More'n one of our young officers been askin' me for a dance."

"Have they now?" I said.

She tipped up her pretty chin and gave me a saucy wink. "I might even consider a match if the right one do ask."

Thomas prepared a baptism feast two days later. I attended,

Will accompanying me to lend support, for I'd confessed to him my heartache. I watched Thomas from across the governor's yard, but he looked away and avoided me.

It is as well, I thought, remembering Will's words. This is what you wanted, girl, to be left in peace.

But what one wants one day may not be what is wanted another. I felt cold to the bone, drained of spirit. Each night I clutched Thomas's quilt, burying my face in its soft folds. I slept with it wrapped around me. His scent slowly faded, replaced by my own.

At last, on the first day of May, the sun came out strong and warm, an omen of spring. I spent an entire morning after the men had broken fast, feverishly cleaning, tending to every whim of Mistress Horton until she found nothing to harp about, then prepared the midday meal and served mess to my men.

I had no appetite. While they ate, I sat on a rock worn smooth by the sea and gazed across the narrow strip of turquoise water dancing in the sunlight—all that separated me from the main island.

At last, feeling a surge of determination, I stood up from my perch. Instead of scrubbing out my pots in the surf, I climbed the hill to the compound and the little cottage where Mistress dozed, drool oozing between her thin, sagging lips. Pulling Thomas's quilt from beneath my palm-bough pallet, I folded it across my arm, ducked out through the door and started walking. I prayed for courage to sustain me.

The ferryman took me across to the main island. I walked up from the harbor to the stockade and the long hut I knew to be occupied by a dozen of the governor's men, including Thomas.

His kitchen boy looked out when I called for Thomas from the doorway. "He be gone to the woods, Miss, diggin' roots."

"Thank you." I turned to go.

"I should fetch him for you?"

"No," I called over my shoulder.

It didn't take me long to find him—at one of the places I had shown him months ago, down on his knees beside a burlap sack bulging with pungent things of the wood. I smelled new-dug mushrooms, bark fungi, roots, nuts, winter berries, and herbs, all fertile and rich with the rusty-dark soil, unspoilt by ages of planting.

I said nothing, could say nothing, my throat was so closed in upon itself. I walked nearly over him before he turned with a start at the rustle of my step on dead leaves. When he looked up his eyes clouded with confusion, for he clearly had not expected me.

I stood before the big man—trembling, eyes stinging, insides tumbling and heaving as if I had eaten bad mushrooms.

His gaze, questioning yet hesitant, fixed on mine as he wiped his dirty hands down the sides of his woodsing smock. He shifted from one booted foot to the other and back again. His feet, I thought for the first time, they are enormous—to match his hands.

"Elizabeth?"

I drew a sharp breath, looking up at him then away. Nothing had changed. I should never have come.

He sighed. "Miranda, it is then. What do you want?"

I made a small brave smile and let my gaze drift down to the quilt on my arm.

His eyes followed. Understanding slowly lit his face, opening it wide to me with that lovely warm smile of his. I did not wait for him to move or even to speak. I flew at him.

I was wicked.

The quilt was generous enough, as I had imagined it would be, covering us as we stretched out upon a thick, waxy bed of fragrant pine needles. I had no fear of snakes or vermin nibbling at my exposed flesh as we lay together, for we still had discovered none on our islands. There was only Thomas to do the nibbling.

His body spread, hard and heavy, atop me. He prepared me tenderly with his strong fingers, releasing my maidenhead with only a quick, passing pain, then moving himself to fill the space he had made.

Once it was done, we rested and he stroked my breasts, my stomach, back and thighs. The soothing warmth of his hands on my flesh, which was all I had come for, seemed now not enough. I wrapped my arms as far as I was able around his great barrel of a chest and drew him back down over me.

This time I led him into me. But instead of only holding himself there, he moved within me, and it was not unpleasant. I did not think of my mother's rape or of screams through thin walls or of the women who came, bruised and battered to seek my father's healing salves. I saw and felt and knew only my Thomas.

After the third time he said, "Do you still fear me?" These were the first words either of us had spoken since my coming upon him in the wood.

I shook my head. "Do you still fear me?" I smiled innocently up at him.

He chuckled low in his throat, and there was pure joy in the sound. Then he rolled on top of me again and this time moved with great industry to release himself, and the motions of his thrusts and withdrawals made me giddy. Gasping, I clutched his long hair by the fistfuls and felt a new pain that wasn't pain, so that when he was finished he had to quiet my excitement with more kisses and stroking until I settled into a drowsy, warm sleep curled against the fur of his chest.

This is what it feels like to sin, I thought.

I am bound for hell.

Thirty-five

For you, in my respect, are all the world;
Then how can it be said I am alone,
When all the world is here to look on me?
—from *A Midsummer-Night's Dream*

You should bathe," he said.

I opened my eyes and stared up into the face of my Caliban turned prince. "Do I stink?"

Thomas laughed. "Aye, you do—of sex, lass. If you return to Somers' Island and your mistress like this, the entire company will know what you've been about."

I felt the blood drain from my face. "Where should I bathe? I would not have them see me." The pond on my island was small and usually not watched by the sailors, who could be counted on either to be working on the ships or drunk to sleep. But if I put my clothing back on to reach it, the fabric would carry the odor of our wildness.

He sat me up and wrapped the quilt around me. "Come this way."

Carrying our clothing and his foraging sack, he strode as naked as Adam through the wood. I averted my eyes from his backside as I followed, but the sight of him drew me back again. I liked the way his body moved, the strength of his shoulders, the narrowing of his waist, though his was not a boyish figure. His bottom was firm and full, and I felt inclined to cup it with my hands. I stifled a laugh at my roguishness.

How might a woman feel both possessed and possessor at the very same moment? An even more intriguing question: Why did wickedness feel so good? Neither priest nor minister had preached on these aspects of sin!

I would need to pray very hard that night to make up for having no priest to hear my confession.

As soon as we entered the clearing, I realized where we were. It was a brackish but serviceable pond nearly at the center of the main island. Surrounded by mangroves and lush with ferns erupting between the massive claw-shaped tree roots, the water was not sweet enough for drinking but would do fine for a bath.

As we entered the clearing, birds flew up in alarm. They had learnt to fear us, their hunters, even as I had learnt not to fear my pursuer.

We washed each other. Thomas let me touch him in all the mysterious places that had made me curious. I allowed his hands to roam my flesh.

We kissed. And kissed more.

"I am spent," he whispered.

"I am not," I said.

He fondled me beneath the water until, laughing and weak-kneed and used up, I clutched him to me and begged him to stop.

Thirty-six

There's small choice
in rotten apples.
—from *The Taming of the Shrew*

*T*wo problems slowed the completion of our ships that spring. Lack of oakum and Stephen Hopkins.

Although much of our dear old ruined *Venture* had been salvaged and reshaped into our new, smaller ships, most of the oakum from between her boards had worked itself free and floated away during the storm that had brought us to this blessed place.

To replace it we had few choices. One barrel of tar and another of pitch did not go far. After that, rags and boiled lumps of tar that washed up on the beaches might hold long enough. Or might not. Then we would fill up with water and sink before we reached Virginia, which Captain Newport estimated to be only seven or eight days distant.

If we made our vessels tight and the weather favored us, we would rejoin whoever among our fleet had survived the storm that drove us apart, along with the settlers of the first and second expeditions who had come to Jamestown. All must sorely miss their governor and admiral, thinking both good gentlemen at the bottom of the sea.

A substitute for oakum, though, became the lesser problem as warm currents brought us more and more tar lumps. Mr. Hopkins, who had argued for months with our minister and governor, again proved irksome by stealing men away from their work to listen to his preaching. At last, Governor Gates censured him for the peace of the community. But even this did little good, Hopkins refusing to be quieted.

Eventually the temporary bonfires in the woods of the man's followers became permanent. They built their own shelters apart from ours and warned the governor's men away with sticks and guns.

"Mutiny, that's what it is," Mistress stated over dinner with the governor and admiral. She sucked on a hog's rib, licking the sweet grease from her fingers. "Didn't I say this would happen?"

These days she regularly invited one or the other of the gentlemen to her new table, which she had paid one of our carpenters to make for her. It was long enough to seat eight, with benches at the sides for her guests and, predictably, a high-back chair of a size and rough grandeur to serve as a throne.

"Mr. Hopkins has not yet attempted to claim leadership of the colony," the governor said.

"He will, if you do not act," she warned, waving the rib at him. "I hear he will petition with his followers to remain on the island when we sail."

"It may be that he and a few others will wish to remain when we leave for Virginia," Admiral Somers said. "But I am certain not the whole of his group intends to part with our company."

"And what if you are wrong, sir?" she asked. "Should he steal away enough of our sailors, who should sail our ships?" How she came by these rumors, I knew not. She kept herself shut away so, and I did not bring them to her.

I served them silently, worried but not commenting, as it was not my place. But I could see concern in the gentlemen's expressions.

"They will tire of him." Governor Gates levered a hunk of meat the size of my fist into his mouth and chewed. "His fervor will exhaust them. They will find it easier to return to our company than abide his foolishness."

"But will you not punish them for desertion?" she asked. "Hanging is no unfair treatment for mutiny."

Ever since the public execution of Robert Waters, she had spoken with great enthusiasm of punishments for this or that crime. Latching the offender in the stocks or ordering a turn in the dunking chair seemed not to satisfy her. I thought she missed the grim entertainment of London's gallows.

"Punishment is due, certainly," the admiral agreed. "But we must weigh carefully our options." He raised a hand to hold back her interruption. "Not that the deserters don't deserve hanging or worse. But if we dispatch our sailors, we face again the same quandary: *who* will sail our ships?"

"Maybe it is for the best," the governor mused as I filled his cup again with my fresh-made ginger beer. "Do away with the rubbish and take only the faithful among us. We would only need the one ship then."

"No," Admiral Somers argued, "we need the pinnace to carry sustenance to Virginia, for our fellows there."

That the governor could not argue against. The mission of our original fleet of eight ships, beyond further populating New Britannia, was to bring desperately needed food and supplies to the starving colonists. Captain Newport's earlier journey there reported the colony incapable of sustaining itself. It seemed that the gentlemen sent there to first hold the land, for her Majesty Queen Elizabeth, then for her successor King James I, were far less capable of fishing and hunting in the wild than on their own estates and preserves, and unwilling to accept hard labor in the fields.

Although the foods *Venture* had carried from England were now either at the bottom of the vast Atlantic or consumed, we had discovered in our sweet Bermudas limitless quantities of healthful foods—the freshest meats, fowl, fish, eggs, berries, and nuts. In recent months our best hunters had busied themselves slaughtering and salting pork and smoking fish so that it might keep for our cousins' use when we came to be reunited.

"No indeed. We cannot spare the men to Mr. Hopkins," the admiral stated, his fist thumping for emphasis Mistress's table. "We must take both ships, laden to the bulwarks with victuals to assure the survival of our colony." He looked to the governor. "Do you not agree, sir?"

"I do," said Gates. "We can do nothing more than wait on their return to our company and welcome them back as prodigal sons."

But, I thought, what if they don't come back?

Thirty-seven

Hasty marriage seldom proveth well.
—from *Henry VI, Part III*

*T*homas came to me at least twice each week. More often than this we dared not attempt, as his presence would arouse suspicion among the men. Even worse, from Mistress.

We used our cooking lessons as excuse. The governor enjoyed Thomas's new additions to his menu and, when told of my instruction, encouraged his cook to continue his education. The admiral secretly gloated over the superior dishes produced by his woman-cook, so obviously sought after by the governor. No small competition grew up between the gentlemen, as to whose table offered the finest spread.

Even Mistress, for a time, seemed to accept Thomas's visits, as long as I returned to her service as soon as the evening meal was finished and the pots and crocks scoured clean with sand.

So it was during the afternoons, on the days Thomas came to me, that we went off together to hunt herbs and mushrooms and dig turtle eggs from the warm sand. But in truth, less time was spent in foraging than in feasting upon each other. On the days he came not, I thought of nothing else but him. On our days together, my whole world *became* him.

I knew the signs, having close watched my mother when she carried my younger brother and little sister. I had no sickness at all, but my breasts tingled and grew sensitive to Thomas's kisses and the calluses of his palms. I had grown to trust him, but also knew that men, even good ones like Thomas, did not always welcome a child. And so I said nothing to him of my condition.

Instead, I sought out my old friend, Will, for advisement.

He looked up before I reached him at his favorite dune. His expression was curious and not a little irritated. "So you choose to join me at last. I see little of you but hear you have been keeping company with Mr. Powell."

I blushed at his hard, searching look that took in all of me, including my stomach, not very much swollen yet, but warm to my senses.

"I did not expect you to miss me," I teased. "Besides, it was a friendship you encouraged."

His blue eyes flashed. "I did not say you were missed."

"Then I will not stay and annoy you further."

He blew out a breath even as I turned away, pretending to leave.

"Wench," he muttered, then louder: "Stay a while, Miranda. Your company is not the worst on this island."

I went and sat beside him, though not as close as I would have to Thomas.

I noted that his journal seemed nearly full and wondered what he would do when he ran out of pages.

"You could have come down to dine at my messes," I said. "Do you no longer care for my cooking?"

"Thomas's table improves greatly, so much so that I mostly eat with the governor."

I smiled to myself, taking it as a compliment. But there was a tightness in his voice that worried me. "Are you still set on returning in haste to England?"

He nodded. "I have had enough adventure."

"And I have had enough of being a servant."

"Ah," he choked on a laugh, "so now you take my word that you have choices!"

I was reminded that at one time I had seen none. "I see possibilities."

"And do these possibilities have anything to do with Mr. Powell?"

I nodded. "I love him." Unaccountably, tears came to my eyes.

"Don't be common," he snapped, suddenly angry.

I stared at him, astounded. "I thought you wanted me to accept him. You pushed me to him, you did!"

"I said you should *marry* the boy, not play the tart! Or get yourself *that* way." He gestured toward my belly. How was it evident to him and not to my lover?

"I am not trapping him, if that's what you think."

"Ach!" He got to his feet, his journal sliding from his lap. He paced away from me then back again, his face working through stages of anger. "Do you not see the difference? He came to you, wooing gently. If you had but said yes, it would be to him as if he'd won, and marry you he would."

"But what have I lost by taking him with the whole of my heart and body? He loves me still."

"So I was right. You *do* lie with him." He was shouting now, his eyes wild, breathing raspy, pacing the sand. I felt as if all of the island must hear him. "You go from innocence to whore in the span of a few days."

Tears streamed down my face. "I am not . . . not what you say." I wouldn't repeat his word. "It is by mutual affection that we are together. He wishes it as much as I."

"Ah, but you should have secured his pledge before giving him what he wanted. If you had not shut yourself away from me, I would have warned you."

I wept openly. "Please. What am I to do? Do I tell him now or wait? What will he say to me?"

He closed his eyes and sat down beside me. "I do not know. If he is a good man, he will marry you and provide for you. But I cannot speak for him, Miranda. I do not know."

I left Will and ran down to the beach, where I collapsed in the sand, alone, shivering, fearful. I suppose, even before I knew that I carried Thomas's babe, the thought had come to me that he might spurn me and a child. But I had chased it away as quickly as it had come. Only Will's words had turned the stray doubt into nagging worry. And now it seemed so very likely that I had behaved foolishly. What would become of me—become of *us*, for I was doubled now?

I knew that Mistress Horton would have none of a serving girl who got herself with child. That was how I had come to be chosen for the voyage. Her Beatrice had only just shown herself with child a week before the scheduled sailing, and Mistress refused to be troubled with the burden of a baby, even if the captain would have allowed a woman to board who might give birth during the sea voyage, which he would not.

I lacked even the smallest of courage to face Thomas and my mistress. Later, I told myself, when the time is right and I know the words.

As it happened, Stephen Hopkins and his followers assisted me in delaying delivery of my news to Thomas. They had gathered in number and made a constant nuisance of themselves plotting raids on our munitions and dwindling supply of sugar, seeds, and other rations. Thomas was preoccupied, along with the governor's marines, protecting our supplies, and so I saw little of him.

When their raids resulted in few successes, Hopkins petitioned Governor Gates to allow his party to form their own community and remain to officially settle the islands, claiming them for His Majesty. The governor refused.

As more men joined the mutinous company, the governor feared our very lives might be forfeited, for the mutineer's demands became more and more warlike. Indeed, some said Hopkins threatened violent punishment on those who refused to join him. The admiral sent two of his men as spies into Hopkins's camp, and they reported he was plotting the murder of Gates, Somers, and Captain Newport.

Every loyal man on the governor's and the admiral's islands was put to guard duty, day and night. More than once our sentries caught Hopkins's men trying to lay gunpowder outside the governor's cabin, and so the mood in our community became most desperate.

"We must take special care to guard our ships," Captain Newport warned. "Even more so than our stores, which can be replenished." We feared the rebels might take it into their heads to destroy our little fleet to keep us from leaving, since they wished to stay and the governor refused to allow it.

With the men thus occupied and the ferry between our islands disabled and under guard, it was easy to avoid Thomas. As the weeks passed, I built up my courage. If Thomas is the good man Will claims him to be, I thought, all will be well. But if Thomas was less good, I would be seen as an adulteress in the eyes of our company and, at best, be cast out.

Stephen Hopkins's conspiracy came to a sudden end. More than half of the men who had departed with him tired of his preaching at them and the lack of good food, and came back to us as a group. (I would like to claim some small thanks for this, their having become accustomed to my excellent messes.) They drifted into camp, hungry, penitent, complaining of having been worked harder by Mr. Hopkins in his forest camp than ever they had in our shipyard, and missing the companionship of friends who had elected to remain loyal to our mission. Each day, more appeared— sober as bishops, begging the governor's pardon.

"He should hang the lot!" Mistress declared with glee.

"Was it not you who once blamed me for the loss of a single man?" I asked, smiling into the laundry tub.

"Insolent slut," she muttered. "Your opinion is neither sought nor of any value."

After that, I fed her gruel for three days in a row, then felt sorry for her when her strength seemed to diminish for lack of proper nourishment.

I expected to feel sick with the child, but never did. Perhaps it was the constant and good fresh air, in this place where no one seemed to take ill of plague. Or maybe I was too busy feeding my men to heed my body's changes. Six weeks into my separation from Thomas I felt healthy and so normal I nearly could convince myself that no babe grew inside me.

When at last the governor released his ban on travel about the islands, Thomas sent a note begging me to join him at our private place. I had yearned for him, even while fearing this meeting.

We embraced and kissed, and were as loving as we ever had been before. Only with so much more hunger for each other. I let him do whatever he would, only wanting to please him, but found equal pleasure in him. Since he didn't remark on any changes he might have noticed in my body, I decided not to spoil our reunion day. Soon enough, he would know without my saying anything.

"Have you told him?" Will asked the next time I saw him, two weeks later.

"No."

"You must."

"Why? So he can abandon me all the sooner?" I stared at him. Each day of silence brought me hours of bliss. I would not lose him.

"He may not leave," Will said. "Give him the chance to do right by you."

Thirty-eight

Alas, how love can trifle with itself!
—from *The Two Gentlemen of Verona*

*Y*ou thrive on your own cooking," Thomas said, his warm palm resting on my stomach.

He lay at my side, still playing with the parts of me he favored most. His eyes heavy with sated passion.

"You should talk, I have seen you consume three trenchers full in one sitting."

"Why should I not enjoy the fruits of my own labor?" he said. "I cook well too, you know."

"Not as delicately as I."

"I cook for a man's fulsome tastes," he parried.

"And that is why your carpenters sneak over to my island to dine?"

He raised his thick eyebrows in pretend astonishment. "Mutinous buggers."

His hand smoothed over my belly, testing its firmness as he would a plump seabird before roasting it. His lazy composure turned to a faint expression of puzzlement, then a frown.

His eyes rose to meet mine and he sat up abruptly.

"Elizabeth?"

He only ever used my old name when he was unhappy with me. In fact, most of the company now called me Miranda, having heard it from Thomas and Will, thinking it was a joke because of my role in Will's play.

I closed my eyes as his hand lifted away and the warmth of it left me. Will was right. I should have told him sooner, but I had so wished to keep him as long as I might.

"Look at me," he said.

Tears seeped unbidden from beneath my closed lids. I turned my head aside and tasted salt on my tongue and down the back of my throat. It filled my nostrils, nearly choking me, and I still did not look at him.

"Miranda." His voice was softer, but he kept his hands from me. I pulled our quilt around me, waiting for his words of disgust and dismissal.

My only defense was to be as angry with him as he must be with me. When he leaned toward me, I pushed him away.

"Did you think we could be like this forever, without making a babe?" I cried.

"But you said nothing about—"

"What did you expect me to say, you silly man? Admitting I am full of your child is wishing you away. I did not wish"—agonized sobs broke from my throat—"did not wish you"—I gasped—"*gone!*"

He stood up and stared down at me. I felt his gaze fixed on me but refused to look up to bear the weight of his censure.

I finally coughed to clear my throat. "If the governor allows it, I will remain on my island. I will have the babe and raise it, even as Prospero raised his Miranda."

Thomas said nothing.

"I don't mind being alone." I wiped tears away with my sleeve. "I don't."

He was still staring down at me. What was he thinking? That I had lain a snare for him?

"It is about time," he said. "Thanks be to Our Lord."

I breathed and sniffled and tried to understand why this tone of joy in his voice. "Time?" I asked.

"I thought I was without seed."

When I looked up he wore a strange half smile.

"I don't understand."

"I have been with other women."

I did not want to hear of his conquests. He was older than I, and so I assumed he had bedded others. But it was not a topic I cared to discuss.

"So?"

"Never has one been with child of mine."

"How fortunate for you," I snapped. Had Will been so lucky, he would have saved himself from an unwanted wife.

"You don't understand. I could not tell you I was seedless. You would not have had me then."

I stared at him, this man I knew more intimately than any other, yet apparently knew so little. This man I thought

I understood down to his very soul. Yet he unfolded secrets before me like layers of pastry dough.

"*I* would not have *you*, Thomas?"

"I feared I could not provide you with children, as every woman naturally wants. The only alternative was to let another take you to his bed to provide—" He stopped as if the words stuck in his throat, his eyes shifting away for a moment, then back to me with such sadness in them my heart went out to him. "How could I bear to let another man touch you, my Miranda, my wife in all but name?"

With a surge of happiness such as I had never known, I threw my arms around his big, strong, sweaty neck. "Marry me well then, my dear Thomas!"

Thirty-nine

Asses were made to bear, and so are you.
—from *The Taming of the Shrew*

*M*arry Thomas, I thought. Nothing in my life seemed more right. In our own way, separate from the others, we had handfasted. Pledged ourselves to each other. But that would not be enough for our good officers or for Mistress. It was to her I went first for permission, as would be expected of a servant.

I found her dozing in the sun, outside our hut. She woke with a start when I approached.

"There you are," she said, straightening up in her chair. "I have nearly starved while you were off." Her eyes narrowed and she pointed her hawklike nose at me, then took in Thomas's blanket, rolled under my arm. "What have you been up to, girl?"

Although she was right, I had been a-sinning, I held my head proud. For how many wives bedded their husbands before their church vows? Certainly our Anna had done.

"I have come to you as your loyal servant," I began, keeping my eyes lowered though it was hard to straighten away my smile for the joy I was feeling. "To ask your permission to marry."

I suppose I knew she would not be pleased, might well refuse my request. Thomas and I had already spoken of this, and he had said if denied we would appeal to the governor.

"Marry?" She let out a crack of a laugh. "Who would want—" She broke off to study my face through slits of eyes. "Ah yes, that worthless poisoning cook, it is. That is who would have a plain girl like you."

I smiled in spite of all efforts not to. Plain or not, the man loved me. Such joy even the old crow couldn't destroy.

"Thomas Powell would have me and I would have him." I decided to hold nothing back, for love had made me brave. "I am with his child and we would wed soon."

I cannot say what she was thinking at that moment. But it suddenly seemed that her face took on another five years, the wrinkles deepening, the sallowness blanching an ivory white so unhealthful that she resembled a corpse.

"I will not have a squalling infant in my home, Elizabeth Persons."

"I was not asking permission to bring the child into your hut," I said as calmly as possible. "I was asking that I be released from your employ, madam. For I expect I will be living with my new husband in Virginia."

She blinked at me twice, then waved a hand at me. "Foolish girl, he shall leave you soon as he sees you as you are—dull and incapable."

There was a time when I easily would have agreed with her. But that time had passed. I was clever with my herbs and stirred magic into my pots. I knew the names of birds and flowers and creatures of our island. I had loved a man and made him happy with me. I felt near to bursting with joy even as she scowled her displeasure at me.

"I will marry Thomas. We will have our child."

She rolled her eyes. "Foolishness! I forbid this marriage. You are bound to me and it is your fornication that is the sin. I shall go to the governor and he will see you whipped and disgraced for your indecency."

The confidence she had in her words suddenly terrified me. Although Anna and her groom had been wed with nary a blink of the eye toward her swelling belly, she was not a servant.

Mistress seemed to feel my fear, and feed on it. "If you do not wish to suffer public humiliation, Elizabeth, you will use whatever crude wisdom of nature you possess to rid yourself of the bastard inside you. Then put your sinful ways aside. I will take you back and things will be as they were. I would not tell the governor that you have strayed."

I stared at her, horrified. My baby? Kill my babe in my womb?

I knew it was done by some. I remembered certain potions my father provided with grim manner when requested, though our faith forbade the ending of a life.

"No," I said.

Her glare hardened. "I am not asking you, Elizabeth. I

am telling you what you must do or face dire punishment. Would you have the governor abandon you on this rock when we leave it?"

The fate that had once seemed appealing—solitude—now shattered me. Being alone meant being without my Thomas. How could I bear that, having known what it was to love and be loved?

She must have seen denial in my face, for her manner of forcing me to accept her will altered as completely as if I were the moon eclipsing her sun, taking away all her power. She sagged in her chair.

"You would leave me," she said. "Leave me helpless, when I was the one who saved you from the streets. Thankless wretch! I see you are not to be persuaded, your heart is so cold to the needs of an old woman who brought you into her home." She shook her head. "You leave me no choice, girl. Do as you will, but the governor will learn of your disrespect and desertion." Her black-bead eyes flashed one last time. "He will hear from me presently."

Forty

Look, how my ring encompasseth thy finger,
Even so thy breast encloseth my poor heart . . .
Wear both of them, for both of them
are thine.
—from *Richard III*

*T*homas smiled the first he saw me, coming down the beach from the ferry cove toward his kitchen. He looked up from his chopping block, a wide grin on his face that faded at the sight of my tears.

Putting down his cleaver, he strode fast toward me. "What is it, lass?"

"Mistress Horton," I said. "She is going to the governor with news of my sin. She refuses to grant us our marriage."

His eyes steeled. "She does, hey? Well, then . . ." His big

arms came around me and pulled me in. "I say we save her some trouble, poor old lady." Was he laughing?

"Thomas! She's a witch and means to ruin us with her evil doings."

"Aye, she is. But I know her type. All she's doin' is lookin' after herself, she is. What she wants is to keep her serving girl, and she thinks by complaining to the governor she will."

"But how do we stop her?"

"I know a secret she knows not." He winked at me, and the knot in my stomach eased, though why I didn't yet understand. "Come, we will have a word with Sir Gates."

I thought him either the bravest of men, or the stupidest. We climbed the hill together, hands clasped, toward the governor's cottage. It was as simple as all of the others, only one room to it, but the view from the top of the hill was beyond breathtaking. Enough trees had been cleared to let in good sunlight, and the governor had squared out for himself a small garden to one side of the building, where he was growing cabbages, carrots, peas, onions, some radish, and muskmelon, from seeds rescued from our wreck.

"Such a beautiful garden," I said.

"He brings his vegitives to me," Thomas said, with pride, "and I make for him a good, rich stock that soothes his aches, as you have taught me."

"Is this then your secret?" I asked, hopeful. "He will favor us for your good soup?"

Thomas shook his head. "Nay, lass. You wait."

Two of the governor's guard stood sentry outside his cottage door and stopped us from going further. One disappeared inside to fetch him when we asked for an audience.

My stomach tossing and turning, I looked up at Thomas. Although he had sounded confident enough, his expression now appeared strained, and he wet his lips as if preparing them for a challenging speech.

Governor Gates stepped outside, with Will following him, both men squinting into the sunlight. "Thomas, how are you? And Miss Eliza—" He smiled. "No, Miranda it is. Prospero's daughter." With a wink toward his friend.

I curtsied for him. "I am not a wizard's child today. We come to beg Your Honor's indulgence."

Then we pled our case.

The Governor listened with solemn expression that seemed to bode our plea ill, but Will gave me an encouraging wink and appeared unworried.

When we were done, the governor took a deep breath, then looked down and away toward Somers' Island, lush and green in the middle of shimmering turquoise waters. The stockade was clearly visible from where we stood, and within it would be the crude houses and storage sheds we had built there.

"Mistress Horton," he said, "has provided this company with a largess that I cannot overlook. Without her funds, and those she procured from her friends, we should have been hard put to find adequate investors. I hesitate to offend the woman."

My heart shattered. He was refusing our plea?

Thomas said, a hint of urgency, "Aye, but does her wealth give her the right to refuse her servant's marriage?"

"Under ordinary circumstances, yes, of course." Gates looked at me. "So long as Miss Persons is beneath her roof."

Will stepped forward. "Very true, sir. But a roof here is not a roof in London. And of necessity, we have provided our own rules and laws as well as palm boughs to replace shingles."

I held my breath, said a silent prayer.

The governor turned and looked long and hard at me, an emotion passing behind his eyes I could not define. "Do you wish to marry my cook?"

I choked over the words, so hasty was I to get them out. "I do, Sir Lord Gates."

He dipped his head once, firmly, and cleared his throat. "Your father, I knew him. Did Thomas tell you that?"

"He did not." I slid my lover a look that promised mischief to him later for his slyness.

"I knew the man well, and I mourned his loss."

I was shocked. No one had spoken of my father since his disgrace.

"He was a good and honest man," Gates said softly. "His end was . . . unfortunate." Not wrong, he wouldn't criticize his sovereign. This was, I supposed, the most he could say in kindness without doing himself harm.

"Yes, sir, he was."

Will stepped forward. "Then having no father to give his permission, I take it upon myself to act in his place." He looked solemnly at Thomas. "I see no better man to mate my adopted daughter."

"Good then," said Gates. "I will charge our Master Bucke with announcing your bans at service this Sunday, but the handfasting should be done now, to seal your betrothal before witnesses."

I would have fallen to my knees in relief had not both Will and Thomas caught me up by the arms and prevented it.

"I am well," I assured them after steadying myself, not wishing to put off our pledges.

"Then you may begin," Gates said, looking at me.

And so Thomas and I turned to face each other before the governor and our good friend Will, beneath God's generous blue sky. Clasping Thomas's big right hand in mine I spoke to my beloved, "Here is my hand, Thomas, in faith forever, whether my mistress wills it or not. Never will I forsake thee."

With a smile and a spark in his eyes that warmed me to my toes, Thomas wrapped both his hands around my one. "And here are my two hands, for I wish to give all I have to my Miranda. I thereby plight my troth, to have no other woman so long as I do live."

For a moment I stood looking up at Thomas, breathless and amazed, smiling giddily at what we had done.

Gates laughed. "Well, lad, do kiss her to make your vows! She is yours."

Thomas flung his immense arms around me and, lifting me off the ground in a crushing bear hug, kissed me full on the mouth before our gentlemen, to my embarrassment and joy. Laughing, I looked at Will. "Thank you."

"For what, girl?"

"For being an old pest and bringing us together."

He shrugged but looked pleased, then turned to the governor. "Will there be no exchange of gifts to mark the occasion?"

"Ah," Gates said, looking around as if he expected a store

of riches to suddenly appear. "No ring is there for the bride, I see."

Will reached up and tugged on the gold loop in his left ear.

"No," I said, "but thank you. It is too small to fit over my finger."

Governor Gates drew a silver coin from his vest. "Here then, this will do." He handed it to Thomas. "My wife and I had no more than you two when we wed. Do break the coin and each take half, as token of your devotion, each being half of the whole."

And so Thomas did separate the coin with his bare hands, to the astonishment of all, and one half I slipped into my bosom to be close to my heart. As close as this dear man had become to me.

"I think it best I break the news to your mistress," the governor said. He looked at Will. "Perhaps you will join me, Mr. Strachey? Over tea tomorrow."

Will nodded, looking altogether pleased with himself. "I shall be your reinforcement, sir."

Our wedding was no less festive than the previous one. But it was not celebrated with the same enthusiasm by all. Mistress Horton clung to the bitterest of moods, as if she were a ship rat set adrift on a timber, although I did all I could to primp and polish her before the event. Her periwig I redyed with macerated marigold blossoms. Her ruff was pleated and newly starched. I straightened the wires of her rebato to stand tall behind her wizened head so that she looked nearly regal. Her best gown I removed out of her trunk and freshened in the air.

No, she did not offer the use of any of her gowns to the bride. But I would have wed Thomas as naked as Eve. Sarah's mistress offered me a simple blue gown that suited me more than well enough.

We vowed before the minister, feasted on the meal we together had made for the company, danced and sang, and at nightfall, went off to do what we loved best—delight in each other.

As we lay on the sand in a little cove apart from our fellows, I turned to my husband and held his dear head between my palms and kissed him on the mouth.

"I do wish our babe to be a boy as strapping, and brave, and wise as his father," I whispered.

"Nay," he said, pulling me down over him, our bodies matching for curve and swell, warming the length of us, humming with the song of our lovemaking. "*She* shall be a lovely lass, like her mother."

"If she is lovely, she will not resemble her mother."

"If she is not lovely, she will resemble her father, and I would wish that not on any girl child." He laughed, deep and hearty, his eyes bright with joy.

If never I do have another moment of cheer in my life, I thought, this one shall last me to my dying day.

Forty~one

Love comforteth, like sunshine after rain.
—from *Venus and Adonis*

*T*he morn of our leaving the Bermudas, only two men remained behind. It was to be their task to watch over the land, having claimed it in the name of King James I of our fair England, while our two ships carried the rest of us on to Virginia and Jamestown.

Knowing these two as I did, I expected they would do only as much labor as was necessary to produce their palm wine and provide sustenance sufficient that they might lift their right arms. I expected the governor chose them as they'd be little use to us in our new home.

I stood on the deck of *Deliverance* and watched our fair isles shrink until they were no more than green specks above the dark ocean. The seas were well and tame, and my husband stood at my side. A new world awaited us, God willing.

On the 17th of May in the year of Our Lord 1610, we saw a change in the water. Our little pinnace bobbed happily behind us from her leash, like a playful pup. The color of the water lightened, and floating debris came to us, so a sailor said, "Land. She's not far and away." And all ascended onto the decks to watch, but nothing came to sight.

A day later, around midnight, a lead put down measured thirty-seven fathoms. "How much longer?" I asked Will, who stood by my side while Thomas slept below.

"Soon, I should hope. The food we carry will not last much longer."

For although we had stored up much in advance of our sailing, there was space on our crowded ships for little more than what we might consume during our trip of estimated eight days. And already we had been at sea for seven.

I slept below with my husband for a few hours that night, then we came above again to marvel at the stars, which were brighter and larger by far than those seen through gritty-gray London air. We watched the sailors put down another sounding, which showed us to be now at nineteen and one half fathoms with a promising sandy ground. But still no sight of land.

I worried. If this New Britannia were as vast as all of our England, or perchance vaster still, how would we ever locate our fellow settlers? But both Will and Thomas spoke of our mariners' skill at navigation and of various signals and landmarks. Yet all I saw was the endless ocean around us, and I despaired of having left my sweet, safe islands.

"It is not for myself I have fears," I confided in Thomas as we lay beneath the night sky, as away from the others as we might be on so crowded a ship. "I am frightened for my babe. He would have thrived on Somers' Island with us there to watch over him, but here in this strange land . . ." I shook my head. "We know not what we shall face."

He shook his head and smiled at me. "Certain I am those who came before us have faced the worst dangers and by now tamed 'em." He kissed the tip of my nose and wound his arms around me until I felt but a cozy little nutmeat within his body's strong shell.

"And if they have not?"

"Look around you, lass. Have we not all of the brawny governor's guard and admiral's marines to secure and protect us? What evil can happen in Virginia that did not in the Bermudas?"

But it was that very night my headaches began again, weak at first, although no rains came or seemed to threaten. An awful dread filled me, and I prayed in silence that our Good Lord might preserve us yet again from a storm.

On the twentieth of May the welcome smell of earth and trees came to us, though nothing, even through the captain's spyglass, appeared on the western horizon. However, the next morn one of the sailors woke us with cries of "Land! Land, ho!" and all aboard made up through passage and hatch to deck.

I seized Thomas's hand, dragging him to the rail, and there in the early pink-and-orange dawn we espied two hillocks, as green and pleasing as any in England. My heart swelled at the hope of this new land offering us comfort.

I pressed my hand over my baby's swell. "We have come, little one," I whispered.

Will stood beside us, having searched out the mate, who knew this wild place better than any, as he had voyaged here before.

"And that point?" I heard him ask the man.

"We call her Cape Henry, sir, in honor of our young prince. T'other over there, she's Cape Charles, after our princely Duke of York."

"And the body of water between?"

"Why, sir, none other than the famous and fair Chesapeake Bay."

And she was wondrously fair to my eyes, nearly as blue and sheltered as our harbor in the islands, guarded by porpoise that led us, leaping and frolicking, into still shallower waters. However, our relief lasted only a short while, for within the hour, the sun disappeared.

I stared up at the sky to see fierce dun-colored clouds building above us. Moments later the maelstrom broke with such crashing of thunder and terrifying lightning bolts that all we could do was scurry below for safety while our mariners made us fast with anchors to prevent our ship from pitching up onto nearby rocks.

"It is only wind and rain," Thomas said, to comfort me as I held my poor pounding head in the crowded, dark hold.

"I'm not afraid so long as you are with me." I leaned into his body. "Storms savage my head. The pain will pass with the weather."

"Ah, lass," he said, holding and rocking me until the rumblings stopped and people began to move about again.

On that same day, the one and twentieth of May, after the ugly skies cleared, we ventured back onto the deck as *Deliverance* rounded into a wide river.

"We have arrived!" Captain Newport shouted down from his station at the bow. "'Tis Point Comfort. And there on the rise sits our bonnie fort."

Cheers went up all around. I could see Mistress, her back to me at the rail, and Sarah and her family further to the stern. Sailors took to the spars and rigging to better see the surrounding land. There was much embracing and slapping of backs in celebration of our safe coming.

But the good captain was as surprised as any of us when the fort's guard discharged a booming cannon shot that fell with a splash terrifyingly close to our starboard side.

"Why is they firing at us?" Sarah cried, rushing toward us from the rail, her eyes wide with terror.

All around, others seemed to be asking the same question, concern showing in every face across the crowded decks. Even Will, standing portside, journal balanced in one hand, pen in the other moving quickly, appeared more alert than usual to what was going on around him.

"That was a warning shot. We have no flag," Thomas explained when he could see that we didn't understand. "They cannot know whether we are friend or foe."

I gripped his hand. "Our ships must look so very queer to them, being they resemble none that left England nearly a year ago."

"And being they are constructed of rubble and virgin lumber." He laughed. "We must be quite a puzzlement to them!"

"Oh, dearie . . . dearie," Sarah wailed. "What'll happen now? After suff'rin' so much, is we to be attacked by our own countrymen?"

"They might mistake us for Spanish," I said.

Thomas shook his head. "The admiral will send out his longboat with a messenger to tell them of the miracle of our survival and deliver a letter from the governor." He reached out for Sarah, squeezing me in one strong arm and her in the other. "Nothin' to worry you, me lasses. All will be well."

Yet, I did wonder about that, for strangely, my headache had only lessened, not gone away. It lingered as a dull warning throb.

Having assured the guard at the fort of our being the survivors of the wrecked flagship *Sea Venture*, from Point Comfort we sailed upriver at no great speed, following instructions gained at the fort. After two days we at last came to Jamestown. With great joy our company left *Deliverance* and her pinnace for land and our new home. My poor head still warned me of evil weather to come, though prettier or fairer days I'd never seen.

Thomas held my hand and guided me down the path from rough wooden docks to the stockade earlier settlers had erected in a cleared patch of forest. Our company of well over a hundred made the trek in stunned silence.

If we had expected a small prosperous city or even a modest village of good order, as we had been promised by the Virginia Company, this was not it.

Master Bucke fell to his knees and prayed at the sight of palisades torn down, gates off their hinges, houses abandoned by owners now dead from injury, famine, or pestilence.

Indeed, many of the still occupied homes were ravaged as well, their materials burned as firewood—as was explained to us by a man who looked near starved himself. "None of us dares venture from our poor shelter into the woods to fetch either food or wood," he said. "The Indians kill as they wish."

"This cannot be our home," I whispered to Thomas, holding my head to ease its dull pounding.

He stared around us, his eyes darkening to the color of charred cedar, his brow creased in a deep scowl. "'Tis a disgrace. Have these people no care of their homes?"

It was true; everywhere we looked was disrepair, desolation, and misery. "They may well care, Thomas my love. Only look at them," I whispered. "They are starving, too weak to do much of anything."

Only the blockhouse, manned by a few guardsmen, stood to protect Jamestown's helpless survivors from death at the hands of nature or savages. I knew not what would become of us.

In the days that followed, some order came to Jamestown, such as it was. Our governor summoned all to the tiny church. Master Bucke, after leading us in prayer and thanks for our safe arrival, gave over to Governor Gates, who delivered a brave speech of reassurance, asking all to dedicate themselves to the hard labor of rebuilding the town.

"Do you believe he means for us to stay in this godforsaken place?" I asked Thomas.

He gripped my hand. "Aye, lass. But we'll make her sound and safe. We are strong from our days in the Bermudas and will work as hard as ever we have to build again her walls and drive away those who would harm us."

I saw Will seated at the very back of the church, through the dim greenish light of dusk, cast through an open window. I could not read his expression. For once he was not writing. He just looked around him as if in utter shock, unable to make any meaning of this place.

In the days that followed, the palisades were restored with stout and strong saplings, lashed together well. Our men never ventured into the woods in fewer than parties of ten, and always with powder and arms. They brought back lumber, killed game as they could, but found no riches of any sort to load onto our homeward-bound ships. No fat hogs came to visit us. No plump birds of sea or air greeted us with the unwitting trust and curious nature of those in our islands. No meaty turtles crept to shore to provide nourishment. We survived, but just.

One acceptable oven had been built in the largest of the houses still standing and occupied. Mary Alder and her husband, who therein lived, welcomed us. We slept with many more of our company laid out on her straw-covered floor like logs before milling. When a hunting party returned with venison or rabbit or squirrel, we boiled up a stew to stretch the meat the furthest and feed all. Our new friends began to look stronger of heart and body, as a result of our company, good cheer, and healthful victuals. They joined in the labor as best they could, fortifying the palisades and houses.

Will worked as hard as any but was back to his writing and, I noticed, had found ways to keep to himself much of the time. One night, after I had noticed our officers in secretive discussion in the yard, Will among them, I went to him.

"How do you fare, Miranda?" he asked, smiling. "The babe is not making you ill?"

"No," I said, "though my headaches come and go, and I do not know why."

"No storms in the offing?"

"None justify this nagging pain in my head." I sighed. "Perchance it's a different sort of storm to come upon us. Starvation . . . madness."

He nodded, looking thoughtful.

"Tell me," I said, lifting my chin toward the little church where the governor had established his headquarters, "what are their plans for us?"

He drew a deep breath and seemed to consider his words. "The company will forbear. The houses will be rebuilt. With the marines and guardsmen to further protect from savages, you should be safe enough."

"You are still determined to return to London?"

"I am, daughter."

I smiled but weakly. Good for him, bad for me. "I shall miss you, Will. You will never see my babe."

He squinted into the dark. "Yes. You are content with Thomas, are you not?"

"I am. Very."

"Then here you belong, with him." He drew a deep breath, letting it out slowly as if to settle himself to a decision made.

"I do," I said. "Besides, there is naught for me in London."

He said nothing to that and already seemed an ocean away. "Then you have a ship to take you?"

"One shall return to England, though without the riches the king may be expecting, except for the ten wild turkeys he requested for his table." Will smiled but was immediately serious again. "I will go to His Majesty's ministers, with the governor's blessing, and plead the colony's case, asking that he send more aid, and quickly."

"But even if the winds are fair it may be near winter before they return with supplies and ordnance."

He nodded in solemn agreement. "That is so. But Governor Gates himself is taking *Deliverance* back to the Bermudas with men enough to hunt hogs, fowl, and turtle, and bring them back to last until sustenance arrives from England."

Reminders of the island brought a wistful sigh from my lips. "Would that I could go with them, back to my beautiful islands."

He shook his head. "The governor is unlikely to allow it, my girl, as you are with child. Besides"—he patted my hand—"how would your fine young husband like waving you off?"

"Oh, he would come with me, of course!" I said quickly. I could not imagine a life now without Thomas, as surely as, less than a year ago, I had sworn to never take a mate. How quickly life changes.

He said, "You are safe enough here, and conditions improve daily. Our men are wary and well armed. It may be that some gentling of the native peoples will come when they are more accustomed to us. Gates already speaks of sending a party to negotiate with their chief for safe hunting passage." He laughed. "I expect you will be safer here than I in London with vengeful Mr. George Wilkens scheming against me."

"Oh, Will," I said.

He shrugged and tucked away his journal beneath his cloak as if to keep it warm, or as though the mere mention of his enemy endangered him and it.

A thought came to me then. "Will?"

"Yes, my girl."

"You are still writing of our adventure?"

"Of course."

"And what will you do with this history of our journey?"

"I suppose what I do with all of my jottings and ideas. Some parts of them will find their way into a play."

An idea grew inside of me, and I found it thrilling. "What if you were to do more with them?"

"How more?" He turned to study me.

"What if this true story of our miraculous survival were presented at court, to His Majesty King James? Presented as a gift to show the travail of his subjects and our brave attitudes in establishing this, his colony, so far from England."

His gaze deepened, telling me I had his interest. "Give my little book directly to the King?"

"Yes. Your hand to his."

He shook his head. "We players of the Globe entertain a fragile favor by His Majesty, but I have no means of approaching him directly."

"Through a friend then?" I looked up at him from beneath my eyelashes. "Perhaps a lady you may know who has the influence to bring to His Majesty your gift?"

"And this gift you believe will buy me what?"

"Your safety from your enemy, of course. For if you are the King's man, who can scheme against you?"

"Who indeed?" He grinned at me, patting his chest wherein lay his precious journal. "Dear girl, I think you have hit on the answer."

Forty-two

True is it that we have seen better days.
—from *As You Like It*

The days grew lighter and longer, and my babe started to feel as a little cahow egg nestled in my stomach with a weight of its own. It would be months, near to autumn before he was born, but I already felt he was a part of me.

"It *is* a boy." I tormented Thomas.

"She is already beautiful, like her mother." He refused to even consider a male child, though I knew he would be happy to have our little man.

Our lovemaking waited for times when the rest of our fold was fast asleep, or at least pretended to be, for we dared not go off alone into the trees outside the palisades.

Thomas left the cooking to me and Mary Alder, and joined the hunting parties most days when he wasn't helping with repairs to the cabins or walls of our little village. Things began to look more like a home, and the desperate, sunken-eyed stares of our new friends turned to an occasional smile.

Each day, I expected my head to stop hurting, for the weather was fair, with barely a cloud above. But it did not. Indeed the pain, after fading for a few days, then seemed to grow worse no matter what herbs I applied to it through poultice or decoction. I wished I might go off into the woods to hunt for a better remedy, but Thomas would not allow it.

"This place is in no way like our Bermudas. Promise me you will stay within the walls. Today while we are out hunting, I will look for herbs for you. Tell me how to recognize them."

"Peppermint, rosemary, and chamomile—you already know by sight." I pressed my hand to my brow and closed my eyes. "If you see lavender, that is best of all. It will have a long stalk with tiny purple blossoms. I don't expect you will find them all, but any one or two will help."

"I'll not come back without them," he promised, and kissed me where it most hurt.

That day I showed Mary how to make my cassava bread, for flour had become as dear to those here as it had been to us on the islands. We worked all morning at a flaming hearth and by noon had enough for our entire community, along with squirrel stew, some lettuces, and wild asparagus.

I heard the men coming back, hallooing the guard in loud voices to open the gates for them.

"They must have done well," Mary said. "To come back so early and so full of excitement."

"I hope they have at least a good meaty buck," I laughed.

"Or I will send them back out again for their laziness. I yearn for a roast of venison."

She shook her head at me, smiling. "Food is always on your mind these days. I see how you eat like a soldier. It is the babe's doing."

"If I keep eating as my appetite dictates, he will be fat and full grown by the time he is born." I wiped my greasy hands on my apron and tucked the loose strands of hair back into my cap, preparing to greet my husband.

"It has never happened before, but I suppose there is always a first time." She cast me an impatient look. "Go and see what your Thomas has for us. You would let the bread burn to charcoal with your distraction. I will tend it."

I smiled at her and rushed out the door into the cool air. My cheeks felt burnished by the flames and heat of the little kitchen. The fresh air cooled them, and I looked toward the far side of the yard and the gates, which had been swung wide to allow our men back inside.

I realized almost immediately that this was no ordinary hunting party returning. Though they carried on their shoulders a covered carcass of some sort, it was not a deer's, and there was much shouting and agitation among the men. Before I could get much closer, someone started ringing the church bell with the urgency of an alarm, and people streamed from sheds, shacks, and cottages.

I searched among the gathered men for Thomas, but at first failed to see him. My head pounded its hardest yet. I pressed a fist to my chest, stomach tightening, eyes wandering and ever more frantic as I counted off men in the group.

Ten had left to hunt. Three I saw approaching the governor. Then four more in a tight group, their weapons resting on their shoulders, expressions dour. And yes, the two carrying their prize, which made nine. But then so many others of our company rushed forward, summoned by the bell from their duties, and I supposed Thomas must be hidden among the crush, though he was so tall he usually stood above them.

I started to run toward the two hunters, still carrying their load. But the crowd blocked my way—a wall of murmuring, pointing people, watching the men lay down their burden with a gentleness no game merited. Only then did I peer between cloaks and limbs to see it was a man they carried. And I became aware of the powerful stench of blood.

The hood of the cape in which he'd been wrapped fell away in the wind. I saw his face. My heart lurched.

"No!" I cried, pushing aside bodies and restraining arms.

Master Bucke stood solidly in my way, his face aggrieved, arms spread as if to embrace me. "Stay, child. You can do nothing."

"He is hurt!" I cried, trying to move him aside. "I need to help him."

Suddenly Will was there, the admiral at his side.

"Miranda," the poet said gently, "come away with me now."

"No!" I screamed. "I can heal his wounds. You must let me."

"Let her go to him," came the admiral's voice, steady and low. "Let her be with her husband, sir."

I flew forward as the crowd parted, falling to my knees by Thomas's side. His beautiful round face, always so rosy from the fires over which we cooked, had turned an ashen gray. With frantic fingers I drew aside the fabric still covering his body.

There was only one wound, but it was deep. The arrow had penetrated his throat, bathing his chest and shoulders in blood; one of the men must have removed the shaft.

I lifted his hand from the ground between us and fitted my fingers between his. He was not yet cold. If others standing around us came and went, or whispered questions or explanations about what had happened in the woods, I did not hear them. There was only Thomas and me, and the babe in my belly who would never see his father.

I lifted my beloved's hand to my cheek, feeling its rough caress one last time. This touch I had never wanted that had taught me to desire and cherish.

Tenderly I laid his arm over his broad chest, then reached across his body for the other arm, to put it at rest as well. When I lifted his right hand, I saw that it wasn't empty. Gripped within his wide fingers was a small bouquet of greenery, tugged up by the roots.

"Lavender," I whispered. "Oh, Thomas."

And then the headache left me, for my storm had come.

Forty-three

When he shall die,
Take him and cut him out in little stars,
And he will make the face of heaven so fine
That all the world will be in love with night . . .
—from *Romeo and Juliet*

*W*e buried my beloved husband within the stockade, as I did not want those who had murdered him to discover his grave and dishonor his body. Master Bucke spoke of Thomas's bravery, risking his life to provide food for our needy company. He spoke of his love for his wife and unborn child. I remember those few words but little else of that black, black day, or the next two that followed. If others had kind words for me, as I am sure they did, I recall not a one.

On the fourth day Sarah came to me and touched my face

with her warm little hands and made me look into her eyes. "Lizzy . . . Miranda, listen to me. You must let me help you bathe and dress. Governor Gates wishes to see you, girl, and you cannot go to him like this."

I shook my head.

"You will starve your babe if you do not eat. Please!" She was weeping, tears flowing down her pretty face. "Thomas wouldn't want you to do this to yourself, to his child. Please, let me wash and dress you. Then we'll go together to see the gov'nor."

I breathed in, out, closed my eyes again. But when I opened them, she was still there.

"I will see him as I am," I said, pushing myself up off the pallet where I had lain, wrapped in my misery, unwilling to think of life without my Thomas and therefore unable to face life at all. "I need not please anyone with my appearance so long as I mourn." And I felt as if that would be forever.

Governor Gates was waiting for me in the church, but he was not alone. When I stepped through the door, Mistress Horton was there as well, and so were Will and Admiral Somers. Mistress sat in the front pew, scowling up at the governor with her most stubborn expression, and I had the impression that they had been arguing. I leaned on little Sarah for support.

Will took a step forward, as if to come to me, but the governor put out an arm to stop him. The church was so small there wasn't even a nave, just a few benches either side of a center aisle and an altar as plain as any could be and still be called proper. A simple linen cloth covered it with one candle lit, flickering as the draft that came between the wall slats played with the flame.

"Sit down, my dear," the admiral said when we had reached him. He gestured to the front bench.

Sarah cast a worried glance toward Mistress Horton, who looked away from us. Sarah settled me on the far end of the bench, then sat between me and Mistress without being told she could. No one said anything for a moment.

I placed my hands on my lap and looked up at the governor. "Yes, your lordship."

The governor rolled his eyes toward the ceiling and shook his head. I thought he appeared not entirely well, but whether this was fatigue or illness or dismay at the condition of Jamestown I could not say. "We are here to help you, Elizabeth."

I felt Will cringe ever so slightly, as if he knew what my response would be.

"Miranda," I said. "It is my name."

"Very well. As you know, I am leaving Jamestown to return to the Bermudas for supplies."

"Yes," I said.

"I do not wish to leave you in such a state."

"My state is unchangeable," I said, "unless you would have me believe you can restore my husband to me."

He looked grave indeed. "You know I cannot do that."

"I told you she would be rude and impossible," Mistress Horton snapped.

"And I told you to hold your tongue, woman!"

Mistress glared at the governor.

He sighed. "My dear girl, we all mourn Thomas Powell's loss. But the survival of this community depends upon each one of us doing what must be done to keep from losing even one more member." His eyes dropped to my stomach. "Or more than one."

"What would you have me do, sir?" I asked. "Do you wish me back in the kitchen with Mary Alder?"

"In good time, of course." He shook his head then looked to the admiral and, lastly, to Will.

The admiral spoke up. "It is our mission to ensure the continuance of this colony. If one member is lost, it is the responsibility of another member to take up the burden our departed member has left behind."

"I don't understand." I looked in confusion at Will, who was frowning but said nothing.

Mistress Horton looked pleased, as if she were being proven right, though about what I couldn't have said.

"The governor is trying to say that it is in our company's best interest that you be provided for, Miranda." Admiral Somers began to pace, as if to better churn out the words. "And by providing for you and your babe, so that both of you thrive in our community, we insure that you will eventually be able again to help others. We each have a role in James-town, and you have shown yourself to be a hard worker of resourceful nature as cook on Somers' Island."

"I thank you, sir." But not having eaten for days had made my head feel unequal to the task of untangling his pretty praise to find the meaning beneath it.

No one said anything for a moment.

"May I go now, sir?"

The governor coughed into his hand and tried again. "You must be aware, Mrs. Powell, that your welfare and that of your child will depend upon your—"

Will broke in. "They think you need to marry again. Soon."

I stared at him, unable to understand why he would say anything so absurd.

"Why?" I asked.

"Your mistress," the governor explained, "has refused to take you back as her servant. That leaves you without home or protection. Before we left England, it was stated most clearly in the contract that the only women on board should be married to men in the company or enlisted as servants. A woman on her own encourages uncivilized behavior and tension between the men."

A surge of anger bolstered what little strength I had. "You are saying, your lordship, that I must return to servitude or marry a man I do not love? And this so soon after the death of my dear husband?"

"For the good of all, including your babe, it is our opinion that only the one choice remains since Mistress Horton declares"—the governor shot her a look of exasperation—"she will not have you."

I turned to Will, but he glanced away.

"No," I said.

"There are many men here in Jamestown who would be happy to wive, even though you carry another man's child."

I opened my mouth and then shut it, feeling the hot flush

of anger rise in my cheeks. Standing up, I turned and, without another word to any of them, walked out of the church.

Mary Alder's Wilde Goose

Into one kilt Goose stuff an Onyon, one Peece of Pork, both Pepper and Salt and a good spoonful of red Wine. Lay Goose into enuff water for Gravy then dredge with Flower and frequent baste in Butter to browne. Cook over hot fier to done and serve with Gravy from thikened juses.

Forty-four

I would not wish
Any companion in the world but you,
Nor can imagination form a shape,
Besides yourself, to like of.
—from *The Tempest*

*S*arah and Mary Alder sat with me by the cooking fire as we pared the last of the carrots we had brought with us from the governor's garden on his island.

"It is the sensible thing to do, my girl," Mary said, wagging her head.

"I will love Thomas until the day I die. How can I marry another man?"

"It may not be too bad," Sarah said. "Meself, I'd prefer the marriage bed over bein' a maid."

"And you wouldn't care who the man might be?" I asked,

wondering at her naivety. She was as bad as I once had been, though I had dismissed all men, whereas she welcomed all.

"Well, not every man. Not a one so old he couldn't keep a stiff—"

"Ah, sweet Jesus!" Mrs. Alder hooted. "What talk is this? There are many men here fine enough husbanding material." She nudged me with her elbow. "Some of them marines the good Admiral brought with him are brawny fellas. Hey?"

I closed my eyes and shuddered. I would forever compare all men to my Thomas and find them lacking. "I shall not marry."

Sarah put an arm around me and squeezed. "The gov'nor sets sail tomorrow, and I don't think he'll take no for your answer. He may choose a man for you if you do not choose your own."

I wrapped Thomas's quilt around my shoulders, imagining his arms in there with me. "No."

"No, what?" a voice said.

I looked up but did not smile. "Will."

He waited for my explanation but I gave none.

Sarah chimed out, "She says she will not marry."

He smiled. "She used to say that all of the time, but then she changed her mind."

"Never again," I said firmly.

He nodded. "I believe you mean it."

"I do. They cannot make me marry. I will have none other than my Thomas, and since I cannot have him, I will have none ever."

"They won't give up, you know," he said gently. "They believe it will help the stability of the community. And in truth, you will need a provider for your child. This place is not like England. Someone must hunt and forage for you and the babe. Someone must build you a shelter. The kindness of your neighbors will last for a while, then they will expect you to become a part of a family again."

"Mistress Horton never married."

Will snorted. "And you would wish to be like her?"

"She has her wealth as a mate," Mary said, a touch of bitters in her tone. "Ah well, we each have our place in life, dear."

And I knew it was true. A young woman lived with her parents until she married, then with her husband. To be a woman alone in the world, without fortune or property, was an impossible situation.

Tears filled my eyes to brimming, and no amount of effort held them back. "But I so loved him . . ."

After all had supped that night, I made for my pallet in the corner where Thomas and I had lain together since our coming to this wretched land. I retired there as weary as I ever had been and know not how long I tossed while others not on sentry duty found places to lie, gradually falling asleep, their snores and chortles sounding like farmyard animals'.

"Miranda," a voice whispered.

I looked up into the darkness. A figure held a lantern over me. The shoulders were narrow, not like my Thomas's, so broad and strong. A glint, as of gold casting back the lantern's orange glow, informed me of my visitor.

"What is it, Will?"

"Come outside for a moment. We must talk."

"But I am so very tired."

He squatted down beside me and whispered. "Are you determined to be on your own with the babe?"

"I am. Please do not try to dissuade me further."

"I will not." He paused. "But I believe I've found a means by which to make your chosen path safe."

I sat up to better see his face in the lantern light; his eyes gleamed, no longer blue in the darkness, but black and shining as hot tar. The only other times I had seen them appear this way he had been consumed with excitement.

"Tell me," I said.

Epilogue

Out of this nettle, danger, we pluck
this flower, safety.
—from *Henry IV, Part I*

*T*o say one event or conversation or night can change a person's life sounds overly dramatic, more like a scene plucked from one of my friend Will's plays. But it was nevertheless true in my case. For had not one day taken my father's life, and another buried my mother and siblings? Had not a hunting trip robbed me of the father of my child?

Yet dark times are not all that change a life. Hope shines through the bleakest hours, if you look for it. That was how I found Thomas Powell, by opening my eyes to a possibility I never had dreamt or imagined. And had I not dug up a pail of sweet clams from the pink sands of Paradise, I might not have become known years later as the finest baker of steak pies in all of Warwickshire.

Sharing my gifts, opening my heart to Thomas and to hope for the future gave me two new lives—my own, and that of my little Thomasina. For my husband had been right after all. Our babe was a girl, as sweet and impish as ever I could imagine.

He was wrong about her appearance, though, for she did not favor me. Thomasina had his beautiful fern-green eyes, his sunny round face, and grew with a speed and sturdiness of limb that let me know she would become a strong woman with a temperament to match her father's. And though I tried to teach her to speak as a lady ought, by the time she turned two years, she had picked up the language of our customers in the tavern, her first words sprinkled with colorful bawdy chatter.

"Are you daydreaming again, Miranda?"

I turned to the teasing voice of my sister. Well, not by blood and birth, but by the companionship we shared these cozy days in Stratford, that village upon the Avon River where Will Shakespeare soon would retire to be close to his family.

"I am working on these pies, and if you are done with wearing out my child you may lend me a hand."

Suzanne looked down at little Thomasina, red-cheeked, dust from the country road in her soft brown curls, and smiled at her. "You aren't tired from our stroll, are you, sweetheart?"

Tommie shook her head, her eyes roaming toward the tabletop, still too high for her to see over. "Hungry," she said.

I broke off a tiny bite of cooled, cooked potato I had saved for her.

"Here, my precious, open wide." I popped it into her mouth.

"Does she ever stop eating?" Suzanne asked. "I bought her a sweet on our walk."

"She eats like her father—constantly," I said with a smile.

The hurt of losing Thomas never left, but even the saddest moments were lit with the little joys life brings. Like my father's counterweights used to measure the fairness of a coin, I weighed the good against the bad in life.

I drew up from my bodice the two pieces of a coin that dangled together on a chain around my throat, and held them together in my hand. The bad—my husband died while hunting for food to feed his family and friends. The good—he lived on in his daughter.

But there was more to it than that. Had Thomas survived, we would have stayed in Jamestown. He was that stubborn about finishing what he started. And who is to say whether we would have survived, the three of us, that last cruel winter before the colony finally began to support itself? Many did perish, Mistress Horton among them. And so Will had been right; my tormentor never again returned to her beloved London. I can't say that news saddened me. But tragic word also came back to us with another returning ship: even with increased supplies of food and building materials, the cold had been too much for those already weakened by illness.

"My father sent word," Suzanne said, helping herself to a plump plum from the bowl beside my window, "he will return to us next week."

Another sunny bit of news. I smiled. "The theatres are closing for the summer?"

"How else would we ever see him?" She laughed. "I do think he comes more often now that you are here, Miranda. You and the little one."

I shook my head, though I was pleased by her compliment. "It is not me or even his little godchild that draws him."

"What then?" She took up a wooden rolling pin and began to work my dough for the pies' crusts.

"He protects his investments. Since he now has property to keep in repair and for which to collect rent, as well as the profits from the Green Turtle, he feels obligated to come more frequently."

"Rent? He actually makes you pay him for all you do here?" She looked astonished.

"It was the bargain we struck in Virginia, my last night there."

"That he profit from your tragic loss?" She whacked the dough with the pin. "The old scoundrel!"

"Not at all." I picked up my child, my babe, my life, and cuddled her to me. "He told me he had invested in several properties with his earnings from the Globe—some in London, more here in the country."

"Just before he disappeared to go off adventuring," she said with a roll of her blue eyes, so like her father's. "The man makes no sense."

Will had never told Suzanne or her sister, Judith, or their mother, Ann, about the dangerous reason he had arranged passage under an assumed name aboard *Sea Venture*. He believed the less they knew of his enemy's plot, the better. To them this adventure was just more evidence of the mysterious, quirky nature of a man who lived more often in his fantasies than in the real world.

"Sensible or not in character, his investments seem sound enough. Among the properties, he explained to me that night, was an old tavern in the town where his family lived, fallen into disrepair but of promise. Since I once had confided to him my dream of becoming a lady victualer, cooking for others as I had done in our months in the Bermudas, he proposed to transport me here to keep the place." The admiral, already having offered Will safe passage back to England so that he might inform the Virginia Company of our survival, agreed I might travel with him as his serving girl. "I provide meals for travelers or townspeople, as might come. In return, I pay him one third of my profits as rent. It is a bargain I shall keep with joy."

"I still think he overcharges you, Miranda. Look at how hard you work."

I gazed around my tidy kitchen with its broad stone hearth, sturdy oak table the size of a marriage bed, chairs and stools and cupboards all of good heavy chestnut wood.

Will had imported tiles in the Italian style of terra-cotta for the floor, and hired craftsmen to lay them, an unheard of luxury for a village tavern or any house but the wealthiest. My larder was full. I kept paid-up accounts with butcher, fishmonger, and sundry merchants in town. My rooms to let each had pretty chintz curtains, a braided rug, and a feather bed to accommodate as many as four.

My heart filled with pride. The Green Turtle Tavern felt more like home than the memory of the old apothecary in

London. Moreover, it was mine, from the name I had given it to the foods I prepared from the good things growing in my garden.

"Hard work?" I shrugged. "Only once in my life can I say I have been happier."

And as I closed my eyes, feeling the warmth of my kitchen, and of friends as close as family, I could believe even *that* kind of happiness might visit me again.

Green Turtle Tavern's Receipt for Steak Pye ala Francaise

(Borrowed from THE ACCOMPLISHT COOK, 1660)

Season the steaks with pepper, nutmeg, and salt lightly, and set them by, then take a piece of the leanest of a leg of mutton, and mince it small with some beef suet and a few sweet herbs, as tops of thyme, pennyroyal, young red sage, grated bread, yolks of eggs, sweet cream, raisins of the sun & c. work all together and make it into little balls, and rouls, put them into a deep round pye on the steaks, then put to them some butter, and sprinkle it with verjuyce, close it up and bake it, being baked cut it up, then roul sage leaves in butter, fry them, and stick them in the ball, serve the pye without a cover, and liquor it with the juyce of two or three oranges or lemons.

Author's Note

The recipes in this novel are not recommended for modern preparation, as measurements of ingredients and instructions for preparation are often left to the imagination and/or knowledge of the cook. However, readers interested in trying modernized versions of some of the dishes Elizabeth Miranda Persons might have been familiar with are directed toward a marvelous cookbook by Francine Segan, *Shakespeare's Kitchen: Renaissance Recipes for the Contemporary Cook*, Random House, New York, 2003. This book and another—*The Williamsburg Art of Cookery,* by Mrs. Helen Bullock, Colonial Williamsburg/Dietz Press, Richmond, 1985 (first published in 1938)—provided inspiration for many of Miranda's receipts.

A Historical Note

$\mathcal{M}$any scholars believe that William Shakespeare's celebrated play *The Tempest* was inspired by an actual shipwreck and true tale of survival that captured the imagination of seventeenth-century London. Two dramatic accounts written by passengers aboard the ill-fated *Sea Venture* made their way back to England: William Strachey's "A True Reportory of the Wreck and Redemption of Sir Thomas Gates, Knight," and Silvester Jourdain's, "A Discovery of the Bermudas, Otherwise Called the Isle of Devils." Some theories hold that Will was one of those people back in London who had access to these accounts before they were published some years after his death.

Many of the characters in *The Gentleman Poet* are named on the ship's manifest, including Elizabeth Persons, listed as the maidservant of a Mistress Horton. No accounts exist describing these passengers in much detail. Portraying Elizabeth as a timid Catholic orphan, and Mistress Horton as a shrewish old maid, are purely the results of a fiction writer's imagination. However, Strachey does mention the marriage of Elizabeth Persons and the ship's cook, Thomas Powell, which naturally leads us to assume that a romance developed while they lived on Bermuda.

In addition, Strachey's journal includes rather exciting, sometimes grim, facts that beg to be woven into a story. For instance, one sailor was reported to have been "villainously killed by the foresaid Robert Waters (a sailor likewise) with a shovel, who strake him therewith under the lift of the ear . . ." And later the ship's historian hints that the fight might have erupted as a result of a dispute over a woman.

Very little information is available from any source to help us imagine the personality or even the physical appearance of William Shakespeare, since he never commissioned a portrait of himself and no autobiography or diaries exist. Even the two undisputed likenesses of him—an engraving (the Droeshout Print) that appears as the frontispiece of the *First Folio* (a collection of his plays published by his friends after his death in 1623) and the bust in his funerary monument—give little sense of the passionate, multitalented man he must have been. Two other portraits—the Cobbe (1610) and the Chandos (early 1600s)—are accepted as probably his and therefore rendered in his lifetime, but some still argue they are not Shakespeare at all!

However, a few interesting clues in his contemporaries' writing give us intriguing glimpses of the man. He seemed not to be a heavy drinker or prone to bar brawls like his fellow playwright Christopher Marlowe, who ended up dying in a sword fight. He was, according to at least one account, a quiet man who preferred his own company.

He also seems to have had a soft spot in his heart for young lovers. If the events in some of his plays (*Romeo and Juliet*, *A Midsummer-Night's Dream*, *Much Ado About Nothing*) aren't enough to prove this, then there is at least one piece of legal evidence. It appears that Will inserted himself into the emotional turmoil of the Mountjoy household in London, on Silver Street, where he'd rented a room. Court depositions made and signed by Shakespeare, as well as corroborating statements by others, indicate that he encouraged the young apprentice of his landlord to marry the man's daughter. In fact, he'd been entreated by the girl's mother to nudge the boy in the proper direction. I thought it not a long stretch to imagine Will acting as a matchmaker between Elizabeth Miranda and her Thomas.

Is it likely that William Shakespeare actually took the name William Strachey and sailed off on his last great adventure to the New World? Probably not, although in the time during which the story takes place, 1609–1610, there is little if any evidence that he was either in London or in Stratford-upon-Avon, his most familiar haunts. His trail fades to nearly nothing through vast patches of his life. But isn't it at least interesting to notice that the two men had the same first name (though a common one) and, indeed, the same initials? How tempting to a novelist!

It's also fun to compare Strachey's account with Shakespeare's play, *The Tempest*. They share certain details and ways of looking at the world. Sea travelers of the time really were fearful of monsters, enchanted objects, witches' spells, and cannibals. Shakespeare employs all of these elements in his play. Prospero, the father marooned with his daughter on an island that some think was meant to be Bermuda (though the geography isn't quite right), is a magician. He uses a magic cape when he wishes to become invisible and directs a sprite called Ariel to create spells and mayhem. Some experts believe that Shakespeare, acting in as well as writing his plays, may have created the role in his own image and actually played it onstage. Miranda might have been modeled after his favorite daughter, Suzanne. Caliban, the deformed and enslaved creature of the island, born of a witch, takes the place of both monster and cannibal. Themes of mutiny, loyalty, compassion, forgiveness, and survival against great odds appear in both Strachey's account and the play.

And what of the *Sea Venture* herself? Her bones lie undisturbed in the pristine waters off the easternmost tip of Bermuda. The few artifacts that have been retrieved from the coral shoals where she floundered are today in the Bermuda Maritime Museum—several cannon, about eighty cannonballs, shot for small arms, and a few household items, including a pewter candlestick and ceramic shards. If you visit Bermuda today, you can see them as well as a replica of the *Deliverance*, which would have taken Elizabeth and Thomas on to Jamestown.

—KKJ, 2009

Kathryn Johnson

Jean Korten Moser

KATHRYN JOHNSON is the author of many books for readers of all ages. She writes and lives in Maryland with her husband and two feline writing partners—named appropriately, Tempest and Miranda. An advocate for literacy, she encourages membership in reading clubs and is available for in-person visits to local meetings and speakerphone appearances at others. Requests can be e-mailed to Kathryn johnson100@yahoo.com. Kathryn enjoys hearing from her readers by e-mail or on Facebook, and tweets to her followers on Twitter (KathrynKJohnson) whenever she has a spare moment.

The lighter side of HISTORY

* Look for this seal on select historical fiction titles from Harper. Books bearing it contain special bonus materials, including timelines, interviews with the author, and insights into the real-life events that inspired the book, as well as recommendations for further reading.

ANNETTE VALLON:
A Novel of the French Revolution
by James Tipton
978-0-06-082222-4 (paperback)
For fans of Tracy Chevalier and Sarah Dunant comes this vibrant, alluring debut novel of a compelling, independent woman who would inspire one of the world's greatest poets and survive a nation's bloody transformation.

BOUND: A Novel
by Sally Gunning
978-0-06-124026-3 (paperback)
An indentured servant finds herself bound by law, society, and her own heart in colonial Cape Cod.

CASSANDRA & JANE: A Jane Austen Novel
by Jill Pitkeathley
978-0-06-144639-9 (paperback)
The relationship between Jane Austen and her sister—explored through the letters that might have been.

CROSSED: A Tale of the Fourth Crusade
by Nicole Galland
978-0-06-084180-5 (paperback)
Under the banner of the Crusades, a pious knight and a British vagabond attempt a daring rescue.

A CROWNING MERCY: A Novel
by Bernard Cornwell and Susannah Kells
978-0-06-172438-1 (paperback)
A rebellious young Puritan woman embarks on a daring journey to win love and a secret fortune.

DANCING WITH MR. DARCY:
Stories Inspired by Jane Austen and Chawton House Library
Edited by Sarah Waters
978-0-06-199906-2 (paperback)
An anthology of the winning entries in the
Jane Austen Short Story Award 2009.

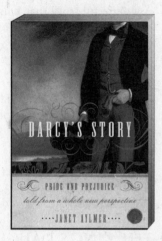

DARCY'S STORY
by Janet Aylmer
978-0-06-114870-5 (paperback)
Read Mr. Darcy's side of the story—*Pride
and Prejudice* from a new perspective.

DEAREST COUSIN JANE:
A Jane Austen Novel
by Jill Pitkeathley
978-0-06-187598-4 (paperback)
An inventive reimagining of the intriguing
and scandalous life of Jane Austen's cousin.

THE FALLEN ANGELS: A Novel
by Bernard Cornwell and Susannah Kells
978-0-06-172545-6 (paperback)
In the sequel to *A Crowning Mercy*, Lady Campion Lazender's courage,
faith, and family loyalty are tested when she must complete a perilous
journey between two worlds.

A FATAL WALTZ: A Novel of Suspense
by Tasha Alexander
978-0-06-117423-0 (paperback)
Caught in a murder mystery, Emily must do the unthinkable to save her
fiancé: bargain with her ultimate nemesis, the Countess von Lange.

FIGURES IN SILK: A Novel
by Vanora Bennett
978-0-06-168985-7 (paperback)
The art of silk making, political intrigue, and a sweeping love story all
interwoven in the fate of two sisters.

THE FIREMASTER'S MISTRESS: A Novel
by Christie Dickason
978-0-06-156826-8 (paperback)
Estranged lovers Francis and Kate rekindle their
romance in the midst of Guy Fawkes's plot to blow up
Parliament.

THE GENTLEMAN POET:
A Novel of Love, Danger, and Shakespeare's The Temptest
by Kathryn Johnson
978-0-06-196531-9 (paperback)
A wonderful story that tells the tale of how William Shakespeare may have come to his inspiration for *The Tempest*.

JULIA AND THE MASTER OF MORANCOURT: A Novel
by Janet Aylmer
978-0-06-167295-8 (paperback)
Amidst family tragedy, Julia travels all over England, desperate to marry the man she loves instead of the arranged suitor preferred by her mother.

KEPT: A Novel
by D. J. Taylor
978-0-06-114609-1 (paperback)
A gorgeously intricate, dazzling reinvention of Victorian life and passions that is also a riveting investigation into some of the darkest, most secret chambers of the human heart.

THE KING'S DAUGHTER: A Novel
by Christie Dickason
978-0-06-197627-8 (paperback)
A superb historical novel of the Jacobean court, in which Princess Elizabeth, daughter of James I, strives to avoid becoming her father's pawn in the royal marriage market.

THE MIRACLES OF PRATO: A Novel
by Laurie Albanese and Laura Morowitz
978-0-06-155835-1 (paperback)
The unforgettable story of a nearly impossible romance between a painter-monk (the renowned artist Fra Filippo Lippi) and the young nun who becomes his muse, his lover, and the mother of his children.

PILATE'S WIFE:
A Novel of the Roman Empire
by Antoinette May
978-0-06-112866-0 (paperback)
Claudia foresaw the Romans' persecution of Christians, but even she could not stop the crucifixion.

PORTRAIT OF AN UNKNOWN WOMAN: A Novel
by Vanora Bennett
978-0-06-125256-3 (paperback)
Meg, adopted daughter of Sir Thomas More, narrates the tale of a
famous Holbein painting and the secrets it holds.

THE PRINCESS OF NOWHERE: A Novel
by Prince Lorenzo Borghese
978-0-06-172161-8 (paperback)
From a descendant of Napoleon Bonaparte's brother-in-law comes a
historical novel about his famous ancestor, Princess Pauline Bonaparte
Borghese.

THE QUEEN'S SORROW: A Novel of Mary Tudor
by Suzannah Dunn
978-0-06-170427-7 (paperback)
Queen of England Mary Tudor's reign is brought low by abused power
and a forbidden love.

REBECCA:
The Classic Tale of Romantic Suspense
by Daphne du Maurier
978-0-380-73040-7 (paperback)
Follow the second Mrs. Maxim de Winter down the lonely drive to
Manderley, where Rebecca once ruled.

REBECCA'S TALE: A Novel
by Sally Beauman
978-0-06-117467-4 (paperback)
Unlock the dark secrets and old worlds of Rebecca de Winter's life with
investigator Colonel Julyan.

THE SIXTH WIFE: A Novel of Katherine Parr
by Suzannah Dunn
978-0-06-143156-2 (paperback)
Kate Parr survived four years of marriage to King Henry VIII, but a
new love may undo a lifetime of caution.

WATERMARK: A Novel of the Middle Ages
by Vanitha Sankaran
978-0-06-184927-5 (paperback)
A compelling debut about the search for identiy, the
power of self-expression, and value of the written word.